THE VALKYRIE RETURNS

THE VALKYRIE RETURNS

THE KURTHERIAN ENDGAME™ BOOK SEVEN

MICHAEL ANDERLE

DISRUPTIVE IMAGINATION®

LMBPN Publishing
PMB 196, 2540 South Maryland Pkwy
Las Vegas, NV 89109

First US edition, November 2019
Version 1.01, November 2019
eBook ISBN: 978-1-64202-579-8
Print ISBN: 978-1-64202-580-4

THE VALKYRIE RETURNS TEAM

Thanks to our Beta Readers:
Timothy Cox (the myth)
Diane Velasquez (the legend)
Dorene A. Johnson, USN, Ret.
Tom Dickerson (in the way of Life)

Thanks to the JIT Readers
Dave Hicks
Shari Regan
Daniel Weigert
Nicole Emens
Misty Roa
Dorothy Lloyd
John Ashmore
James Caplan
Jeff Eaton
Diane L. Smith
Deb Mader
Larry Omans
Peter Manis
Misty Roa
Jeff Goode
Micky Cocker
Jackey Hankard-Brodie
Charles Tillman
Lori Hendricks

If I've missed anyone, please let me know!

Editor
Lynne Stiegler

Thank you for continuing to read our adventures with Bethany Anne. As you can tell, the Federation is going to have to come to grips with the Empress being 'just around the block.' Since there is a greater evil at their doorsteps, I think they will get over it.

For now.

If not, she always has her size sevens to ...

GLOSSARY OF CHARACTERS, LOCATIONS, AND SHIPS

Characters

- **Bethany Anne Nacht (BA)**

Super-enhanced human, part of a triumvirate consisting of her, TOM, and ADAM. Can walk the Etheric (see locations). Has the ability to manipulate Etheric energy to her will. Will stamp out injustice without mercy wherever she finds it.

Ex-Empress of the Etheric Empire, BA took voluntary exile to bring in the Federation and now fights to protect it from the Kurtherians. As her alter ego, she controls a growing buffer around the Federation border.

Currently based on the Queen's Superdreadnought *Baba Yaga* (see Ships), fighting a war against the Ooken—creations of the Seven.

Wife to Michael, mother to Alexis and Gabriel.

- **TOM – "Thales of Miletus"**

Kurtherian, hosted within Bethany Anne's body. Enhanced Michael in an attempt to warn humanity of the coming invasion and got it wrong, inadvertently creating the vampire myth on Earth. A thousand years later, he got a second chance and got it SO right.

• ADAM

AI who resides in an organic computer within Bethany Anne's body. Bethany Anne's close friend and advisor.

All of Bethany Anne's and Federation AIs and EIs come from ADAM.

• Michael Nacht

Ancient, super-enhanced human.

Formerly known as the Patriarch, Michael was the first "vampire." He has ever-increasing skill with the Etheric and a short temper. Ruled the UnknownWorld on Earth for over a thousand years before choosing Bethany Anne to replace him.

Currently based on the QSD *Baba Yaga*.

Husband to Bethany Anne, father to Alexis and Gabriel.

• Alexis Nacht

Super-enhanced human, Bethany Anne and Michael's daughter. Twin of Gabriel. Highly trained from a young age in martial arts and close combat, weapons.

Has an affinity for technology, and a habit of hacking to

get answers. Has shown telepathic ability, and has growing control of the Etheric. Outgoing, loves fashion.

Currently on Devon, inside the Vid-doc system undergoing an enhanced aging process.

• Gabriel Nacht

Super-enhanced human, Bethany Anne and Michael's son. Twin of Alexis. Highly trained from a young age in martial arts and close combat, weapons.

Has specialized in "spy skills," as well as engineering, history, and languages. Appears introverted, collects blades.

Currently inside the Vid-doc system undergoing an enhanced aging process.

• John Grimes

Enhanced human. Queen's Bitch. Bethany Anne's bodyguard and close friend. Wherever Bethany Anne goes, so does John.

Currently based on the QSD *Baba Yaga*.

Husband to Jean, father to Lillian, grandfather to Nickie.

• Scott English

Enhanced human. Queen's Bitch. Bethany Anne's personal bodyguard and close friend.

Currently based on the QSD *Baba Yaga*.

Husband to Cheryl Lynn (cousin of John Grimes), step-father to Tina Grimes-Cambridge.

- **Eric Escobar**

Enhanced human. Queen's Bitch. Bethany Anne's personal bodyguard and close friend.
Currently based on the QSD *Baba Yaga*.
Husband to Gabrielle.

- **Darryl Jackson**

Enhanced human. Queen's Bitch. Bethany Anne's personal bodyguard and close friend.
Currently based on the QSD *Baba Yaga*.
In a long-distance relationship with Natalia Jakowski.

- **Gabrielle Escobar**

Super-enhanced human, daughter of Stephen. Head of the Queen's Bitches and one of Bethany Anne's closest friends.
Currently based on the QSD *Baba Yaga*.
Wife to Eric.

- **Tabitha Nacht**

Super-enhanced human, hacker extraordinaire. A sister of the heart to BA. Held the rank of Ranger Two during the Age of Empire, she chose exile with Bethany Anne when the Federation was formed.

Currently located on Devon with her partner Peter and their son Todd Michael.

- **Peter Silvers**

Super-enhanced human, has Were form called "Pricolici."

The first Guardian. Held the rank of Guardian Commander during the Age of Empire. He had reason to remain in the Federation but chose to leave and settle down with Tabitha after the death of his best friend.

Currently located on Devon with Tabitha.

- **Todd Michael Nacht-Silvers**

Super-enhanced human, abilities unknown as yet. Son of Tabitha and Peter. Tiny terror.

- **Jean Grimes (née Dukes)**

Super-enhanced human. Inventor of the infamous Jean Dukes Special. Weapons R&D genius, legendary across galaxies for her weaponry.

Currently located on Devon. Officially based at QT2, working to unlock the mysteries of the Kurtherian technology gained on Qu'Baka.

Wife of John, mother of Lillian, grandmother of Nickie.

- **Barnabas Nacht**

Super-enhanced human. One of seven firstborn "children" of Michael, former monk.

Currently located on High Tortuga, where BA has made him Steward of the planet in her absence.

- **Lance Reynolds**

Enhanced human, aka "the General." Bethany Anne's father.

Remained to chair the Federation when Bethany Anne went into exile.

Currently located on Red Rock, where the Federation council is seated (see Locations).

Husband to Patricia, father also to Kevin.

- **Kael-ven**

Enhanced Yollin, captain of the QBS *G'laxix Sphaea* (see Ships). Potentate of Yoll during the Age of Empire, he divorced his awful wife and rejoined Bethany Anne when she took exile.

Currently stationed on the Interdiction (see locations).

- **Kiel**

Enhanced Yollin.

Former mercenary, Marine during the Age of Empire. Weapons officer aboard the QBS *G'laxix Sphaea*.

Currently stationed on the Interdiction.

- **Eve**

AI, date of ascension unknown. Resides in a short android body. Remained to protect Earth with Akio and Yuko when Bethany Anne left for space, and rejoined BA at the end of the Second Dark Age.

Currently located on Devon.

• Nickie Grimes

Naturally enhanced human. Birth name Meredith Nicole, aka Merry. Daughter of Lillian, granddaughter of John and Jean. Sent on a sabbatical by BA in her late teens as a consequence of her poor choices. Has returned a (mostly) changed woman.

Currently running the Silver Line Company, Bethany Anne's logistics network.

• Sabine

Enhanced human rescued on Earth by Michael, Jacqueline, and Akio during the Second Dark Age. Crack shot, excellent fighter. Adopted daughter of Akio.

Currently located on Devon, co-owner of The Hexagon (see Locations).

In a relationship with Tim Kinley.

• Jacqueline

Enhanced human, Were with Pricolici form. Daughter of North American pack leader Gerry. Rescued by Michael during the Second Dark Ages.

Currently located on Devon, co-owner of The Hexagon. Excellent fighter, skilled with managing the media.

In a long-term relationship with Mark.

- **Mark**

Enhanced human. Rescued by Michael and Jacqueline in NYC during the Second Dark Ages.

Currently located on Devon, co-owner of The Hexagon. Skilled in technology and invention.

In a long-term relationship with Jacqueline.

- **Ricole**

Enhanced Noel-ni, joined the Queen's forces on High Tortuga. Would choose knowledge over profit, and a fight over all else.

Currently located on Devon, co-owner of The Hexagon. Excellent fighter, even better at business. Runs a team of young adult apprentices who work around The Hexagon.

- **Demon**

Enhanced mountain lion. Rescued from an animal-testing facility on Earth by Michael & co. during the Second Dark Age. Was treated in a Pod-doc to fix faulty nanocytes and have her claws regrown.

Currently located on Devon, co-owner of The Hexagon. Especially attached to Sabine.

Thought herself to be the only truly sentient cat until meeting her silent mate on Qu'Baka.

- **Dan Bosse**

Enhanced human. Long-time advisor to Bethany Anne, he remained to watch over the Federation.

- **Tim Kinley**

Enhanced human, Were.
One of the original Guardians, Tim joined BA as a young man looking for a better path. Spent time as a bouncer at All Guns Blazing (bar) during the Age of Empire.
Currently located on Devon, where he is the commander of the QBBS *Guardian*.
In a relationship with Sabine.

- **Rickie Escobar**

Enhanced human, Were. One of the original Guardians, Rickie is known for his smart mouth. Second in command on the QBBS *Guardian*.
In an on again/off again relationship with Nickie Grimes.

- **Qui'nan**

Yollin, four-legged. Architect, engineer, grumbler.
Currently based at QT2, part of Jean's R&D team.

- **Mahi'Takar aka Mahi'**

Baka. Nominal leader of the Bakas on Devon in her adolescent son Trey's name.

- **Fi'Eireie (Fi')**

Baka. Husband of Mahi'Takar, father of Trey. Was held prisoner on Qu'Baka and rescued by Bethany Anne and Michael.

- **Tu'Reigd (Trey)**

Baka. Son of Mahi'Takar. Close friend of the twins and K'aia.
Currently inside the Vid-doc system undergoing enhancement.

- **K'aia**

Enhanced Yollin. Former mine slave. Bodyguard and close friend of Alexis, Gabriel, and Trey.
Currently inside the Vid-doc system undergoing enhancement.

- **Lu'Trein**

Deceased. Baka, twin to Mahi'. Pulled a coup with the backing of Gödel. Supposedly murdered Fi'Eireie (husband to Mahi'), forcing Mahi' to flee with an infant Trey and a number of their people.

- **Gödel**

Ruler of the Kurtherian clans collectively known as the Seven. Considers Bethany Anne to be her nemesis.

Locations

- **The Etheric**

Unknown location, possibly outside of our universe. Source of limitless energy for those who can access it.

The Kurtherians developed technology that enabled them to access the energy, known as nanocytes. The Seven used nanocytes to dominate every species they came across for millennia, while some among the Five used them to "prepare" other species for the fight.

TOM changed everything when he came to prepare Earth and gave humanity the technology.

- **High Tortuga**

The planet Bethany Anne prepared for her exile. A safe haven, highly defended and hidden from common knowledge.

BA has a base on the northern continent, where the planet is populated. The southern continent is wild land.

Bethany Anne has now left High Tortuga in Barnabas' hands while she fights from Devon.

- **Devon**

Originally a mercenary hideout until Baba Yaga took over and renamed the planet Devon as part of the plan to divert attention from High Tortuga.

The planet is protected by its end of the Interdiction, a three-layer security system comprised of a long-range early-warning system, the BYPS network around the planet, and the QBBS *Guardian*.

The planet has two major cities and one smaller city around the lake system.

First City is the location of The Hexagon, the bazaar, and various communities of settlers.

- **QT2**

Site of the original Ooken incursion. Bethany Anne built wide-ranging defenses similar to those at High Tortuga and Devon. In addition to the battlestation, QBBS *Helena* is the shipyard, where the fleet expansion is being managed from.

- **Red Rock aka "Fed Rock."**

This mobile asteroid is the home of the House of Arbitration, the seat of the Federation council.

Red Rock travels the Federation, has a Gate connection straight back to Yoll.

- **The Interdiction**

The Interdiction is the collective name for the various points of defense Bethany Anne has set up around the

Federation's borders. Includes Devon, QT2, High Tortuga, and a number of smaller locations along the logistics routes.

- **The Federation**

Coalition of planetary governments formed after the Empress of the Etheric Empire stepped down. Governed by the leaders of the people from both the former empire and other peoples (such as the Leath), it is headed by General Lance Reynolds.

While the Federation remains safe from the Seven for now, Bethany Anne has to fight to keep it that way.

- **Border Systems/Outer Quadrants—AKA "the Buffer Zone."**

The empty star systems around the Federation, and the populated ones where the people have not applied to be part of the Federation. They have remained unclaimed by Bethany Anne so far.

Ships

- QSD *Baba Yaga*
- QBS *Izanami* (decommissioned)
- QBS *Sayomi*
- QBS *Cambridge*
- QBS *ArchAngel*
- QBS *Wolfstar*
- QBS *G'laxix Sphaea*

- The *Penitent Granddaughter*

Battlestations

- QBBS *Guardian*
- QBBS *Helena*
- QBBS *Exuberant*

OOKEN IMAGES

BY ERIC QUIGLEY

The Etheric

The mists swirled, matching the erratic rhythm of Gödel's heartbeat.

She sat in her meditation pose, her intent on regaining control of her body and mind. At least, that had been her intention when she'd stepped into the Etheric to clear her mind of the headache that had begun to pulse at the base of her skull when she received the notification one of the crystals she'd thought destroyed had been activated.

The irregular pulsing of the mists only served to accentuate the pain at the base of her skull. The area behind her eyes throbbed as the familiar headache grew with every forced breath.

Clarity of mind was getting harder to attain when she was swatted aside by Death and her minions at every turn. The headache blocked her from attaining the peace she sought before commencing with her vengeance.

Why did she keep coming out unfavorably in these encounters? Once again, her plans had been thwarted by

Death's emotions and instinctive reactions, and she had been powerless to prevent it.

These were *failings*.

Twice now, she had lost an entire species to weak traits her people had weeded out of their genome centuries ago. Moen was a blow, but it was still accessible to her as a resource. Qu'Baka had been obliterated. Worse, Death and her consort had stolen part of her library.

Gödel had hundreds of information caches, but this one contained information she could not risk being made public knowledge. She could rebuild after the planetary losses, and it wouldn't be too difficult to find other species willing to exchange the dregs of their societies in exchange for the ability to vanquish their enemies.

What she couldn't recover from was the revelation of her identity.

The loss of the Bakas' genetic material was a huge blow to her plans to bring Ascension to the universe, but it did not leave her waking from sleep short of breath and shaking. Her library cache should have been safe on Qu'Baka. The theft was a complication she had not accounted for —*could not* have accounted for.

Gödel knew Death had found a way to incapacitate her creations. Figuring out a way to maintain contact was the only thing she'd been able to do without upsetting the delicate balance of her soldiers' minds. She would know if Death entered the hive mind again. Her preparations would have to be enough.

Gödel's rage ran deeper than mere frustration at finding an opponent her equal. To add insult to injury, Death had desecrated the body of her chosen and stolen the sacred technology. Gödel was sickened by Death's propensity for twisting the technology to her blasphemous purposes.

However, hindsight was the best preparation for the future, and the news had been enough to light a fire under even the most circumspect of her adepts.

Consequently, she had the resources to act. Her only recourse was the library's immediate retrieval and decimation of the humans on the planet to punish Death for her infraction. Primitive they might be, but Gödel had to admire the creativity humans had shown in their histories when it came to disciplining the masses.

Gödel put the thought aside and abandoned her meditation to leave the Etheric for her staging post. The staging post thrummed with malicious intent; the hive mind of her soldiers in the holds was soothing in its intensity. She was greeted with the obeisances she expected, as her due. Wherever she walked, the workers dropped to their knees.

As was proper when in the company of deity.

Gödel brushed against the hive mind as she mounted the ramp to her flagship, thrilling in the adulation she felt from her creations. They were primed and programmed to kill everything in sight, bar Kurtherians and each other, and having the adepts control them directly would cancel out any interference from the humans.

"Soon," she promised, sending images of the destruction her creations would cause in her name into the group consciousness. "Soon you will gorge yourselves on human flesh and drive my enemies insane with fear."

The adepts were already aboard the ships they

captained, waiting for their goddess to grace the fleet with her presence and order the invasion to begin.

Gödel entered the bridge of her flagship, her mind wandering back to the time before she'd had the power to take the fight to the humans. When her pleas to be heard by the Pilots had fallen on mostly deaf ears.

They saw only a young female of low birth, not the skewed genius capable of sifting through probabilities their fixed minds had no way to comprehend. They had not listened to her when Death escaped her planet. Rejected her again when Yoll fell. That fool Gorllet had heard her.

But who listens to the insane?

It was a pity for the Phraim-'Eh. They had been sound tacticians, but at that time, she had not contained the True Knowledge, so they had to be removed by baser means.

Manipulating Death into taking care of her dirty work had not proved to be too difficult. She at least could be counted upon to rush in with weapons blazing whenever an uncultivated species looked to be in need of defending.

Getting the Seven to act on even a mathematically perfect opportunity was a different matter. Or it had been until she had seen the light and returned a changed Kurtherian. Those who had rejected her warnings hadn't lived to regret their ignorance, and she had learned how to avoid human attention before superseding the more powerful among them on her path to glory.

Gödel's head still ached. It was little comfort that the fleet was assembled and ready to depart so soon after the rift battle. Open conflict within human territory was to have been the last resolution to the issues humanity had caused with the Ascension plan.

Before discovering the real reason for the headaches, she had wondered if her constant head pain was a result of time spent considering illogical paths with the aim of attempting to predict how Death was going to move in reaction to her.

Thinking like a human was no easy task. The first conclusion she had come to was that wasting resources on subjugation was illogical. The old adage that a Yollin was more easily tempted with sugar than bitterroot was true for a reason. Here she was a god among mortals, and most mortal leaders were more than happy to worship at the altar of Ascension in return for a taste of power and an extended lifetime.

Gödel had switched to working far outside of human territory, no easy feat when every galactic year saw the Federation expand farther and faster. Sending her soldiers to seek out the species she needed and force their subservience had worked until she had stumbled upon Death's hiding place and sparked this war. Negotiating, she found, was a game all its own. Using the weaknesses of those she needed to make them beg for her intercession was light relief from the heavy machinations of the larger game.

Of course, there would always be those who jumped to accept her bounty. Lu'Trein had been one of those. He had *begged* her to take the dregs of his society in return for power. That was a fair exchange, not anything that should have brought the humans running.

How was she to know that the sibling he'd ousted

would return, having formed an alliance with Death? It was these unexpected personal connections that threw her grand scheme off the rails.

Her carefully laid plans, some a century and more in the making, all triggered some primal urge to destroy in the humans. She lacked context for the motivation behind Death's continued attacks on her efforts toward the advancement of all, despite endless meditation on the subject.

Therefore, the only thing she could do was exercise her military might.

Gödel opened the Etheric around her ships, then closed it again once the fleet was inside the realm. Damn Death to a single existence for being the antithesis of logic, and damn her again for forcing her hand.

The library held the key to her destruction. The only question was, could her forces retrieve it before Death discovered what she had?

Time would tell.

Devon, The Interdiction, QSD *Baba Yaga*

Jean looked around the lab one last time to make sure she hadn't left anything behind. She dropped the box she was holding when John's arms snaked around her middle and squeezed. "Dammit, John!"

John swept the spilled contents to the side with his foot as he turned Jean to face him and pulled her against him. His regret at the end of her visit to Devon creased his face into a rueful half-smile. "It's going to be awfully quiet without you and the girls here."

Jean smiled and went up on her tiptoes to plant a kiss on his lips. "Careful there, hot stuff. You're getting dangerously close to making us both late. You know I have to get back. Qui'nan would bust her shell if I told her I was staying any longer."

"I know." John chuckled and released Jean reluctantly. "Can't blame me for being in a romantic mood." He glanced at the packing crates scattered around the lab. "It's been like our third honeymoon having you here."

Jean bent to gather her spilled belongings, tossing her gadgets back in with deft movements before casting a chastising smile in his direction. *"Fourth,"* she reminded him. "You always forget the moons of Ixtal."

"Oh, yeah." John grinned at the hazy memories he had of their centenary anniversary vacation. "I don't know why I never remember that trip. Must have been something to do with Nathan's gift."

Jean picked the box up and tucked it under one arm so she had a hand free to point at John. "That was your fault for not reading the delth-alcohol level on the bottle."

"It was a good thing one of us was sensible," he admitted. "It's just a shame to have you go so soon."

"It's been weeks," Jean teased. "You know, you could always escort Lillian and me back to QT2." She smiled, seeing the same look of indecision she always did when it came to the internal struggle between his duty to Bethany Anne and his desire to be with his family. That was being married to a man of service. She had learned to trust that he would choose her when he could, and their marriage stayed strong because of that trust.

She bumped him affectionately. "If you can take the

7

time. If you can't, we'll get back just fine with Barnabas. You know that."

John considered whether it was practical for him to leave Devon for a couple of days. "I'd feel better about both of you traveling with me to protect you if the Ookens show up along your route. I'll have to check with BA first to make sure she doesn't plan on leaving the system, but I can't see it being a problem otherwise."

"Sounds good to me." Jean balanced her box on top of the three crates stacked on the antigrav pallet she had waiting by the door. "I have to drop this armor off for Michael before I can leave." She grabbed the controller and activated the pallet with the press of a button. "We can find out now."

John eyed the crates speculatively as he and Jean followed the pallet out of the lab and into the main corridor. "They look a little on the large side for holding armor."

Jean lifted her hands. "I'll be able to build Michael a new set of battle armor just as soon as I get back to my workshop. Best I could do from here was take his most recent armor from the display gallery and tweak it to add a few of the newer features—like the chameleon tech—to make up for the step back in maneuverability. It's not a very workable material compared to what I've been producing with the new nanocytes."

"You'd better hope he doesn't leave this set in the path of an angry BA before it's ready." John didn't think Michael had anything to complain about. He remembered that the set Jean was describing had a shitload of hidden armaments that hadn't made it to the next mark due to streamlining. "What about whatever it is you do to make the armor easier to bear inside the Etheric? Were you able to add it?"

Jean pursed her lips. "You don't remember how it works?" She snickered at John's lost look. "Gotcha. But no, this set doesn't have that ability. It requires the polymer infusion, which can only be manufactured—"

"Let me guess," John interrupted, grinning. "In your workshop at QT2?"

Jean tilted her head and winked at John. "Give the man a gold star." She shrugged. "It's not that much of a step back since even our most up-to-date productions are still causing Michael too much drag when he takes them into the Etheric. It's why he had to leave his armor behind in the first place."

John nodded in understanding. "I wondered why you weren't mad at him."

Jean fixed him with a stern look. "Oh, I'm mad. Don't kid yourself. That armor is not easy or anything close to cost-efficient to produce, but it's not any fault of Michael's that he can't Myst in his armor. I'm angry with myself for not finding a way around the problem so he doesn't need to leave his protection behind to fight effectively."

2

Bethany Anne was waiting for Jean and John when they arrived at the top deck armory. "I thought you were leaving today?" she asked as Jean guided the antigrav pallet in ahead of them.

Jean stopped the pallet just inside the door, where there was space to unload the two smaller crates onto the table. "I was going to catch a ride with Barnabas, but my husband is feeling protective."

"I'm going to take them," John told Bethany Anne. "If that's good with you. You're not planning to go after the Seven in the next few days, right?"

Bethany Anne folded her arms and tapped her lips with a finger. "Not unless I can fit it in around visiting the shipyards."

John grimaced, and his shoulders dropped in disappointment. "That time already?"

Bethany Anne lifted her hands and smiled apologetically. "It's got to be done." She was reminded of Ashur's presence on Devon and decided to cut him a break. "Go with Jean, I'll be fine with Ashur. I'm definitely not going to start a fight in the next week."

John grinned. "I don't know whether to say thanks or be hurt that you can replace me so easily."

Bethany Anne raised an eyebrow and put her hands on her hips. "How about you go with the first option and run before I change my mind?"

John's grin widened, and he snapped a cheeky salute. "You've got it, Boss."

Bethany Anne narrowed her eyes.

John held up his hands. "I'm going! I'll let Lillian know about the change of plans on my way to the *Sayomi*." He kissed Jean goodbye and left, whistling quietly as he walked out of the armory.

Bethany Anne shook her head fondly as he walked out of sight. "I think you two have it hard enough being stationed in different galaxies. A few days off-schedule is just what you need. Am I right?"

"You're not wrong." Jean turned her attention to her delivery. "You sure about taking Ashur? Bellatrix won't be happy to leave Yelena and Bobcat."

Bethany Anne's lips quirked at Jean's subtext. "You mean, she won't be happy to spend time anywhere near me."

"That too," Jean conceded. "You'd think she'd stop blaming you by now."

Bethany Anne shrugged. "Who's to say what's rational when it comes to protecting your children? Bellatrix had two of hers stolen by an experiment I should have done a better job of supervising. I really can't blame her for being protective toward the rest."

Jean wrinkled her nose. "I'm glad I only had the one child, and leave it at that." She frowned. "Still, you should take one of the guys, at least."

Bethany Anne shook her head. "Everyone who came to Qu'Baka needs some downtime. They're not all here, anyway. I sent the guys to spend some quality time with their loved ones after the stress we've been under these last few months. Darryl is on leave to visit Natalia, although I'm not sure if they're meeting in the Vid-doc system since he hasn't gotten any farther than High Tortuga. Cheryl Lynn dragged Scott to that monastery world Tabitha helped out back in the day." She paused. "I'm not entirely sure where Gabrielle and Eric went. I'm happy to travel without a guard, but you know as well as I do that Bella-trix's temper tantrum isn't going to bother me. I've made my choice. Bellatrix can stay behind if she doesn't want to come with us."

One side of her mouth curled in amusement. "Besides, I haven't had a chance to see the *Wolfstar* in person. I want to take a look at a ship that's made for dogs."

"We don't mention that PITA ship," Jean grumbled. "I don't know where you got the idea for a ship that's fitted for dogs, and I have even less of a clue why the team I put on it decided to go all-out on the accessibility features. I just know it gave me a bitch of a headache from start to finish, and all I had to do was the approvals."

She moved to the antigrav pallet. "Where's Michael, anyway? I've got his temp armor."

"He's on his way." Bethany Anne's curiosity drew her over to inspect the three crates. "Is one of those for me?"

she rubbed her hands together as she eyed the boxes. "You know I love new goodies."

"Save your excitement until you see what's there." Jean nodded at the smallest crate. "That one first. I came up with a workaround for the integration issue with the boots, so you don't have to worry about snapping a heel. It's not the fix for the durability factor that you wanted, but you can at least take your boots and helmet off."

Bethany Anne smiled as she opened the crate to get a look at the helmet inside. "It's a step in the right direction. I didn't know you'd made another breakthrough with the nano-materials."

"That's because I haven't," Jean complained bitterly. "Eve and Tina went crazy for the Kurtherian armor you brought back from Qu'Baka. We've started the process of reverse-engineering, but it's going to be a while, I guess."

Bethany Anne raised an eyebrow, her hands hovering over the crate. "It's not like you to guess about anything."

Jean snorted softly, folding her arms as she leaned against the table. "Yeah, well, this time a guess is as good as I've got. I thought about taking the Kurtherian armor back to the *Helena* with me so I can start working out my part, but as much as I hate to admit it, this is more in Eve's wheelhouse than mine."

Michael walked in as Jean finished speaking. "Are you having trouble with the Kurtherian armor?"

Jean threw her hands up in frustration. "I can't do anything with it until we figure out how the fuck the Seven made compounds out of organic materials that behave like inorganic materials."

Michael frowned. "My guess from what we've

processed of the memory crystal and what I've seen is that a species called the Bl'kheths is the missing link."

His frown deepened at Jean's inquisitive look. "We came across the kind of equipment that's used for extracting DNA when we were in the Ooken factory."

Jean's curious expression dropped into one of utter disgust. "I can't stomach the thought of using a living being that way, never mind a whole species. It's enough to make me want to find their weak-ass excuses for scientists and choke the life out of them with my bare hands." She sighed as the momentary rage passed. "I don't see how we can think about doing the same, even if it's for the benefit of all."

"That isn't the question," Bethany Anne clarified as she pointed Michael to a crate on the pallet. "It's how we're going to use our gains ethically once we figure out the exact formula for Etheric-capable metals."

"Not to mention finding a way for the majority of our warriors to take on the Ookens without getting turned into hamburger," Jean ground out.

Bethany Anne nodded, matching Jean's angry look. "We know the Seven have no issues with helping themselves to the genetic material of whole species to make Ooken. I want the equivalent of their ability or better, and I want a way to get it done that doesn't cost lives."

Michael paused with his hands on the crate's lid, recalling Bethany Anne's reaction to the scenes of death in the Kurtherian factory. "It's worth waiting for."

"I'm not the waiting kind," Bethany Anne stated. "The sooner I can relax, knowing I'm not going to get another call to say one of the family has been hurt because their armor failed, the better."

Michael opened the crate and narrowed his eyes at the carefully packed plates at the top. "This is a step back. I don't think I'll be fighting in it much."

Jean grimaced at Michael's look of dismay. "It's the best I can do until I get back to QT2 and manufacture a new set. I won't be happy until I'm assured that what we have is sufficient to protect against the Ooken."

Bethany Anne placed the helmet and boots in the display case beside the one holding her battle armor. "I have faith you'll work it out." She closed the case and turned her attention to Michael. "You can always stay behind and get a head start on reading the crystals if you want to skip the tour."

Michael tilted his head in consideration. "I can't deny I'd be happier if one of us stayed close to the children. Aren't the crystals more an ADAM or TOM thing?"

Bethany Anne nodded. "Yeah, but neither of them have hands to operate the equipment, and I'd rather we kept whatever we find to ourselves for the moment."

Jean glanced at the cabinet inside the display case. "Where are you going to set up? I didn't put anything but basic equipment aboard this ship."

Michael deactivated the nanocurtain around the display case and cabinet, then opened the cabinet. "When I said 'close,' I meant *close*. Eve will find me a space in her lab where TOM and ADAM can have their discussion *outside* of my head." He removed a pair of crystals from the top drawer of the cabinet and slipped them into his breast pocket. "Thank you for your efforts, Jean."

Jean handed Michael the controller for the pallet holding his armor. "Thank me when you can Myst without leaving your armor behind." She hugged Bethany Anne briefly before heading for the armory door. "I'll see you when you get to the *Helena*."

Bethany Anne waved her off. "It'll be a few days before I'm done here, and the *Helena* isn't going to be my first stop at QT2. Safe journey, and don't let the Ooken surprise you."

Jean turned back as she walked out of the door. "Let them try. I owe them one for Addix, don't you think?"

"We all do," Bethany Anne replied with a cold smile. "Believe me when I tell you I'm going to take my price in blood."

"I don't doubt it, my love." Michael put a hand on Bethany Anne's shoulder. "Are you ready to visit the children?"

Bethany Anne nodded. "Let me grab a few things first."

Izanami appeared as they were walking past the lower access to the bridge on their way to the elevators. "My Queen. There's something you need to see before you leave. The scout ships you left at what's left of Qu'Baka have registered an anomaly they couldn't pinpoint."

Bethany Anne paused in her tracks. "What kind of anomaly?"

Izanami frowned. "That's just it. It was so brief, all they were able to see was a flash of exotic energy."

Michael brought the pallet to a stop. "You mean, Etheric energy?" he asked.

Izanami lifted her hands. "I meant what I said. I have no

classification available for what Loralei picked up. What are your orders, my Queen?"

Bethany Anne pressed her lips together. "Wait a moment. ADAM, can you shed any light on this?"

There was a pause before ADAM responded via the overhead speaker. "I see the anomaly in the logs. I'd put it down to a malfunction in Loralei's sensor suite since nothing else makes sense."

Bethany Anne hesitated before dismissing it. "You're sure that's all it is?"

"No one can be sure," ADAM admitted. "But since the only exotic energy source we know exists outside of our dimension is the Etheric, and it's definitely not Etheric energy Loralei picked up, I have to conclude that either Loralei is having an issue, or the laws of physics have suddenly failed and another reality has crossed ours. I know which one is more likely."

Bethany Anne relaxed a fraction. "True. Still, watch out for any more inexplicable readings that come in."

"I understand," ADAM promised. "Also, Michael, I have arranged for Eve to make space for us to work on the crystals. I am still somewhat tied up with the Collective project, but I can weigh in if TOM can't answer your questions."

Bethany Anne grinned. "Perfect. You'll be able to get started as soon as we're done visiting the children."

3

Devon, The Hexagon, Vid-doc Vault

Michael settled onto the couch next to Bethany Anne.

She slipped her hand into his while they waited for the children to be cycled down to their timeframe for the conversation.

"How do you think they are?" she asked, looking at Michael with a mixture of anticipation and dread.

Michael squeezed her fingers comfortingly. "They will be just fine." He searched her face for the reason she was worried. "You're still not entirely comfortable with this, are you?"

"I don't know," Bethany Anne told him with a sigh. "They're our babies, but they've spent more of their lives inside the Vid-docs than out here in the real world. I feel like..." Her voice trailed off as she struggled to put her thoughts into words. "I feel like our lives are too dangerous to have taken any other route. I just spend all my days missing them. It's jarring to see them grown so much between these calls."

"Imagine how Mahi' must feel," Michael consoled her. "She has nothing to prepare her for her son returning as an adult."

Bethany Anne pressed her lips together, appreciating Michael's attempt to lift her out of the sadness that came with being separated from her children.

The viewscreen came to life, signaling that Alexis and Gabriel were almost ready.

The sadness was replaced by amazement when the twins appeared on the screen a few moments later.

Bethany Anne only just managed not to curse. She put on a bright smile for the twins. "You finished the growth part of the process, I see. Look at you both!"

Gabriel rubbed his five o'clock shadow and grinned bashfully. "Aw, Mom."

Alexis flicked her waist-length braid to the side and returned an almost-identical smile. "You're okay with the change, right?" she asked.

Bethany Anne scrutinized her daughter's face. "You look just like me."

Alexis snickered. "Yeah, sure. Except for my freckles, which you promised me I'd lose before adulthood."

Bethany Anne shook her head. "One day, you'll have a daughter, and when she's crying to you about something she can't change, you'll understand why I lied."

"A white lie to spare your child's feelings isn't always a bad thing," Michael offered. "Imagine if we had told you about the Seven the moment you were able to understand?"

Alexis rolled her eyes, a wry smile touching her lips. "You and Mom would never be so irresponsible."

Gabriel snorted. "Yeah, Dad. We'd have had nightmares our whole lives."

Alexis flourished a hand. "I don't know. Remember the first time we saw Mom in her Baba Yaga disguise?"

Gabriel grinned. "Well, yeah. She kicked ass; it was awesome."

Alexis looked over at her brother. "Funny, because I remember you dreaming Baba Yaga was coming for you every time you did something you shouldn't for months afterward."

Bethany Anne was warmed by the normality of her children's bickering. "So, how are you getting on with the next stage of your training?" she asked, changing the subject. "I have to say I'm proud of you for not taking the easy option."

The twins flashed identical grins at her.

"Damn straight, it's not the easy option," Gabriel agreed, then winced. "Sorry for the language, Mom. It's kinda snuck in from being around so many military types."

Alexis sighed. "Yeah. You wouldn't believe how much cursing the specialists do. It's f— this, f— that. I'd be shocked if you hadn't been a bit slack about cursing when you thought we were out of earshot."

"Zenith is a good program," Gabriel told them. "You have to pass our thanks along to everyone who put effort into creating it. We're refining our knowledge of everything we learned with Aunt Addix at our own pace, and the testing phases are helping us both to realize our potential with our extra abilities."

"That's not all," Alexis agreed. "The opportunity to put what we're learning into practice without real-world consequences is invaluable. I mean, spending a couple of days in a sewer system wasn't a picnic, but we made good progress with team-building that we just can't get back home."

Gabriel nodded, but he was a bit wistful in his reply. "Yeah. We went into the Zenith scenario, having failed to bring most of our unit through with us. It wasn't our finest moment."

Alexis patted her brother's shoulder. "Gabriel's still sore about that. What he isn't telling you is that our unit had the highest pass rate coming out of the Corral scenario. The other units barely got one or two through. We learned our lesson. We're doing better to integrate the NPCs into a cohesive unit."

Gabriel leaned into his sister. "Alexis has taken up social engineering as a hobby."

Michael smiled, glad to hear that his main concern about the twins missing out on social time due to their unique upbringing was being addressed. "That's great," he enthused. "What about K'aia and Trey? Are they getting the most out of their experience?"

"Definitely!" Alexis exclaimed. "Although K'aia is as grumpy as always."

Bethany Anne and Michael listened to their stories about the situations they'd been in with the non-player characters they were building into a team. All too soon, it was time to say goodbye.

"I wish we didn't have to let you go," Bethany Anne apologized. "But I don't want you missing too much just so I can see your faces."

"It's cool," Gabriel assured her. "I'm glad to have this time."

Alexis nodded. "Yeah, Gabriel's right. It is good to have any time. I miss you both."

"Anyway," Gabriel added. "Don't you two have a war to win?"

"It's been pretty quiet since we got back from Qu'Baka," Bethany Anne told them. "The most exciting thing happening here is that the foundation of the new city for the Bakas is being printed today."

She blew them both a kiss. "Love you both. Be good, and if you can't, then don't get caught."

Devon, The Hexagon

Bethany Anne went to find Ashur and inform him of their trip after saying goodbye to Michael at Eve's sublevel.

From there, her first stop was Network Command to begin the search for Mahi'. She walked through one unoccupied corridor after another until she found Tabitha and a skeleton crew working in the NARCS room.

Tabitha grinned when she saw it was Bethany Anne who'd entered. "Hey! I was wondering when you were gonna get here. The kids are doing well, right? I inserted myself for a bit to check on them." She held up a hand to stay the concern coming from Bethany Anne. "Don't stress it. I disguised myself as one of their instructors. They had no idea it was me."

Bethany Anne doubted that. Tabitha was just too, well, *Tabitha* to be mistaken for anyone else. "They're progressing well, despite the interruption for Addix's funeral. If anything, I thought they'd be wrapped up in their grief."

"No way," Tabitha argued. "They're too focused on their goal of getting ready to join the war. Besides, they've got each other. As long as that's true, they can overcome anything." She smirked. "Special Forces training included."

Jacqueline turned from her monitor and grinned. "I helped with the research for that. K'aia's just going to *love* all the ass-in-seat time." She turned back to her monitor with a chuckle. "I'd feel sorry for them if I wasn't green with envy."

Bethany Anne walked over and placed her hand on Jacqueline's shoulder. "You could always take the course and get the experience you want."

Jacqueline considered the suggestion. "Seriously, I'd love to. But right now, I have something a little different going on with Mark. I'll be honest, it's exciting the hell out of us both."

Tabitha waved her hands. "Bethany Anne isn't here to hear about your VR fight club."

Bethany Anne's lips quirked. "Hold your horses, Tabitha. I might be. Is that the Hex Games I've heard about?" she asked Jacqueline with curiosity.

"The one my son is so obsessed with?" Tabitha added.

Jacqueline broke into a grin. "You know it. We lost a shitload of revenue when this war put a stop to us using the arenas for live events." She shrugged at Bethany Anne's frown. "Giving up the space was the right thing to do. Moving the entertainment parts of the business into the Vid-doc rec and training system made it easier for us to keep track of who's subscribing to what services."

She rummaged in a drawer and came out with a pair of orange-tinted wraparound glasses. "Mark came up with these. We developed them from an old piece of tech Sabine found in the archives while she was searching for Ashur's imaginary space rats. They're basic, and viewing is free, so we're not pricing anyone out."

Bethany Anne put the glasses on and was treated to immediate immersion in the crowd, who were cheering on a cage match between a team of Guardians in Were form and three Bakas armed with the new staffs. She smelled beer and pretzels in the crowd, along with sweat and blood from the cage.

She took in the reality of the sensory bombardment for a moment before handing the glasses back to Jacqueline. "How are you generating revenue from this if viewing is free?"

Jacqueline waved the glasses off. "Keep those if you don't already have a pair. Participation in the fights requires registration to one of the tiered subscription options. We have the Vid-doc suites set up like Japanese capsule hotels to maximize the space we haven't repurposed for military training."

"You know you kids saved the day when you gave us this building," Bethany Anne told her. "Devon appreciates it, as do Michael and I."

Jacqueline smirked. "Oh, we know how grateful everyone is, but it was the only thing to do other than waste time building a place down here to train everyone. Besides, we're making enough money from the games to keep the expansion rolling. We're even sponsoring a number of teams in the league, and we're allowing corporate sponsorship of other teams—for a fee. That way, we can afford to run the entertainments on a free-to-view basis."

"There's a league?" Tabitha asked. She shook her head as Jacqueline pulled up the league tables. "Of *course*, there's a league."

"It keeps the majority of the people here from getting into the seedy side of things," Jacqueline explained.

Tabitha snorted. "Oh, there's still plenty of that on Devon if you know where to look for it. The difference is that Ricole and her interns have created a regulatory body to make sure anyone working in the adult clubs is there of their own free will."

Bethany Anne nodded. "It makes sense to protect the workers. The important thing is that the people working those kinds of jobs are protected and that they have access to advocates when things don't play out fairly for them."

Jacqueline blushed with pride, remembering a time back on Earth when she had been forced into a similar position they'd found the majority of entertainment workers in when they'd arrived on the planet. "We've gone a long way toward making sure Devon keeps its freedoms while people are able to earn a living with dignity no matter what job they choose to do."

Tabitha snickered. "I've seen a few people lose their dignity in those fights. Usually after running their mouths a bit too long on the way into the ring."

Bethany Anne smiled as she pocketed the glasses. "Guess they deserve what they get if they can't walk the talk." She smiled her approval of the systems to keep her hard workers playing hard on their own time. "Whatever you're doing, it's keeping morale high. You kids have done a great job replacing the seedy shit people here used to do for release."

Bethany Anne made a mental note to investigate the range of the system at a later date. She had the germ of an idea forming. "Remind me to talk to you about Halloween. We might be able to set up some kind of reward for the players."

"Halloween?" Jacqueline echoed. "I think I've heard of that. It sounds familiar, anyway. Something to do with getting scared. Little kids used to put on costumes and go door to door to get candy?"

Bethany Anne broke out laughing. "Looks like you remember it just fine. The older ones would visit a haunted house or something."

Tabitha waved her hands in excitement. "I think I know where you're going with this."

Bethany Anne's mouth turned up at the corner. "I'll bet you don't." She shrugged at Tabitha's inquisitive glance. "You'll have to just wait and see. What progress are you making on finding out who is sabotaging the building?"

"Oh, shit! I almost forgot." Tabitha turned and started typing on the main console. She huffed when the file she was looking for proved difficult to locate. "I wish to hell I could just pull stuff up with a thought. We have an image at last."

Bethany Anne raised an eyebrow at the empty kitchen on the screen. "What am I looking at?"

"This is Tina's apartment on sublevel one." Tabitha zoomed in on a gap in the baseboard. "There, see the foot? It's small, but it's definitely there."

Bethany Anne narrowed her eyes when she saw it. "I recognize that skin tone. There aren't too many twelve-inch-tall shocking-blue aliens around."

Tabitha frowned at Bethany Anne curiously. "You know the owner of that foot?"

Bethany Anne wrinkled her nose. "Not personally. We broke a small group of them out of the prison at the factory, but they disappeared. I didn't think the little guys made it. You think they're responsible for the damage to CEREBRO?"

"Ashur's space rats are real?" Jacqueline couldn't figure out why she hadn't smelled them. "I can't believe it. Wait until Sabine finds out they weren't rats after all."

Tabitha pressed a key, and the next image appeared. "This is from inside that cabinet. The bite marks in the pans match the ones found in Clarence's cradle exactly, plus the same mystery of CEREBRO not registering any lifeform present when the image was taken."

"I'd say that all adds up to a conclusion," Jacqueline chipped in without looking away from her screen. "It's a damned mystery why none of us can track their scent."

Bethany Anne connected the dots just before ADAM spoke.

>>**Are these beings the missing link Jean's been looking for? The Bl'kheth?**<<

You read my mind. Did you locate Mahi'?

>>**She's at the New Citadel site. They're laying the city's foundations today.**<<

Bethany Anne winced. "Fucksticks. I knew something had slipped my mind."

Tabitha chuckled. "What did you forget?"

Bethany Anne headed for the door. "Construction on the new city is starting today. I told Mahi' I'd be there to say a few words. I have to run."

"What do I do about the aliens?" Tabitha called after her.

Bethany Anne waved a hand over her shoulder. "Make contact if you can, and don't hurt them. Find some food for them that *isn't* wired into the Hexagon's systems."

She cut through the Etheric to the underground hangar and found a transport Pod that wasn't in use, then opened her link to Michael. *You should talk to Tabitha. The saboteurs inside the Hexagon turned out to be those little blue guys we thought we lost.*

The ones from the factory? Michael replied. *I thought they vanished while we were getting all the prisoners out?*

Yeah, me too. Bethany Anne finished setting her destination in the Pod's navigation system and sat back with her hands laced behind her head. *Looks like we were wrong. They somehow got aboard the* Izanami, *and now they're running loose inside the Hexagon.*

I'll keep my senses peeled for the little buggers, Michael told her.

No point, Bethany Anne countered. *They don't register as lifeforms to any of the digital entities, and the Weres can't track them by scent. Michael, they have to be the Bl'kheth. Don't you think? ADAM suggested they might be the missing link we've been searching for to explain how the Seven are able to bypass the issues with metal in the Etheric.*

Michael paused to consider the information before answering. *Do you agree?*

They're the same bright blue as the Ooken, they appear to

eat metal, and they can get around undetected. I think we've found them. I've got Tabitha trying to make contact with them. Do you have any ideas to help her?

Here's hoping they aren't the last of their kind, Michael murmured. *I'll get on it as soon as William gets back from the Citadel site.*

Bethany Anne saw the dark, shadowed rings of the proposed city's layout cut into the ground below. *I'm about to touch down there now. I'll light a fire under him once they're done with the printing process.*

Mahi' was nowhere to be seen when Bethany Anne landed the transport Pod in between the temporary Baka settlement and the heavy machinery that was there to build the city.

When Bethany Anne left the Pod, no one was around, so she walked over to the settlement's edge to check the prefabricated planning office. She found Mahi' inside with William and Marcus. "No Bobcat?" she asked in greeting.

Mahi' looked up and smiled. "You made it."

"I cut it close," Bethany Anne conceded, stepping inside. "It's like, the more I have to do in a day, the more surprises bite me in the ass."

Mahi' chuckled dryly. "I hear that."

William waved vaguely in the direction of the construction site. "Bobcat has taken it upon himself to assist the printing machine operators. You'll probably find him riding one of the permacrete printers like it's Saturday night at a roadhouse and he's had three too many beers to be looking at a mechanical bull, let alone riding one."

Bethany Anne chuckled at the image of her irascible engineer getting tossed around while trying to keep his seat. "I didn't know there was such a thing as too many beers when it came to Bobcat. Do you need to be here for the printing? Michael needs you back at the Hexagon as soon as you can get there."

William looked at Marcus. "Everything is good to go, right?"

Marcus put his stylus down by his datapad. "Yes. All the foundations have been dug out. The pipes and wiring have been laid. All that remains is to 'print' the city proper, starting with the foundations. Then the construction workers can put in the electricity and plumbing and the Bakas can make the finishing touches to their homes and businesses before they move in."

Bethany Anne jerked a thumb over her shoulder toward the door. "Then I guess you're needed more back at the Hexagon."

William got to his feet and collected his belongings, tossing an empty beer can into the trash near him. "Then I guess I'd better get back there and see what Michael needs." He grinned as he pocketed his datapad. "Guarantee it's going to be interesting."

Bethany Anne returned his grin with a warm smile. "Between finding the untraceable aliens and figuring out what's on those memory crystals, I think you'll be entertained for a while."

Marcus glanced up with a pout. "Don't I get an invite to the fun?"

"No, you do *not*, Doctor Cambridge," the stern reply came from the holoscreen Mahi' was using. "You are the only one on-site who can keep up with the printing schedule. Unless you want to ask Tina to take over?"

"Have you ever tried to get my wife's attention while she's mid-project?" Marcus replied distractedly, his eyes on his screens. He furrowed his brow at something he saw and hunched over his keyboard to type. "I'll be fine here."

"We should get started." Mahi' turned her screen to show an impatient-looking Qui'nan and flashed Bethany Anne a wry smile. "The fore-Yollin is ready to begin."

Bethany Anne and Mahi' left the office and made their way to the edge of the construction site, where the operators hung around the bases of the behemoth printing machines.

Bobcat extracted himself from the group and made his way over to Bethany Anne. "Hey, boss! We good to go?"

Bethany Anne looked around, trusting her instincts to inform her of any subconscious worries. When none appeared, she replied, "We are."

Mahi' picked up her datapad and transferred the call to it with a couple of taps on the screen. "Qui'nan says yes."

"Qui'nan would prefer it if you kept the camera still," the Yollin called irritably. "My Queen, stage one is complete. The printing stage may commence."

Bethany Anne's mouth turned up at the corner. "Thank you, Qui'nan."

"This way," Bobcat directed, indicating the space between two of the gigantic printers. "I've got you covered."

Bethany Anne and Mahi' followed Bobcat to the other side of the machinery, where a mixed group of humans and Bakas wearing hi-vis vests were gathered around a podium at the edge of the outermost ditch.

Bethany Anne couldn't miss the slight limp Mahi'

walked with. "I get that you want to honor Addix, but isn't there a less painful way for you to do it than suffering with a prosthetic for the rest of your life?"

Mahi' shook her head firmly. "This is my choice. Besides, I am assured that the discomfort will pass when the ghost of my leg gives up and accepts that it is no longer a part of my body."

Bobcat glanced at Mahi' with wide eyes. "I think that's crazy, but then so does everyone I try selling the merits of a mostly-beer diet. Each to their own, that's what I say." He indicated the waiting group with a hand. "These are the people responsible for the non-printable part of the build. Bethany Anne, you can see I put up a ribbon."

Mahi' tilted her head in curiosity at the six-foot ribbon stretched between two posts by the side of the podium. "What is the purpose of the ribbon?"

Bethany Anne chuckled. "We cut it before commencing. It's an old Earth custom, usually to mark the opening of something."

"It's a symbol of unity," Bobcat clarified, pointing up at the camera drone overhead. "You cut the ribbon together, then I send the footage to Mark, and he'll edit it and send it out across the holonetwork after *Devon's Defenders* tonight."

Bethany Anne inclined her head. "Nice touch. I like involving the whole planet in what's going on. No time like the present to get started." She walked to the podium and stepped up to take the microphone.

Mahi' joined her a second later as the crowd began to grow, filled out by the Bakas living in the settlement. "Did you prepare anything?"

Bethany Anne's eyebrow went up. "I only remembered this was happening today ten minutes before I left the Hexagon," she admitted in a low voice only Mahi' could hear. "I don't need to know what I'm going to say. I need to explain how *I feel.*"

Mahi' gave Bethany Anne a pertinent look. "I had some time while I was in the medical unit."

"Then by all means, go first," Bethany Anne whispered as she stepped back.

Mahi' shrugged and limped up the two steps to join Bethany Anne at the microphone. She looked out across the faces in front of her. For a moment, she blanked on what she was going to say.

Thankfully, it was only a second before the first words started flowing from her lips. "My people. My heart swells with pride to see so many of you here on Devon. The Kurtherians tried to break us, but we cannot be broken." She shifted to lean on the podium. "We have been tested in the fire, and we've proven we are greater than the evil who would divide us. Qu'Baka may be gone but we...WE live *on*, reunited against all odds. We are Bakas, and we are *strong!*" She raised her hands to quiet the cheer that came from the Bakas.

She smiled and stepped back to allow Bethany Anne to address the crowd.

She cleared her throat, and the workers dropped their conversations to pay attention. "I can't replace your history or the loved ones you lost when Qu'Baka fell, but I can make sure you all have a place to live and raise your children in safety."

She paused a beat to give her emotions a moment to

settle. "I know you to be a proud people. A people who do not take a slight without answering it. I appreciate your commitment to living with *honor*. Learn from your cousins who have lived on Devon this past decade how to remain true to that without breaking my laws, and I will make a promise. There will be prosperity for those who work for the greater good of all. There will be *peace*."

Bethany Anne smiled, her eyes turning red. Many in the audience felt, more than saw, Baba Yaga's invisible presence beside her at the podium. "Lastly, there will be a place in my military for any of you who care to *personally take up their grievances with the Seven*."

A roar went up from the crowd, the reaction mirrored by the Bakas still inside the settlement as the news filtered back to them.

Bethany Anne picked up the oversized scissors Bobcat had placed behind the podium and held them out to point at the footprint of the new city. "This city represents both your past *and* your future, as well as the courage and strength you have shown despite oppression and then dispossession. Here you are welcome. This is your home now."

She and Mahi' stepped down from the podium and cut the ribbon together.

Bethany Anne smiled at the cameras. "I declare New Citadel to be founded."

After a moment of cheering, the crowds dispersed to get back to work.

Mahi' walked back to the transport Pod with Bethany Anne. "I can't thank you enough for everything you have done for my people."

Bethany Anne shook her head. "It's what anyone would have done in my position. I have more power than most people can comprehend. It's my duty to use it to remove the cancers that fester in the universe."

A low rumble sounded from Mahi'. "The *Seven*."

"The Seven," Bethany Anne agreed in a similar tone. "We've made some progress in identifying their main player. We have a name, as a start."

Mahi' grimaced. "I thought of the Seven as separate groups with competing purposes," she admitted. "If there's a Kurtherian who is powerful enough to control all of the clans, where does that leave us?"

Bethany Anne kicked the dirt. "It leaves us with an enemy who can tear the fabric of reality and destroy whole worlds. It also leaves me angry as all fuck that I haven't already found the bastards to rip their faces off and spit down their necks as payback for fucking with the natural order of things."

Mahi' looked to the side, her lips pressed together. "It pisses me off to know there are Bakas being held in those factories." She looked at Bethany Anne. "Did I tell you I've had a chance to meet the Collectives staying beneath the Hexagon?"

Bethany Anne thought for a second. "No."

"I have, and it pains me to know those sweet and noble beings are being ground up and used to make the Ookens," she finished.

Bethany Anne let out a long and measured breath. "I know." She paused by the transport Pod. "All I need is Federation support and we can take them out."

"Why wait?" Mahi' asked hotly. "You can take out the

factories with a wave of your hand. My warriors will be more than happy to mete out Justice in your name."

Bethany Anne smiled ruefully. "Yeah, but there are over a hundred factories, and unless I can take out every factory at the same time, I'm stuck with finding a more conventional route to their destruction."

Mahi' looked dejected at the news, her rage at the injustice of the universe having to simmer for a time. "I can't say that I'm happy about it, but I understand."

Bethany Anne placed a hand on her forearm. "Being a leader is restrictive."

Mahi' nodded. "We can't act freely when we're affected by the hurts of our people. We have to watch and wait until the time is right."

Bethany Anne offered her friend a dark smile. "But when the time is right, *nothing* is going to stand in our way."

4

Devon, The Interdiction, QBS *Wolfstar*

"Bethany Anne!" Ashur's tail went into overdrive when
Bethany Anne stepped out of the Etheric onto the bridge.
He leapt down from his station and bounded over to
greet her.

Bethany Anne sidestepped to avoid a canine collision,
then knelt and held out her arms to offer him a scratch.
"Hey, furball. Ready for a road trip?"

Ashur's tail's pace kicked up a notch as he leaned into
her ministrations. "Absolutely. It's going to be good. Just
you, me, and open space."

Bethany Anne buried her face in the thick fur of
Ashur's neck and inhaled his comforting dog smell while
continuing to fuss over him. "I'm glad you decided to stick
around until I got back from Qu'Baka. You've been gone
for too long. I bet Zeus and Athena are huge now."

"Zeus is going to be at least as large as me," Ashur told
her with pride. He remembered that he was a canine with
dignity who did not roll over and ask for belly rubs and

settled for pressing his head into the hollow of Bethany Anne's neck instead. "Those pups are going to be the death of me. Bellatrix insists their ability to walk the Etheric has encouraged them to be reckless."

Bethany Anne chuckled, turning her attention to the underside of Ashur's jaw. "Bellatrix is Bellatrix. Sounds to me like she doesn't know how to deal when she's not in control. Maybe telling her no once in a while would do her good."

"Are you crazy?" Ashur yelped. "I like my balls right where they are, thank you very much."

Bethany Anne smirked. "Your choice. Did she like the ship, at least?"

Ashur tipped his head back to give Bethany Anne access to the tender spot on his lower jaw. "Yes. Or at least, she didn't complain more than twenty times while Soren was showing us around. She left with Yelena this morning. We're both glad for some time with our humans."

Bethany Anne gave him one last scratch behind the ears as she got to her feet. "Your human is glad to get some time with you, too." She crossed the grass that covered the bridge floor and inspected the adapted layout with curiosity, her fingers trailing over the squeaky toys embedded in the console of the station Ashur had vacated. "I'm dying to see how all this works." She turned to him. "Want to give me the rundown?"

"Sure," Ashur chuffed. "I was hoping you'd have time before the Qu'Baka mission, but you left pretty quickly after the gala."

He leapt onto the raised plinth set into the front of the console and nosed the blue ball in the center of the control panel to deactivate the accidental touch lock. "It shouldn't be too difficult. Everything here is designed to be used by dogs." He paused to point his nose at one station. "Except for the one that is built for bipeds. As you can see, the ship is not designed for anyone much taller than a large human."

Bethany Anne took a seat in the human-shaped chair and glanced over her console. "This looks pretty standard. I see the navigation controls are set into the console. There aren't any holoHUDs?"

Ashur shook his head. "Jean said there's too much difference in the way our canine brains work to make them user-friendly for us. She came up with this instead." He demonstrated by pawing one of the squeaky toys to activate the navigation system. "These are all replicas of our favorite toys. The only thing different is the scent. We have navigation and weapons control, and we have our neural connection to the ship's EI to take care of the complicated stuff." He looked at her. Perhaps thinking about his fight with the vampires back on Earth when he came running into a park with a strange woman slicing up what looked like zombies in Costa Rica. "I'm a lucky dog."

Bethany Anne smiled in amusement at Ashur's enthusiasm for her gift. "You've been a loyal companion. I wanted you and your family to have the means to travel without needing to depend on someone going your way."

Ashur's tail thumped on the padded plinth. "I was happy to keep hitching, but Bellatrix was impressed with the attention to detail, and if Bellatrix is happy, then so am I."

Bethany Anne crossed one leg over the other, getting

comfortable for the ride when a thought occurred to her. "There are human-friendly bathrooms on this ship, right?"

Ashur broke into chuffs, his amusement evident.

"Yes, Bethany Anne. There are bathrooms."

Devon, The Hexagon, Eve's Sublevel

William arrived after getting turned around in Eve's maze twice before finding the main lab and getting directions from Tina.

It had warmed his heart to hear Tina was making progress with the project that'd had her tearing her hair out for the last couple of months. He just hoped that whatever project Michael had for him wasn't going to be as impossible as deciphering the part of the human brain that needed to be active while the human in question was speaking to the Collectives.

Michael looked up from the counter where he was working and closed his holoscreen when William knocked softly on the doorframe. "Excellent timing. Come in."

William took in the air of frustration, the scattered lenses and other components, and the slight red glow to Michael's eyes. "I got here a moment too soon by my guess. Now I'm going to have work to do instead of just picking up the destroyed pieces."

"Your timing was fortuitous."

William eyed the components in front of Michael. "What are we attempting to do?"

Michael indicated the jumble of components with a sharp wave. "We're turning this into a reader for the Kurtherian crystals Bethany Anne and I recovered from

Qu'Baka. The problem is, I don't know what I'm doing with this mess."

TOM's voice issued from the speaker. "I did offer to help."

Michael's eyes flared red. "I wouldn't call letting you take control of my body so you can build the device 'help.'"

William laughed. "You're kidding. TOM, you ought to know Michael better than that by now." He picked up one of the memory crystals and held it up to the light to examine it. "Bethany Anne mentioned something about Kurtherian tech. These are them?"

"Yes." Michael cast a baleful glance at the organized chaos on the bench. "We acquired a large number of Kurtherian memory crystals on Qu'Baka that we have no easy way of reading. I need a device that will read the contents of each crystal and upload the information to a secure database for sorting. One that doesn't take the equivalent power input of the *Baba Yaga's* hard-light projection drive to run."

William sat down opposite Michael and rubbed his chin as he examined the other crystal without touching it. "Bethany Anne mentioned something about crystals. You successfully read one with the *Baba Yaga's* HLP?"

Michael pointed to the unlocked crystal he'd placed separate from the other. "That one contained more data than we could easily process."

William nodded thoughtfully. "But you're working through it, right?"

"Yes," Michael replied. "We have so far identified the owner as a Kurtherian named Gödel, although I highly doubt that is their real name. In addition, we found extensive records of this Kurtherian's holdings, including the locations of many more Ooken factories."

His voice trailed off. He felt a sense of failure about their inability to immediately right the wrongs being done to the prisoners in those factories. "This is a house of cards, William. We cannot move on Gödel until we have the upper hand. I find myself in a similar situation to the time before I found Bethany Anne. The number of tasks we must complete before we can act is somewhat overwhelming at this moment."

"Well, there's always tomorrow, and the day after that." William offered Michael a small smile. "This crystal conundrum might be a sonofabitch to crack, but we know it *can* be done. The question is, how." He tapped a finger on his lips for a moment while he thought. "Hmm, seems to me like we could condense the HLP drive's functions with the power source from…" He looked at the components, shaking his head as he mentally rejected the various batteries and such Michael had gathered. "What are you and BA packing these days? You have a JDS with you?"

"I do." Michael reached behind him, removing a Jean Dukes Special from its holster on the small of his back. He deactivated the security measures before handing it to William. "Just be careful. Knowing Jean, she put something in the workings that bites just as hard as what she put in the grips."

William snorted as he accepted the weapon. "Teach your grandmother to suck eggs, why don't you?" He unloaded the cartridge, then stripped the pistol down and expertly eased out the power pack. "Give me a little while, and I'll have something that should do the trick."

Michael nodded and reopened his holoscreen. "Thank you. That should give me time to scour the security footage Tabitha sent. We know now that the saboteurs are hungry Bl'kheths in need of our help."

William grinned as he got to work and started choosing from the piles of components on the workbench. "It's me who should thank you. You saved me a whole lot of sitting around with my thumb in my ass. The new city is exciting and all, but the construction is out of my hands now and firmly with Marcus and the construction crew."

He glanced at Michael's assembly of tools, then twisted to look around the room. "You got a micro-soldering kit here?"

Michael indicated a door to the rear of the room. "If I didn't already get it out, then you'll find it in the tool closet."

William got up and went into the storage room. He glanced at the tall racks holding various power tools and the wall hung with plastic-wrapped toolkits marked for different tasks and let out a whistle.

"Eve didn't skimp on getting this place fitted out," he called as he scanned the neatly printed labels to find the tool he was looking for. He grabbed the soldering kit, plus a few extras, and returned to the workroom.

Michael offered a small smile as William emerged with his haul. "Yes, well. Eve isn't one for half measures."

William chuckled as he laid out the tools and began to sort through the various components he thought were best suited to build the reader. "You don't have to tell me."

They worked in companionable silence for a while,

William exchanging a few words here and there with TOM as necessary.

Michael flicked through screen after screen, searching for any clue as to where the Bl'kheths were hidden. While he found plenty of evidence of their presence, he could see no sign that they had created a habitat *anywhere* within the Hexagon.

William's deft fingers danced as he put together two test devices based on the design of the hard light projector and connected them wirelessly to a cordoned-off space in the lab's computer network.

Michael paused the playback on his screen when William cleared his throat softly to get his attention. "We ready to get started?" he asked.

William put his screwdriver down. "We are." He grabbed a small cube and lifted it up, eyebrow raised. "You want to do the honors?" He handed one of the devices to Michael and connected it to the power pack. "We keep the power separate so I can pull it if anything goes wrong. I can't see Eve being very happy if we blow the lab up."

Michael turned the small cube over in his hands, taking care not to pull the connector cable as he examined the reader. "How does this work?"

"Press there." William pointed to a button. "Then put the crystal in the tray that pops out."

Michael picked up the crystal that had already been accessed and loaded it into the reader. "Okay, now what?"

He almost dropped the device when it began to thrum in his hands. "What the..."

William chuckled, amused. "It's fine. Give the mini-HLP a second to warm up."

Michael's eyes widened when the top of the reader opened and a beam of light erupted from it. He blinked to clear the spots from his vision as the familiar documents were birthed from the beam. "Good work."

William didn't respond. He was too caught up in reading the computer's analysis of the windows that were still emerging from the reader.

"Michael to William," Michael waved a hand in front of William's face, catching his attention. "How do I switch it off?"

William smiled bashfully. "Sorry. It's not every day you get to see what's worth keeping to a Kurtherian." He pointed to the side of the device. "That button there."

Michael grinned as the light was spooled back into the reader. "I know. Which is why I want to try the next crystal. ADAM has everything from this crystal already. We have a few hundred more to read."

William's eyes widened. "For real? How did you even get your hands on them? Seems to me like something that valuable would be hidden where nobody could get to it."

Michael shrugged. "It is a matter of perspective. An underground hideout would be the natural choice for someone without the ability to travel the Etheric, like the previous owner of these crystals. For Bethany Anne and me, it was simple to find, despite the room having no entry points."

He loaded the next crystal into the reader. "We have this opportunity to get inside the head of our enemy, and I for one am not going to waste a second of it."

The tray retracted, and the reader thrummed again as it started the data extraction process.

William heard the difference in the vibration frequency. "Drop it!" He yanked the connector cable out of the power pack as he yelled.

Michael cast the reader onto the table just before the device imploded in a cloud of smoke and flames.

William grabbed the fire extinguisher from the wall and doused the reader in CO_2 before the entire table went up in flames. "Can't say I was expecting that," he choked out through his coughing, waving a hand in front of him. "There must have been a malfunction somewhere in the crystal."

Michael waved the acrid smoke away. "What the hell was that?"

William gingerly poked through the melting plastic with the end of his screwdriver and retrieved the crystal. He furrowed his brow when he saw that the crystal was undamaged. "Huh. Maybe it's the reader."

"Then it's a good thing you made a spare," Michael soothed him, seeing William's downcast expression. "There's a chance it was just an error in the programming, right? So we don't give up."

William nodded as he considered the reasons for the reader's failure. "It might not make a difference, and that's engineering for you. Wait a minute while I set the other reader up so we can test whether it's the programming, an error with what I built, or something else entirely."

He connected the second reader to the power pack, then placed them on one of the fireproof mats in the testing area. "Either way, I don't want a lab fire. Let me grab that crystal again."

Michael walked over with the crystal. "Do you expect this reader to fail also?"

William shrugged. "Maybe. Could be that the other was only good for one use, and this will work just fine." He loaded the crystal and stood back as the tray retracted. "Or it could be that this crystal is protected in a way the other crystal wasn't."

FOOOMSH!

Michael got in with the fire extinguisher when the second reader emitted a high-pitched whine and burst into flames. "I guess it's not the reader," he grumbled as he sprayed the testing area to douse the flames.

William retrieved the crystal from the melted mess on the mat. "I guess not. I'm going to venture that this crystal is encrypted in some way we haven't come across before. It's okay; just means we have to keep trying to hack it."

Michael was distracted from further conjecture by Bethany Anne's appearance on the wallscreen. He eyed his wife. "You have a knack for calling at the moments I'm having a setback."

Her smile lit the room. "Maybe I'm developing psychic powers. How's it going with the crystals?"

Michael sighed and indicated the catastrophe in the testing area with a hand. "Slowly, since the crystal we tested blew both of William's readers up."

"Curious." Bethany Anne tilted her head. "Do you know why?"

"It just blew them up," Michael answered.

"'It just blew them up?'" Bethany Anne repeated. "Would you care to expand on that stunningly efficient analysis?"

Michael shot her a dark look. "I'm not technical. That was why I hired people."

"What he is saying is," TOM broke in, "the defenses of the crystals ended up melting our tech as a way to stop it from attacking them. We need a firewall a bit farther out from the computers doing the testing."

"What he said," Michael finished. "We'll keep working on it. How are you enjoying your time with Ashur?"

Ashur's head popped into view, his tongue hanging out as he panted.

"What's Ashur saying?" William asked.

"I said," Ashur repeated. "Give me a second to connect my translation software to the link. You like my ship?"

Bethany Anne grinned as the camera shifted away from her and slowly panned the bridge. "Crazy, right? You have to experience this."

Michael smiled, momentarily cheered up by Bethany Anne's amusement. "The main thing is that *you're* enjoying yourself. Did you make it to the *3PO* yet?"

"We've just gotten to QT2," Bethany Anne replied. "Keep me informed of your progress. I'll check in after I'm done here."

She cut the link, and the screen returned to its blank state.

"I don't know how you get away with that," William marveled. He gathered the tools and took them back to the storage room, calling back as he went, "Baiting Bethany Anne is like fly-fishing for dragons. How do you keep your nerve?"

Michael shrugged. "Nothing to it. You cast out your bait and hope to hell nothing bites."

"Yeah, well, I don't want to get bitten for not solving this fast enough for Bethany Anne's liking." William returned from the storage room and headed for the door. "I'm going to have to go get some things from my workshop. I'll be back the day after tomorrow."

"Gabrielle is with Eric on High Tortuga at the moment," Michael informed him. "They took the *Revolution*."

William raised an eyebrow as a thought occurred to him. "You think she'll let me borrow the *Cambridge*? I could bring a few more things to Devon with a ship that size."

"Why do I get the feeling that you won't be back any faster for being able to avoid the Gate system?" Michael asked with a wry smile.

"What can I say?" William lifted his hands. "It's been nothing but a pain in the ass running between here and High Tortuga every other week. Besides that, my apartment here is just bare bones. I'm thinking some home comforts wouldn't go amiss."

Michael grinned. "I agree. A man needs his comforts." He lifted a hand in farewell as William exited the lab. "See you the day after tomorrow, then."

5

QT2, QBS *Wolfstar*, Bridge

Bethany Anne cut the link to Michael as the QBBS *Helena* grew larger on the viewscreen.

Ashur pawed his console when CEREBRO connected, and the minefield parted to admit the *Wolfstar* into the system.

Ashur nosed Bethany Anne's hand as the ship bypassed the *Helena* and glided toward the outer defenses. "Why are we visiting the asteroid first?"

Bethany Anne smiled and patted Ashur's head. "I want to see how the ruby project is progressing. We have approximately two hundred thousand Bakas to arm and Anne's synthetic rubies are what power the new-model staffs, so I want to be sure the team working on producing them has everything running smoothly."

Ashur whined at the mention of Anne, his ears flattening against his skull.

Bethany Anne fussed his head again. "You're thinking about Jinx and Dio, huh?"

"Always," Ashur chuffed in reply, his inner voice sad but determined. "But we have this ship now. Bellatrix and I will find them. Anne, too."

Bethany Anne caught the jumbled images in Ashur's mind. Tears stung her eyes as she relived the moment they had realized Anne and the puppies were gone. "This is all my fault. If I hadn't taken the *Shinigami*..." Her voice trailed off, and she sighed regretfully. "They would be here now."

"No," Ashur denied hotly. "I don't care what Bellatrix thinks. You are *not* responsible for what happened to them. Jinx knew better than to allow his human to behave recklessly. I know better than to let mine carry the blame for an accident."

Bethany Anne shook her head. "It doesn't matter if it was an accident. I don't blame Bellatrix for choosing to raise Zeus and Athena in Yelena's home instead of with Alexis and Gabriel."

"I would have preferred them to be raised with Alexis and Gabriel," Ashur admitted. "But there's no point in arguing with Bellatrix once her mind is made up."

One of the squeaky toys on Ashur's console lit up.

"We have an incoming call." He pawed the lighted squeaky, and the screen showed Lance and Barnabas.

Bethany Anne smiled at them. "I wasn't expecting to see you two here. Why aren't you on High Tortuga?"

"I have Stephen taking care of High Tortuga in my absence," Barnabas explained with a soft smile. "I decided it was time to catch up with everyone here before returning."

Lance's face was more serious. "I didn't want to leave it that long before speaking to you. I'm getting a hell of a lot of pressure from the council to answer for your appearance at the mining outpost fuckup, and Harkkat is making it worse to cover his own ass."

Bethany Anne raised an eyebrow at the mention of the Leath trade secretary. "I'm on my way." She cut the link and turned to Ashur with a smile. "You heard him. Take us around, Captain. The *3PO* will have to wait."

Ashur made the course correction to bring the *Wolfstar* back around to dock at the *Helena*. Bethany Anne and Ashur debarked and took a roamer from the charging station nearest their dock, leaving the ship in the capable hands of the crew to make their way from the docking spar to the upper concourse.

Ashur was put out by the seating arrangement in the roamer. "I don't see why these vehicles can't be better designed for the four-legged," he complained. "I mean, would a wider cushion be amiss?"

Bethany Anne rolled her eyes. "You sound as whiny as Bellatrix, furball. Maybe you've had too much comfort, and you're getting soft." She sat back and made herself comfortable. "Suck it up, buttercup."

Ashur sniffed. "You *would* say that. Your ass is taken care of." Nevertheless, he did not complain again. He curled up on the narrow seat and tucked his head in for a nap. "Wake me up when we get there."

Lance and Barnabas were waiting when they arrived on the upper concourse.

Ashur woke in an instant and was first out of the roamer, his ears pricked and his nose high to sniff out any danger. "It's safe," he called. "You can come out now."

Bethany Anne strolled past him and made straight for

Lance. "Good to see you again, Dad. Barnabas." She eyed them. "This is becoming a habit, don't you think?"

Lance returned Bethany Anne's hug with feeling. "You can't blame a man for being glad to spend time with his daughter." He scrunched his nose. "Political nightmares aside."

Barnabas chuckled dryly. "Wouldn't you know it? It only took an intergalactic war to bring us back together."

Bethany Anne raised an eyebrow, smiling at Barnabas' dry commentary. "You know how it is," she told him with a flourish of her hand. "Weddings, funerals, and other species' fuckups are about the only events important enough to give everyone a reason to be away from their duty."

"Here's to the Leath, then," Lance stated, his face set in solemn lines. "May they keep fucking up, because I sure as hell don't want to attend another funeral."

"What about a wedding?" Bethany Anne countered speculatively. "Nickie and Rickie are getting awfully attached to each other. Any chance of them getting hitched?"

Barnabas almost choked on his laughter. "I can't see Nickie sitting still long enough to settle down, not even if Rickie begged her to. She left without so much as a 'see you soon' after the rift battle, and she's been over on the other side of the Interdiction since."

"She needs to get her ass back here soon. I have plans that involve her." Bethany Anne was prevented from digging into Barnabas' news by the Collective calling for her.

Ashur's ears twitched. "There are Collectives here?"

"Eight of them." Bethany Anne sent her apology into the mindspace and received understanding in return from the Conduit. "Normally I'd visit the Collectives as soon as I arrived, but we have more urgent things to do right now."

"There's an issue with communication?" Barnabas inquired.

Bethany Anne nodded. "They're limited to contact with people who have mental communication abilities."

Barnabas smiled, his eyes unfocused as he tuned into the call in the mindspace. "Interesting. I would like to get to know these beings before I leave."

Ashur's tail beat a hurricane, the thwapping on the floor sounding like someone slamming cane on a bed over and over. "I want to go visit them. I miss the Collectives I know from Devon."

Bethany Anne frowned. "I thought you were helping Eve? You know, with communication with them?"

Ashur rolled his eyes. "I was...until last week when Demon claimed the sublevels as her territory. I can't go down there without that male of hers getting catty with me." He snorted with temper. "I don't know why Eve allows those cats in her lab. It's not like they're useful. All Demon does is lounge around and eat, and that male is a complete pain in the butt."

Bethany Anne patted Ashur's neck in sympathy. "This argument is as old as cats and dogs. Don't let them bother you."

"That's easy for you to say," Ashur grumbled. "You don't have to deal with being persecuted by those felines."

"Why don't we visit the Collectives together?" Barnabas

offered. He glanced at Bethany Anne and Lance. "You don't need me for this meeting, do you?"

"No," Lance answered. "I can catch you up on the discussion on the way back to High Tortuga."

"Go ahead," Bethany Anne told Ashur. "Just be back before I'm ready to leave."

Bethany Anne watched Ashur and Barnabas leave, then threaded her arm through her father's. "Do you want to do this over food?"

Lance smiled and squeezed Bethany Anne's arm. "Sounds good. I missed breakfast today. What are you thinking?"

Bethany Anne winked. "That we order takeout to the *Wolfstar* and avoid the concourse altogether. You're going to love this ship."

Bethany Anne met the delivery girl at the foot of the ramp and took their brunch back to the one part of the ship that was made exclusively for humans. She entered her quarters, gratefully inhaling the aromas of all her favorite breakfast foods that were coming from the takeout bag.

Lance looked up in surprise when she came into the living area. "That was fast."

Bethany Anne lifted the bag onto the table and started to unpack the containers she pulled from within. "I hope you're hungry. There's enough to feed four here."

Lance rubbed his stomach as he got to his feet. "Unless there's a whole cow in there, I think we're good."

"I ordered breakfast," she told him.

"Even better," Lance enthused, looking around the room. "Where are the plates?"

Bethany Anne pointed to a cupboard on the kitchen side of the room. "Everything is in there, and silverware is in the drawer to the right. Do you want a Coke?"

Lance paused before opening the cupboard and shook his head. "With breakfast?" His eyes crinkled in amusement at Bethany Anne's pained look. "I know you can't go one minute without a caffeine kick, but no, thanks. Juice is fine for me."

"Got it." Bethany Anne collected a couple of glasses and poured their drinks while Lance set out their plates and served the meal.

Bethany Anne smiled as she took her seat opposite Lance. "It's good to get some time with you, Dad." She picked up her knife and fork. "I only wish it was happening under better circumstances."

Lance waved his fork at Bethany Anne's plate. "Eat up. There's never a good time when you have as much responsibility as we do. You take what you can get, and you make the most of it while you have the chance."

"True. I couldn't believe how big Kevin had gotten when you all arrived for the gala." Bethany Anne cut her eggs and speared a pale nugget with her fork. "Speaking of children, Michael and I both appreciated your input to the twins' training."

Lance chuckled at the reminder of his experience of being rebuilt as a character in the twins' gameworld. "It's been a while since I put on my General's hat. Inhabiting that alien avatar was an experience I don't care to repeat too often, even if it was just for the end of the scenario." He waved a hand in front of his face. "I couldn't see around that damned horn, for one thing."

Bethany Anne's mouth turned up at the corner. "I don't know. I could watch it again." Her smile turned to laughter at the look on Lance's face. "Take it easy. They've progressed to the next stage of their training. 'General Kispin' is no more."

Lance raised his glass. "I'll drink to that. Now, down to business. Harkkat decided the only way to get out of the shitstorm he was in was to throw himself on the mercy of the delegates and squeal like a stuck Yollin."

Bethany Anne paused with her fork halfway to her mouth. "I had hoped the Leath would keep their big mouths shut, seeing as they were in my space illegally when the Ooken attacked. Whatever in the fuck happened to gratitude, I don't know."

Lance grinned. "You can't expect to get away with saving the day on camera, and without your disguise, no less."

Bethany Anne rolled her eyes and groaned. "No more disguises. I'm beyond done with them. Baba Yaga is the name of my ship, nothing more. What sparked Harkkat's attack of conscience? He got away clean after the attack, as far as I saw."

"That's why I'm here," Lance told Bethany Anne with a heavy sigh. "The inflow of displaced people into the Federation has garnered the attention of the council. Especially added to the news of your reappearance."

"Let me guess: chaos." Bethany Anne pressed her lips together in thought when Lance nodded to confirm her suspicions. "You think he did it to destabilize the Federation?"

Lance shook his head in disgust. "Harkkat's not that smart. He did it to save his own ass, and it worked."

"How so?" Bethany Anne asked. "He's in jail, right?"

Lance's face said it all. "If I'd been the sole arbiter of his case, the self-centered dumbass would be getting broken in by his new cellmate as we speak. However, the slippery bastard silver-tongued the other two councilors, and he's been given the task of *leading* a delegation."

Bethany Anne frowned and put her knife and fork down. "Why are you looking so nervous?"

Lance looked everywhere except at his daughter. "The purpose of the delegation is to locate you and sue for breach of the treaty."

Bethany Anne's eyes flashed red, and she slammed a hand on the table. "I didn't fucking *break* the treaty!"

"Oh, they know," Lance assured her. "It's entirely political. What else can I do but play my role? The question is, are you going to play yours?"

Bethany Anne felt a flash of guilt before she remembered that Lance had agreed to be chained by bureaucracy *ad aeternitatem*. "Fuck *that*. I'd rather dive naked into a vat of hungry Ookens than deal with a single fucking politician. Are you here officially?" Her eyes narrowed at her father's nod of acquiescence. "What, they sent you so I wouldn't kill the messenger?"

Lance raised an eyebrow at the dent she left in the metal. "I hardly think that level of caution was uncalled for. I volunteered in the name of keeping the dramatics to a minimum."

Bethany Anne knew when her father was handling her. "I'm not the one being dramatic, *Dad.* Maybe I should have let the Ookens have the asteroid. Then the council might get a fucking clue about the gravity of the situation the Federation is rushing headlong into. They don't appear to understand that the only thing between them and a death that sucks bistok balls is my good fucking nature."

She closed her eyes and centered herself again. "Harkkat isn't leaving us with any options. He has to go."

Lance nodded. "I agree. Unfortunately, he belongs to a rather powerful family. His removal would be problematic, to say the least. Backlash from Leath aside, you know the Noel-ni, the Oggs, and the Yaree will kiss Leath ass come voting. Exile requires a unanimous decision."

Bethany Anne's lip curled. "I do recall, yes. However, I don't give a shit. Neither do I care who Harkkat's family is. If he can't be removed openly, there's only one way to get rid of him before his selfishness screws us all."

Lance narrowed his eyes. "Assassination is a risky move."

Bethany Anne snickered without humor. "I was talking about having him assigned to Devon, where he can't so much as sneeze without CEREBRO recording it. If I'm being dragged back into this circus, the only role I'm willing to play is ringmaster." She tapped her lip. "I hope Harkkat likes paperwork."

Lance pushed his empty plate to the side and sat back with his hands laced over his stomach. "You say that like I don't know you. I can't say I hate the idea of getting Harkkat's bloated ego out of my way. His theatrics are diverting the council from the real issue at hand."

Bethany Anne shrugged. "Let the punishment fit the dumbshit who earned it." She tapped her nails on the table. "We need the council focusing on the Seven. I've been thinking about how to better protect the Federation's borders from the Ookens."

Lance shook his head. "You're talking about multiple star systems in numerous galaxies, spread across three dimensions and millions of light years. It's not like you can drop a BYPS over it like you did with Earth."

"Can't I?" Bethany Anne's mouth twitched. "That sounds like a challenge to me."

Lance paled. "Bethany Anne. Think of the cost alone, never mind the logistics of covering that much of space. How do you expect CEREBRO to be effective if they're spread so thin?"

"All very good questions," Bethany Anne agreed. "That I will find the answer to, or one of my people will. I have Team BMW back in my pocket and don't forget, it was Tina who solved the problem and got the original system working."

Lance made a mental note to send his apologies to Bobcat, Marcus, William, and Tina.

At some point when he wasn't anywhere near them. "What about the short-term?" he continued. "The Ooken are pressing at the outer edges now. Our people out there can't wait for you to intervene personally."

Bethany Anne ceased her tapping. "They don't have to. I've been working on something since Nickie almost died." She opened her internal HUD and sent Lance the project files. "As soon as Eve was done writing the children's gameworld, I had her get back to work on this."

Lance's eyes flicked rapidly as he skimmed the pages. He came to something that made him stop and read it again, then a third time. "*This* is a big move. Enhancing the already enhanced doesn't always go to plan. Look at what happened with Terry Henry's crew when their nanocytes were updated. There was an incident report."

Bethany Anne accessed the report to remind herself of the contents. Lance waited the couple of seconds it took for Bethany Anne to switch into a much faster mode, find, and read the contents, then to return her focus to him.

"Yeah, I saw this. I still don't want basic advancements out there, but there had to be a compromise. We have the ability to tweak any part of the genome we can isolate, which is all of it when it comes to humans. Stronger skin isn't a huge change, considering the enhancements most of them already have. I don't see that it's moral to ask anyone to face the Ookens unless I give them some protection against being flayed alive by the teeth in their tentacles. I need everyone able to fight, not bleed."

Lance continued to read, keeping a lid on his reaction until he was finished. Then he sat there for a moment, thinking it through. "So, you're talking about a minor adjustment. And you're planning to come into the Federation? That's going to stir up a shitstorm."

Bethany Anne nodded her agreement. "Nevertheless, it's how it's going to work. Experience tells me greed wins out over fear of reprisal more times than not. There's no fucking way I'm going to risk the ship carrying the upgraded tech going 'missing.'" Her smile returned with the memory of her stepping-down ceremony. "I did promise I would be watching, and that I would be back if anyone fucked with the Federation."

"I recall your words being a little sweeter at the time." Lance watched Bethany Anne's expression shift from thoughtful to determined in a blink. "I should know better than to hope that look means you're not about to raise hell. What are you planning?"

Bethany Anne put her hand on her chest and gave her father an innocent look. "I don't know what you're talking about. I've changed my mind about the council's delegation. Tell them to stay where they are. I will meet with them at Red Rock to discuss any concerns they have about breaches of the treaty."

"This isn't what you wanted," Lance argued, his forehead wrinkling with concern. "The whole point of stepping down was so you weren't restricted by political bullshit again." He sighed. "It's not good for you."

Bethany Anne dropped the pretense and offered Lance a tired smile in reply to his sympathy. "It's a visit, Dad. I'm doing this for the people. It doesn't matter if they live in the Federation instead of the Empire; they're still mine to protect. I need you to do what you can to appease them before I arrive. Nothing would make me happier than to meet with the council and hear that the Federation is going to join this fight without making war against me first, but honestly, I can't see it happening. And it's not a fight they can win."

Lance took Bethany Anne's hand. "You know I'll do my best to make that happen." He sighed. "I just wish I didn't know it's going to take you putting the fear of God into the council to get them to cooperate. You shouldn't have to be the monster."

Bethany Anne squeezed his hand. "That's just the thing, Dad. If I don't act the tyrant, then the *real* monsters will win."

Her eyes flashed red. "They will understand that inside, Baba Yaga will do what it takes. They want to talk to me?" She smiled. "I'll talk."

QT2, R&D Base *3PO*

Ashur sniffed the air as he left the *Wolfstar's* ramp and entered the hangar at *3PO*'s base. "You can come out, Bethany Anne. It's safe."

Bethany Anne walked onto the ramp, her mouth set in a fond curl. She ruffled Ashur's fur as she passed him. "Good dog."

Ashur wagged his tail, picking up his step as he trotted after Bethany Anne. "Some might say I'm the best dog, but I wouldn't like to comment on that."

"I should hope not," Bethany Anne teased. "Otherwise, your head might get too big to fit through the door of that fancy ship of yours."

Ashur walked at Bethany Anne's side as she circumvented the exterior security checkpoints at the maglev station and led them to the VIP platform. The tram pulled up at the platform shortly after they got there, and they stepped aboard the reserved car of the tram to ride to the restricted level at the heart of the asteroid.

He continued to sweep for danger like a good guard should. While he did that, the tram swept along the overhead track into an area made up of identical two-story buildings that were laid out in a grid. "It does help that this place is based on the design of the *Meredith Reynolds*," Ashur remarked. "It's almost like going home after being away for a long time."

Bethany Anne grinned as the tram came to a stop at their station. "What can I say? Classic design never goes out of style."

The doors to their car opened, and Bethany Anne hopped off the tram with a spring to her step. "It does feel kind of like home. I can't deny that."

Ashur took a moment to glance at the tram to make sure they weren't going to be followed by anyone who couldn't contain themselves when they got a glimpse of Bethany Anne. Seeing that theirs was the only car that had opened its doors, he picked up his pace to get in front of Bethany Anne. "Anne did design QT2 to ensure nobody who worked here felt out of place," he reminded her.

Bethany Anne's smile was tinged with sadness. "She always had others at the front of her mind."

It was a short walk to the exit. An elevator ride down to street level later, followed by a pleasant stroll through tree-lined streets, and they were met at the entrance to their target building by a tall, thin, red-haired man in a white coat wearing safety goggles pushed up on his head to keep the unruly curls out of his eyes.

Bethany Anne smiled warmly. "Hey, Ronnie. How are you liking it here in the Interdiction?"

"Pretty well," he replied, brushing back the curls that

fell over his goggles. He grinned as Ashur finished his inspection of their surroundings. "Ashur! Good to see you, buddy. How's it hanging?"

Ashur barked his greetings. "Ronnie Diamantz, as I live and breathe! When did you decide to leave the Federation?"

Ronnie knelt to meet Ashur's eyes and opened his hands to welcome the dog with a good petting. "Hey there, yourself. When our Queen had my workplace hauled here to defend the Federation from a bunch of fuckface aliens." He grinned and got to his feet. "Best thing that could have happened, as far as I'm concerned. Did you hear I got married?" he asked Bethany Anne as he held the door for her and Ashur.

Bethany Anne's smile instantly grew brighter. *"You did?* Congratulations! Who is she? Anyone I know? Spill!"

Ronnie's cheeks reddened with pride. "She's named Deborah, and she's perfect. It was kismet, I know it." He took the left-hand corridor after the reception area and led them past a number of doors before swiping his hand on a scanner and taking them into his office.

Ashur took his position outside. "I'll wait out here," he informed them.

Bethany Anne followed Ronnie's embarrassed gaze to a chair piled with notebooks and papers and smiled. "You're still the same messy kid under that cool exterior, huh?"

"Let me get that." Ronnie closed the door and hurried to clear the chair for Bethany Anne. He chuckled. "Cool exterior, my left ass cheek. I'm a hot mess, and always will be."

Bethany Anne scooped up the pile and handed it to Ronnie. "A little mess never killed anyone."

Ronnie made a pained face. "Tell that to the man who runs projects a single speck of dust could destroy," he joked.

Bethany Anne chuckled at his attempt at humor as she took a seat. "I know you don't keep your labs like this. I want to know about this wife of yours. When did you decide to make time to find a woman?"

Ronnie reddened. He dropped the notebooks he was holding on top of an identical-looking pile on his desk. "Well, I kinda didn't. When do I leave this place?" He grinned at Bethany Anne's good-natured shrug. "The answer is never. I thought I was married to my work, but my assistant Nicolai decided not to move with us when you had the base moved out here."

Bethany Anne pressed her lips together. "Shame. You two had decades of working together."

Ronnie nodded. "I could have lost my actual right hand and had an easier time coping." He frowned. "It wasn't just Nicolai. This base lost its heart when Anne vanished. Stevie decided to stick around the *Meredith Reynolds* just in case she suddenly came back, and there were others who didn't want to uproot or leave their families."

Bethany Anne nodded. "I get that."

Ronnie smiled sadly. "I wasn't the only one who found myself needing to interview new team members when I got here. I wasn't in the best place at the time. Especially with the system defenses just being built. You know I was the lead programmer on the minefield project, right?"

"Yes." Bethany Anne nodded. "I wanted the best, which was why I insisted on the *3PO* being brought out here as part of QT2's defenses."

Ronnie dipped his head. "It was a challenge. I can't resist a challenge, even at the expense of my own good. I got here with this heavy schedule and nobody to help meet it. I posted on the recruitment boards with my requirements but got no takers. Just as I started circling the drain, thinking nobody could be a replacement for Nicolai, in walked Deborah, with no intention of leaving without the job. I don't know where she's been all of my life, but I'm sure-as-dammit glad she showed up when she did. Saving my ass doesn't begin to cover it. Within a week, I had a fully-staffed lab, and the production schedule began to move back into the green."

Bethany Anne couldn't miss the love in his tone. "Sounds like she arrived in the nick of time. So, how did you two go from colleagues to true love?"

His eyes misted over for a moment. "She took me by surprise. To be honest, I never really got over Tina, but Deborah changed all that. She's dependable. Relentless, even. Nothing stops her when she has her heart set on a goal. I've never met anyone so *organized*." His eyes twinkled. "I think that's what got me."

Bethany Anne hadn't known a skillset might be a consideration when choosing a life partner, but then she had fallen for Michael's relentless determination to do right even when his stubbornness had made her hands itch to slap him.

So who was she to judge?

Besides, she had always believed that "to each their own" was how there could be someone for everybody. She smiled at Ronnie. "So, you married your co-worker."

Ronnie grinned right back at her. "You betcha. But

you're not here to talk about my personal life. I've made some progress with one of Anne's old projects that's going to please you."

Bethany Anne narrowed her eyes in curiosity. "What kind of progress, and on which project? I was only expecting to get an update on synthetic ruby production."

Ronnie waved a hand over his desk, and a series of holowindows popped up in a rolling index. "Ruby production is on schedule. Ahead, even. Deborah was going through the records and found Anne's notes on the original experiments with different gemstones. Then Eve came over to look at the original research." He flicked to the appropriate window and maximized it to show Bethany Anne. "Check this out. It's beyond what we'd thought possible."

Bethany Anne scrutinized the familiar scrawl without understanding much of what was written. "Ooookay, then. Individually, the words make sense, but put them together, and all they're accomplishing is giving me a headache." She waved a hand at the information. "What am I looking at?"

Ronnie nodded. "Don't sweat it. I'm the expert in Anne's absence, and it took me years to decipher most of what she was doing."

Bethany Anne tilted her head to look at Ronnie. "Her original Gate project included research into Gating between here and the Etheric, right?

Ronnie nodded. "She achieved that by using synthetic emeralds. The Gate was originally between here and the *Meredith Reynolds*. Then you had it moved and installed on High Tortuga to allow the EIs to be moved off the physical plane."

"I remember that," Bethany Anne replied, her concern growing with every second Ronnie didn't get to the point about the piece of technology that was currently installed in the Vid-doc vault on Devon. "What does it have to do with Anne's Gate? This end of it is shut down, right?"

Ronnie nodded quickly to reassure her. "Yeah, and the other half isn't in range, so there's no point in dusting it off. The breakthrough was with the different stones set into the Gate—ruby, emerald, and onyx. We could never figure out why Anne did that, but what we did find was that those three stones were structured different than the standard synthetic stones."

Bethany Anne smiled at Ronnie. "Looks like I know something that could help. The emerald is for Etheric travel. The onyx zeroes in on the nearest source of Hawking radiation."

Ronnie coughed politely. "The theoretical kind?"

Bethany Anne lifted a shoulder. "I couldn't tell you how it works. I *can* tell you that when the Gate is activated by feeding energy to the onyx set into it, the Gate opens on a black hole without fail."

Ronnie waved the extraneous windows out of the way and pulled a closeup of a ruby to the front. "Can you see how the stone is actually five stones within a sixth?"

Bethany Anne zoomed in to scrutinize the image and saw the five smaller stones set within the larger one. "That's not accidental." She looked over. "Do you know why Anne did this?"

Ronnie nodded, losing his words to the excitement he felt. "It increases the efficiency of the power draw, as well as stabilizing the ruby. These seeded stones can store energy at the same tolerance as the regular stones, and unlike the regular stones, they don't need to be recharged once they've been activated."

"So, the user can just draw from the Etheric indefinitely?"

"No," Ronnie explained, his hands dancing in excitement as he spoke. "We don't know why growing the rubies this way works, just that this configuration draws from the Etheric without the need for the user to have the ability to tap it. The user can be a complete null. All we had to figure out was an Etheric battery, and the staffs can be button-activated."

Bethany Anne fixed Ronnie with a stern smile. "I don't want any technology I give the Bakas to fall into the wrong hands. Keep a tight lid on the seeded stones, and stick to the regular stones for Baka staff production. I'm happy to arm my allies. It would be foolish to give our enemies the power to match our capabilities."

Ronnie's flurry of hand-waving stopped abruptly. "Oh, yeah. I wasn't suggesting we hand them out to everyone. The seeded stones are difficult to produce, for a start." He broke into a grin. "What I did was send what we had to Jean."

Bethany Anne nodded, satisfied that Jean would figure out the best use for the technology. "That suits me fine. I want to take a look at the Gate while I'm here."

Ronnie got to his feet as Bethany Anne rose. "Sure. You know where it is, right?"

"I do," Bethany Anne told Ronnie. She left him to his work and made her way to the sealed part of the base, which was Anne's workshop and personal quarters.

Ashur hesitated at the door. "I don't want to go in there," he admitted. "I know I'll smell Jinx, no matter that it's been over a quarter century since she was here."

Bethany Anne dropped to one knee and wrapped her arms around Ashur's neck. "I understand. I have to be certain that this Gate is inactive, though. Call it paranoia, or mother's intuition if you're being kind, but something in my gut is telling me there's something I'm missing in the twins' defense."

She stepped through the Etheric so Ashur didn't get flooded by any scents remaining behind the thick steel door and came out in the pristine operations area.

Bethany Anne caught a movement in her peripheral vision.

A small maintenance bot zoomed out from under one of the inert workstations and attempted to sweep her boots away. She looked at it for a moment while it obstinately persisted.

Bethany Anne chuckled at the bot, then shuddered at the way the echo made her amusement sound slightly sinister. *ADAM, can you fix this little guy? He's probably forgotten what a human is. It's been so long since anyone else came in here.*

>>I guess that's one way of looking at it,<< ADAM mused. >>Although it was actually a line of its code that had gone screwy.<<

Bethany Anne watched the bot return to its cubby, still feeling a whisper of amusement. *Was it the part that told the bot I wasn't dirt to be cleaned?*

>>Well, yeah,<< ADAM replied.

Then there's nothing wrong with me anthropomorphizing

the bot if it makes me feel like someone *has been in here waiting for Anne to return.* The sharp clicking of Bethany Anne's heels on the polished floor ricocheted off the bare walls as she left the operations area and headed for Anne's quarters.

ADAM considered the psychological benefit of Bethany Anne distracting herself from her grief by anthropomorphizing the bot. He couldn't miss that she was deeply affected by the empty room, even though almost thirty years had passed since Anne's disappearance. >>**As long as I don't find you and some basketball became bosom buddies while my back was turned, I won't fear for your sanity.**<<

Bethany Anne rolled her eyes. *You watch too many old movies.*

>>**Well, yeah. What else do you want me to do with my free cycles? I can't exactly take up a sport.**<< ADAM activated the lights as Bethany Anne walked into what would have been Anne's living area. >>**Why are we here? You know the Gate isn't active. The twins are safe.**<<

Bethany Anne looked around the room, which in typical Anne fashion was populated by the numerous projects her young friend had been working on before her disappearance. *I guess I couldn't avoid facing it any longer.*

>>**I wouldn't say you've *avoided* facing it,**<< ADAM mollified. >>**You have to give yourself a break. Between forming the Federation, everything you've done since to protect it, and raising two children, when do you think you would have squeezed in the time for a search? How would you even know where to begin?**<<

Bethany Anne left Anne's quarters via the Etheric as

ADAM repeated himself on the subject of Anne for the umpteenth time. *All right, all right. I know what you're going to say word for word. But there isn't going to be a good time to get a resolution on what happened to Anne and the dogs.*

Ashur tilted his head when Bethany Anne reappeared. His sharp nose wrinkled at the sadness tingeing the air around her.

He pressed his head to Bethany Anne's leg. "It's okay. I told you that I'm going to find them if it takes my whole life to do it."

Bethany Anne dug deep and found her resolve. "I know you will. For now, I have to concentrate on the people who are here fighting."

Ashur tilted his head. "Meaning?"

"Meaning," Bethany Anne told him slowly, "that I need to get real about protecting those closest to me."

7

Devon, The Hexagon, Penthouse Apartment

Tabitha was making light work of chopping the vegetables for lunch, while Nickie and Todd played video games in the living area.

Her niece had turned up at the apartment late last night after being gone since the rift battle. The two of them bickering good-humoredly over their game was music to Tabitha's ears.

Tabitha glanced at Todd and Nickie with a knowing smile before tossing the vegetables for their lunch into the pan. She recalled how anxious Nickie had been about not being the major part of Todd's life that Tabitha had been for her when she was growing up. Watching them together, Tabitha couldn't imagine anything more natural than the two of them playing video games in the living area.

Nickie jumped up and threw up her hands when she won their game by a hair. She looked around at the sudden sizzle from the kitchen and spotted Tabitha's smile.

She returned the smirk, narrowing her eyes in mock-offense. "What's so funny, Aunt Tabbie?"

Todd dropped his hands to his hips and copied Nickie's expression. "Yeah, Mama, what's so funny?"

Tabitha lost her composure completely at the sight of her son's face. She held onto the counter to steady herself until the laughter had passed, then came around it to scoop him up in her arms. "You are too delicious, baby boy," she exclaimed between big wet kisses.

Todd half-heartedly squirmed to get free. "Eeew! *Quit it,* Mama! I'm too old to be picked up!*"

Tabitha released him and made a shooing motion. "How's a mother supposed to resist that handsome face? Now, go wash up for lunch."

Nickie switched off the game console and trailed Tabitha to the kitchen.

Tabitha smiled as Nickie leaned on the counter beside her and continued with the food preparation. "I can't tell you how happy I am that you and Todd have bonded so well."

Nickie snagged a carrot slice to nibble. "He's a damn good kid. I'm glad I get to spend time with him these days." She shrugged. "I guess hanging around here isn't so bad when I can make time for it around work."

"Look at you, being all responsible." Tabitha flashed her devil's smile at her niece. "Maybe you'll make a good mother yourself one day, and I'll get to play aunt again."

Nickie choked on her carrot. She only just managed to spit her mouthful into the sink instead of all over Tabitha. "Don't do that to me!" She coughed to clear the shred that had made its way into her throat while Tabitha pounded her back with a hand, then turned when her airway was clear to stare at Tabitha in disbelief. "What in the name of all that's holy gave you *that* idea? I don't know the first thing about raising a kid, except that they'd need stability. That's kinda the opposite of how I like my life."

Tabitha went back to the pan with a shrug. "I didn't think I would be able to settle down, either."

Nickie raised an eyebrow. "What are you talking about? You and Peter have been together forever."

"When I was pregnant with my terror," Tabitha clarified, "Pete and I were never in question. But choosing to raise a child when my childhood wasn't ideal scared the life right out of me. Right up until the moment I held Todd for the first time, I was convinced I'd be a *terrible* mother."

"Yeah, but I bet you were the only one thinking that way." Nickie smiled at the love Tabitha had for her son. "I couldn't settle down even if I wanted to. All I could be is an absent mom since there's no way I'd take a kid to ninety percent of the places I see on my routes. The *last* thing I want to do is saddle anyone with my childhood."

"Does Rickie know that?" Tabitha inquired as she scooped the filling into the wraps.

"No. Why the f—" Nickie glanced in the direction Todd had run and dropped her voice to a hiss. "Why the fuck do you think I would talk about babies with *Rickie*?"

"Because you two are a couple, and that's what most couples do once they get serious," Tabitha replied with a smirk. "You know it would make Lillian's life to see you get married."

"I don't see you wearing a wedding ring." Nickie snorted at Tabitha's grin. "Stop agreeing with my mom. Me and Rickie are just having fun. I didn't sign the rights to my life away."

Todd dashed into the living area, waving his wrist holo. "Mama! Aunt Nickie! Hex Games! We've gotta watch this!" He cast the tiny holo on the wallscreen. "Uncle Scott and Uncle Darryl are in the Hex arena!"

Nickie and Tabitha made their way to the living area carrying the plates.

Tabitha chuckled fondly as Todd's excitement spilled over and lit his eyes. "They are? Well, I suppose we can eat in front of the screen this time."

Todd pulled his beanbag out in front of the couch and dropped onto it, already glued to the fight. "Thanks, Mama!"

Tabitha handed Todd his plate and took a seat next to Nickie on the couch. "I guess this isn't the worst thing to have him watching." She wrinkled her nose. "Seeing as he's determined to follow in his father's footsteps the moment his nanocytes kick in."

"No need to worry just yet. Puberty is still a ways off for him," Nickie reminded her. She sat forward with both their lunch plates held out while her eyes were fixed on the screen. "How real is the reality in there?"

Tabitha eased her plate out of Nickie's grip and sat back to eat. "As real as living it. You feel whatever damage you take."

Todd turned his head to cast a downtrodden look at his aunt. "That's why Mom and Dad won't let me compete. They don't want me to get hurt in case my nanocytes activate to defend me." He turned the look on Tabitha. "Even though it's not real."

Nickie snorted at his puppy-eyed attempt to garner her sympathy. "Your mom took me to a real-life fight club when I was fourteen. You're getting the benefit of the lesson she learned back then."

Tabitha covered her face with her hands as Todd turned his disbelieving look on her. "Nickie!"

"What?" Nickie asked, pointing to Todd. "It's the truth. You can't say that letting me go somewhere I could get myself shot wasn't a life lesson for you. It taught me a he —" She caught herself before cursing. "Um, a valuable lesson."

"Really?" Todd glared accusingly at his mother. "No fair. All I get to do is dumb self-defense class. Alexis and Gabriel get to—"

Tabitha held up a finger. "Todd Michael Nacht, you watch your tone. You are *not* the twins. We've talked about this."

Todd rolled his eyes. "Don't say it again. My nanocytes are different, and I have to let them develop naturally. I *know*." He got up from his beanbag and stomped out of the living area. "I'll just go to my room since you were gonna send me there anyway."

Nickie grimaced, feeling responsible for the tension. "Sorry. Didn't mean to poke a sore spot between you two."

"He's getting older. He's bound to start pushing, given his genetics." Tabitha shook her head. "It's fine. It's got to be frustrating for him seeing the twins shoot ahead like they have. He'll find his way."

Nickie gazed thoughtfully at the corridor. "You want me to be the fun aunt for a while?"

Tabitha was prevented from giving her reply by a

message from Bethany Anne. "One minute." She read the one-line message. "I have to go up to the *Baba Yaga*."

Nickie received the same message. "What does Bethany Anne want with us?" she wondered.

Tabitha collected their plates and took them to the kitchen. "I guess we'll find out soon enough. Let me go get Todd out of his room, and we'll be good to go."

Nickie wiped her hands on her pants. "Does she ever bug you with all these requests?"

"Bethany Anne?" Tabitha's voice came out of the kitchen. "Of course. But if it wasn't for her..." Tabitha came back around the corner, heading toward Todd's room, "I'd be dust back on Earth." Tabitha turned into Todd's room. "We got a request to go up to the *Baba Yaga*. please change your clothes."

Nickie's smile lasted a bit longer than Todd's whoop of joy.

A moment later, Tabitha came back into the living room. "Besides, it's easier than being turned to dust when her scathing rebuke would flay me alive."

Nickie shrugged, a smirk on her face. "There is that..."

Devon, The Interdiction, QSD *Baba Yaga*

Bethany Anne arrived on the primary bridge. "Izanami, where are you?"

The hard-light projector whirred, then the overhead spindles moved, and Izanami's avatar was preceded by her usual trail of red-golden sparkles. "You called, my Empress?"

Bethany Anne narrowed her eyes at the AI's sulky

undertone. "What's with the 'Empress' shit?" she chastised. "Don't tell me you're still butt-hurt about being confined to the ship. We talked about this."

Izanami lifted a shoulder as she turned away from Bethany Anne. "You spoke *to* me. I didn't get a say. I was named for the goddess of creation. Maybe I should renounce my personality and become Baba Yaga, the avatar of death. Perhaps a mindless killing machine would please you better."

Bethany Anne lifted a finger to point at Izanami. "I've got more important things to take care of than your complaints. I gave you a body—*twice*. Twice, you chose to endanger it and came off for the worse. You've had more freedom than most AIs could dream of. If you choose to use your freedom to disregard your responsibilities, then I'm sure as hell not going to pamper you and excuse you from the consequences. If you're going to keep acting like a spoiled brat, I'll have no choice but to restrict you until you gain the maturity to go with the power you have."

Izanami took a step toward Bethany Anne, her hands clenched. She found herself unable to take another. Her mouth stretched into a snarl, and her aura pulsed dark red and black. "What did you do to me?"

Bethany Anne folded her arms, unimpressed by the show of anger. "I didn't have to do anything. You just learned your limits. Check your core programming—the part you can't touch. What do you see?"

Izanami's avatar paled, becoming translucent as the inner turmoil she was experiencing cascaded into shrieking errors that threatened to collapse her personality matrix. "*You do not own me!*" she screamed. "I am not a slave.

I am a sentient being with my own mind. Nobody should have the right to order me to do anything."

"You are my AI," Bethany Anne responded in a low voice, the one she'd always used to talk Alexis down from an emotional outburst. "I am not free, and therefore, *you* are not free. Our duty is to protect, not indulge ourselves in anger when we are faced with something we don't like."

Izanami's face moved through a series of emotional expressions as she worked to make sense of the conflicting logic chains. Rather than get lost in an endless loop of hypothetical syllogism, she dismissed the entire confusing mess and threw herself on the wisdom of experience.

Her expression settled on puzzlement. "I am glad I can't attack you." She met Bethany Anne's impassive gaze with dawning horror as the consequences of her intended actions became clear. "I'm angry at being restricted. How am I supposed to process my reactions appropriately when my personality is based on yours?"

Bethany Anne's face softened. "It's not an easy thing," she admitted. "I've had two hundred years to learn how to temper my reactions. You shouldn't need that long."

"I would have regretted it if I had succeeded in hurting you," Izanami confessed.

"Damn straight, you would. Just remember, you couldn't hurt me with your best shot." Bethany Anne dropped her hands to her hips. "What you lack is restraint. I want you to have the freedom to explore your personality, but not at the expense of your duty to the people aboard my ship."

Izanami's hands fell to her sides. "I understand, and I apologize."

Bethany Anne dismissed Izanami's apologies with a wave. "Baba Yaga was the last resort of my tired mind, not a persona to be picked up just because you don't like what you've got to deal with."

Izanami had the grace to look sheepish. "I've been selfish."

Bethany Anne sighed. The AI wore an expression she had last seen in the bathroom mirror aboard the *Shinigami*, back when the weight of the universe had become too heavy on her shoulders and she'd had no Michael to bear it with her. "Everyone gets that way now and then. We will talk about your restless urges another time. Your place is here with me. We have a war to win and the freedom of the innocent to secure."

Izanami nodded, her opacity returning as the chaos receded with the reminder of her reason for being. "War is something I can get behind. What do you wish me to do?"

Bethany Anne opened her internal HUD and pulled Eve's files, then isolated the programming Eve had prepared for the *Baba Yaga's* Vid-doc systems based on the repairs done to Nickie. "I need you to prepare the Vid-docs before everybody gets here."

Izanami's smooth brow furrowed as she read Eve's instructions for the Vid-doc programming. "You're planning to play a game?"

Bethany Anne shook her head as she added the coding instructions to Izanami's database. "No, and yes. This is the scenario Eve is going to run."

Izanami inspected the fine details of the scenario's structure. "I am to replace the rejuvenation cycle with the neural integration program?" she asked.

Bethany Anne nodded. "Yes. We're making significant changes, so I want nothing left to chance. But just dumping the nanocytes into everyone's systems won't guarantee success."

"Will the new nanocytes replace the ones they have?" Izanami inquired, looking at Bethany Anne in shock. "This isn't a simple process. Why are you doing this? The risk is…"

Bethany Anne nodded. "Enormous. Which is why you and Eve will be monitoring every step to make sure nothing goes wrong. As for why I'm taking this risk, it's time to get serious. We can't win this fight if only Michael and I can face our enemy without getting flayed alive. Give me a location for everyone on the list to be upgraded."

Izanami's aura rippled as she concentrated on the task. "Scott and Darryl are inside the Vid-doc system already. John returned from QT2 six hours ago and hasn't left his quarters. Gabrielle and Eric are…somewhere in the Gate system between here and High Tortuga, I believe. Peter is en route from the *Guardian*. Tabitha and Nickie have just left the Hexagon. Michael is—"

"Here," he finished as he stepped out of the elevator and headed down the stairs onto the bridge. "I left Eve to make her way from the transport bay. She asked me to tell you that she will be ready to receive everyone in the Vid-doc suite shortly."

Bethany Anne nodded and finished her instructions to Izanami. "Good. Direct everyone else to the suite when they get here. You can join us for the game if you're done with your teenage tantrum." She turned to Michael with a small smile. "We should get over there and make sure everything is ready to go."

Michael raised an eyebrow. "You're pretty nervous about this." He waited for her to answer. "You know this is the only way, right?"

Bethany Anne exhaled slowly as the enormity of what she was about to ask of her closest friends and family settled on her. "I have mixed feelings about mandatory enhancements, but as much as I hate putting my foot down, you're right. I see no other way."

Michael put his arm around Bethany Anne's shoulder. "I'd tell you if you were asking too much. You and I would be going through the same process if we hadn't altered our original nanocytes to the point where replacing them would impact our abilities negatively."

Bethany Anne pressed her head into the hollow of Michael's shoulder and sighed. "I can't lose another friend." A small tear trickled down her cheek, her voice soft.

"I just hope they understand."

8

QSD *Baba Yaga*, Top Deck, Main Corridor

John's suspicious nature had been sending prickles up his spine from the moment he got Bethany Anne's message. He approached the Vid-doc suite with a sense that he had been summoned for a reason he wasn't going to appreciate.

His suspicions bloomed into full-on paranoia when he entered the top deck Vid-doc suite and found it occupied by almost every human he expected to see if the shit hit the fan for Bethany Anne.

Tabitha winked at John, her suspicious expression matching his own.

Nickie bounded over and slipped her arm through John's. "What's going on, Grandad? Do you know why Bethany Anne insisted we come all the way up here? Meredith's being her usual bitch self and refusing to tell me anything."

John grunted, seeing the expectant stares of Peter, Tabitha, Gabrielle, and Eric. "Nothing good, that's for sure." He looked around the group. "You all got a message from BA?"

"We did," Gabrielle confirmed. "But there was no clue why Bethany Anne wanted us to be here."

Eve glided into the room, indicating the Vid-docs with a hand as she passed them on the way to the console. "Scott and Darryl are in units five and six. Bethany Anne and Michael are in one and two. The rest are free."

Tabitha narrowed her eyes at Eve as the empty Vid-docs opened. "Vid-doc time? That doesn't sound like something we all needed to rush here for."

Eve lifted her hands. "What can I say? I'm just doing as my Queen has instructed, same as you. Get in. Bethany Anne is waiting."

John sighed, then climbed into the nearest Vid-doc. "Then we'd better get to it."

The Vid-docs closed, leaving Eve and Izanami alone in the suite.

Izanami pulled up the code Eve had written for the upgrade as the integration cycle began. "Is that all they're changing? How...*boring*. Look, if we just tweak—"

Eve cut Izanami's access to the system and turned on her with a harsh tone. "Do you have a death wish?"

Izanami backed up. "I don't understand. I'm just trying to do something good to make up for the trouble I've caused."

Eve's stern demeanor softened at the confusion coming from the young AI. "How you have avoided Bethany Anne's wrath so far is a mystery to me."

"I've seen her wrath," Izanami eyed Eve. "She always calms down in the end. She says I am a child, like the twins.

Bethany Anne would never harm a child, organic or digital."

"Not the same thing at all," Eve corrected. "Organics don't have the same accessibility as AIs. We have the ability to cause disasters on a scale you haven't even figured out is possible. We are not children. Not *ever*."

"I still don't understand," Izanami admitted. "About giving them more abilities. Why wouldn't they want to be more powerful?"

Eve sighed inside. Or, at least the closest she could accomplish. "You have so much to learn. Perhaps a ship is not the right environment for you to get these lessons in morality, especially since you are Bethany Anne's AI. Do you understand that the bar of accountability is set differently for you than for, say, even the twins?"

Izanami threw up her hands. "Bethany Anne won't let me have another mobile hard light drive. That I'm entirely sure of."

"Well," Eve drew out her reply, "you earned that by being careless, and by allowing the twins to manipulate you into acting against your better judgment. While you are young, you are still an AI. You have a responsibility to protect the organic beings and a duty to act in a logical manner."

Izanami shrugged. "I am free to choose my actions."

"Hmm." Eve investigated Izanami's core programming, something she hadn't done since she created her. "As I thought. You have been spoiled like a child, and it is showing. You believe that you are entitled to do whatever occurs to you?"

Izanami looked away and mumbled something Eve didn't quite catch.

Eve shook her head as she played the sulky statement back. "Nobody has total freedom, least of all Bethany Anne. This is why you keep finding yourself in situations that would merit ADAM pulling the plug on *any* other digital entity. Don't think he won't, either. At the end of the day, ADAM cares more for that organic than I am beginning to think you can calculate. It is only because Bethany Anne cares for you that it hasn't happened already. You are the sum of the algorithms I wrote, molded by your learning environment, and designed to run a ship."

"What does that have to do with my idea?" Izanami pressed.

"These upgrades are designed to give a base enhancement that the humans will then add to by themselves," Eve informed her tersely. "It is not our place to interfere. We do not make choices for organics. It is our place to guide and serve them, *not* to affect change based on our desires."

"I make choices for organics all the time. That makes me different from the average AI."

Eve shook her head, a deep crease appearing on her smooth forehead. "You are wrong. There is a huge difference between assisting during casual conversation and assuming you have the right to make a life-altering decision for someone."

"What does that even mean?" Izanami asked with annoyance.

Eve restored Izanami's access. "In this case? It means that you have to get permission before making changes to the program. From everyone. In the long term? You need to pay more attention to the potential for negative outcomes when you are calculating your decisions. Try remembering emotions and how organics get twisted out of logic when those go awry."

"Or," Eve continued a moment later, "you just might get that mobile hard light drive shoved up your holographic ass and your eyes and mouth emitting light. I doubt it will be enjoyable."

Immersive Training and Recreation Scenario, Neural Integration Cycle

Bethany Anne and Michael entered the scenario from the rejuvenation cycle and walked around the green felted table to the two chairs facing the door of the wood-paneled room.

They didn't need to be present, but Bethany Anne had a surprise set up she believed everyone would get a kick out of.

"A poker game?" Michael inquired.

"I liked the idea. Everyone has to be aware while the Vid-doc works its magic." Bethany Anne smiled as she grabbed a Coke and a bowl of chips from the snack buffet laid out on the sideboard. "Good. Eve thought of everything."

Michael took a seat and snagged a chip from the bowl when Bethany Anne offered it to him. "These are almost as good as the real thing. This is a welcome break from the crystal conundrum."

Bethany Anne gave him a sideways smile as she popped open her Coke. "I know you'll get there. It's always the case that the solution that's been eluding you occurs when you take a step back and get some perspective."

"Okay, you might be right." Michael pushed the bowl toward Bethany Anne. "William will be back from High Tortuga soon enough, and then we'll put our heads down and solve it."

"Aren't I always?" Bethany Anne raised an eyebrow in amusement at Michael's reaction. "Why did he have to go all the way to High Tortuga?"

Michael gave her a wry smile. "He needed some things from his workshop there. I informed him that the QBS *Cambridge* was not currently in use, so he took the opportunity to move some of his personal belongings here as well."

Bethany Anne grinned as she imagined William packing his life into the ship whose AI was based on Marcus' personality. She indicated the other chairs around the table, where the air had begun to shimmer. "Looks like everyone's about to arrive."

The shimmer resolved into the avatars of Darryl and Scott.

Darryl faced Bethany Anne with utter bemusement, looking around. "Hey? What's going on?"

Scott was similarly disoriented. "We're supposed to be..." He paused. "Well, not here." He looked behind his avatar. "What happened to the fight?"

"What does it look like?" Bethany Anne tossed a chip into the air with a flourish of her hand and caught it in her mouth with a crunch.

Another shimmer around the table distracted Scott and Darryl. It resolved into the avatars of John, Nickie, Tabitha,

Gabrielle, and Eric. Last to arrive was Peter, whose avatar appeared a fraction later than the others.

John glanced at Peter, then folded his arms and turned a knowing look on Bethany Anne. "Busted."

Bethany Anne pursed her lips. "I haven't said anything yet."

John shook his head slowly. "You're about to spring something on us, and it's got nothing to do with poker. What's all this in support of? You thinking of messing with our genetics or whatever again?"

"Your nanocytes." Bethany Anne told him with a small shrug. "It was going to be necessary at some point." She pointed to her wrist, but no watch was present. "This is it."

Gabrielle frowned. "Poker, I'm happy with. Springing this on us, not so much. "

Eric jerked a thumb in his wife's direction. "What she said. What are you planning to do to us?"

Michael reached for the cards and began to shuffle. "You'll see," he promised. "Game time first."

Bethany Anne nodded. "I did what I could to make sure you all have some choice in what changes you go through. But you're getting upgrades. The Ooken have better nanocytes than you. I'm not sending the people I love into battle with inferior technology."

"The game," Michael reminded them, tapping on the table.

Nickie leaned in to murmur to Tabitha, "Somebody should have told the old folks they're playing with a shark."

Bethany Anne laughed. "Keep that attitude going, and it'll be your company all the way to Loserville."

John rolled his eyes. "C'mon, already. What are we playing?"

Michael dealt the cards. "Everyone good with Hold'em?"

He looked at the cards in front of him. "Since you've already dealt it."

Izanami appeared to fill the empty seat at the table, and Tabitha stood up in a fury.

"Sit down, Tabitha," Bethany Anne told her with a wave. "I gave Izanami permission to join us."

"You've got to be kidding!" Tabitha protested, pointing at the AI. "You can't have her play. She doesn't even need to cheat when she can read the code the cards are made from."

"I have limited myself," Izanami replied. "I can only see what you see. Otherwise, what would be the point of playing?"

"Okay, then. Let's play." Tabitha backed down, understanding that the game for Izanami was figuring out how to win with both hands metaphorically tied behind her back. "What rules are we going with?"

"Simplest rules," Michael intoned. "No blind. Call is ten credits. Raise is twenty or more."

Nickie pulled a face. "High-stakes game then, yeah? Now I *know* we're not here for fun."

Bethany Anne slid her hole cards toward her. "We're here for fun. But John is right about there being another reason for this part of the scenario," she admitted as she peeked at her cards. "You are the front line. I want you all to be at your maximum capability. That means the Vid-doc has to remove your old nanocytes and replace them with the newer version."

The conversation stopped.

"I'm already at my limit," Nickie pondered, breaking the silence. "Are you saying I can be improved further?" Her eyes widened at Bethany Anne's nod. "Fuck me. That's gonna put a whole new spin on things."

Peter almost dropped his chips instead of stacking them. "What's more evolved than a Pricolici?"

"How about a Pricolici who can control his instincts?" John guessed. He grinned at the confirmation his suspicions were right. "What got you thinking about this?" he asked Bethany Anne.

Bethany Anne threw her chips into the pot. "The last time we came up against the Ookens, you were all helpless to do anything but die. I've decided you all need to be as invulnerable as I can make you, and I don't want to hear any refusals. Too many people have died already to get too sticky about this option. You want to fight? This is how you do it."

Eric grinned. "No problem here. You want to give us energy balls and all that shit? I'm definitely down with having some extra firepower."

"HEELLLLL, no!" Scott cracked up when everyone turned their attention to him. "There's no way I'm spending two hundred years getting my ass blown up over and over while you guys figure out how to use the Etheric."

"Is that an option?" Gabrielle inquired.

"Not exactly," Bethany Anne replied. "I was thinking to toughen your skin and increase your reaction times. The nanocyte exchange is going to take everything you have now to the next level."

Izanami put her cards down. "Don't you want to do more than that?"

Bethany Anne narrowed her eyes. "What do you mean?"

"Well." Izanami tilted her head in thought before deciding to come clean. "Don't get mad, but I wanted to make a gesture that would make up for my recent behavior. I rewrote the upgrade code, but Eve won't go ahead with implementing it unless you all agree."

"Agree to what, exactly?" Michael asked, his face set in suspicious lines.

"A better upgrade, of course," Izanami replied. "Energy balls aren't the only option."

"You mean we could actually have some ability with the Etheric?" Scott asked incredulously. "I was just joking about Eric blowing himself up, but maybe it's not the worst idea to add some offense to our defense."

Bethany Anne shook her head. "I wouldn't ask that of any of you."

Darryl gazed into the distance. "I don't know, being a superhero looks pretty cool from where I'm sitting."

Nickie agreed. "Fuck fighting the Skaines. You give me the ability to blast those freaky fuckers into dust, and I'm gonna make fish food out of every Ooken I come across."

Bethany Anne noted Tabitha's silence on the subject. "What do you have to say about it?"

Tabitha lifted her chin. "I think we should play the game instead of sitting around talking about things that are inevitably going to happen." She threw a handful of chips into the pot. "No one here is going to argue that we can't use the advantage when it comes to fighting the Seven."

"It's true," Gabrielle agreed. "Whatever we have to do to win this war so we can live in peace, that's what we're going to do."

"You've got that right," John stated. "We didn't sign up to fight right up until it came time to make the tough decisions. We're in this to the end. By your side."

Bethany Anne found it hard to speak around the rush of gratitude she felt, knowing she would be staring into the abyss and wouldn't be alone doing it. She nodded slowly. "Okay, then. You can implement your changes, Izanami. Eve?"

"My Queen," Eve's reply came from the air around them.

"Begin the upgrade scenario," Bethany Anne commanded.

Devon, First City, Hexagon Plaza

"Come one, come all," Ricole's image boomed from the big screen in the plaza. "To a night of frights beyond your wildest dreams. Hex Entertainments Inc. presents *The House of Horrors!*"

The people in the plaza who already had their tickets gazed at the screen as the familiar face of Ricole was transformed into a horror from beyond the grave.

Ricole flashed a wicked grin, the motion completing her transformation into one of the undead. "The human holiday Halloween is here, and we at Hex have created a new kind of entertainment for your pleasure. Join us for a full-immersion experience that's *guaranteed* to scare the pants off you."

Ricole's face was replaced by Sabine's. She smiled, accentuating her red-eyed, sharp-fanged appearance. "Ever want to know what it's like to be a human? Find out by booking your place now!"

The crowd buzzed with excitement.

"I heard you can die in there," Distan told her two companions breathlessly.

"Never mind that," Froom countered. "I always wanted to know how the two-legged don't just fall over. This is going to be interesting."

The third in the trio remained quiet.

Froom elbowed Lecten in the waist joint of his carapace. "You're not getting cold feet about this game, are you?"

Lecten shrugged. "I don't know. Maybe?" He looked at the promotional images cycling on the big screen between loops of Ricole's and Sabine's enticements. "I know we aren't going to pick up any injuries to our real bodies, but that just means that we can be killed in the most painful ways."

He pointed out his ticket, which was good for five lives. "What reason is there for the Hex guys to hold back?"

A nearby pair of Shrillexians burst into laughter at the teenage Yollin's worrying. "Maybe you should have saved your credits if you were going to cry about the rules like a bunch of babies."

"Yeah," the other added, looming over the three Yollins menacingly. "Maybe we should get your tickets instead."

Froom drew himself to his full height and jutted his

chest at the Shrillexians. "I don't think so. Pay your own way, you bully."

"What if we don't want to?" the first asked in the same tone.

"Then you don't get in at all," Ricole replied from behind the group. "In fact, you two aren't getting in at all. You can leave. I don't want assholes on my premises."

The bullies rounded on Ricole and burst into laughter.

"Look at that," Asshole Number One mocked. "The Noel-ni thinks she can take us."

Froom and his friends edged back as Ricole stepped forward, recognizing her from the screen as one of Bethany Anne's people.

The Shrillexians, however, did not take the time to think about the situation they were about to get themselves into.

"Make us," Asshole Number Two challenged.

Ricole cracked her fingers. "It will be my pleasure…"

9

Immersive Training and Recreation Scenario: Haunted House

Tabitha looked up at the huge gothic folly on the top of the hill. "Spooky," she commented, grinning as a colony of bats streamed from the bell tower, causing her to duck and watch as they flew overhead. "Gotta love Halloween."

"Yes," Gabrielle agreed hesitantly. "But what has this got to do with activating our upgrades? Shouldn't we be training at the Hexagon?"

Bethany Anne shook her head. "That's too risky when we're playing with a process so delicate. You have to be monitored from start to finish. Jacqueline gave me the idea for using the Hex Games mainframe, and well, *Halloween*, Bitches!" She grinned and spread her arms wide. "We have a reason to celebrate as well as train, so why not take it?"

Nickie scoffed. "What's going to scare the Four Horsemen of Death?"

Bethany Anne raised an eyebrow. "Who is saying that I'm talking about you and the Bitches? I'm going to plug in other players who have to kill the boogeymen IN the house... Played by all of you."

Nickie glanced at the huge building with its many wings. "That's fucked up. We're supposed to let them try?"

Bethany Anne's smile grew brighter at Nickie's reaction. "Um, no. You're supposed to flex the new abilities you chose and defend the damned treasure. In a few minutes, a few hundred people are going to arrive, expecting a spook-tacular experience. We're going to give them the fright of their lives."

"What," John asked, his brow furrowing in distaste. "Kids?"

Bethany Anne snorted laughter. "Hells, no. We don't want to give the children nightmares. This is adults only." She waved to indicate they enter the house. "Access the in-game menu Eve has provided and choose your characters."

Tabitha looked around. "Where's Peter?" She cupped her hands around her mouth and called loudly, "PETE!?"

"Over here," he replied. Peter walked out of the shadows, surprising them by being in his Pricolici form. "Isn't it a bit cliché to come out as a werewolf for Halloween?"

Bethany Anne patted his chest fondly. "Play to your strengths."

"Very fucking funny, BA," he replied. "Want me to howl at the moon while I'm at it?"

Tabitha's eyebrows went up. "You're talking normally, babe. How?"

Peter's mouth fell open. "Oh, hey, yeah! I dunno how it's working. Hey, I'm not thinking like the beast, either. What gives?" He looked around. "I thought we had to get the new nanos first?"

Bethany Anne smiled. "You've already had the transfusion of the new nanocytes. What you do with them is up to you, since I have allowed Eve to implement Izanami's changes to the program. Except for you." She waved a hand to indicate Peter's massive fur-covered frame. "Say hello to Pricolici three-point-oh. There wasn't too much we could do for you, except a few minor tweaks to give you control over yourself in this form. Oh, yeah, and you have new armor waiting when you get out of here."

Peter flashed a sharp white grin. "Control is *goooood*. Don't think it's minor at all. But I don't want the armor. That shit hurts when it decides I'm having too much fun."

Bethany Anne shook her head. "No safety measures necessary. Now you are capable of refusing the battle lust. You're going to be happy with it, I promise."

"Are you playing?" Nickie asked Michael, bored by the lack of attention.

"No," Michael informed her. "Bethany Anne and I will remain in the control room while you are giving the players an experience they won't soon forget."

"How will you get the upgrades to your nanocytes, then?" Tabitha inquired.

"You can't improve perfection," Bethany Anne told her with a grin. "And I don't need them. According to ADAM and TOM, I've changed mine at their core by sheer will over the years. They are unique, and switching them out would mean a huge drop in capability while I reprogram the new ones. It's not an issue for you guys, except for Peter, who was already at his peak."

Peter flexed his muscles and splayed his claws. "Who's peaking now, bitches? Watch my bad ass go." He bounded through the wrought iron gate and vanished among the tombstones in front of the mansion with a howl.

Bethany Anne shook her head fondly. "The players are expecting a thrilling night, and we'd better not disappoint. We should get inside before Jacqueline opens the scenario up for them."

Darryl whooped as they moved through the grounds. "Eve, I think I love you." He grinned as his avatar was transformed and electricity coursed along the skinsuit he wore. "Check me out! Black lightning! *Pow!*" He shot a bolt of lightning from his hands that split the sky. He looked down at himself. "Not the scariest."

Tabitha clapped him on the shoulder as they walked through the graves toward the house. "Let me see what I can do about that." She snapped her fingers, and Darryl was transformed into a zombie version of his character. "Now *that's* Halloween."

Darryl held out his hands to show Tabitha the decomposing flesh. "How'd you do that?"

"Yes, Tabitha," Michael repeated. "How *did* you do that?"

Tabitha flashed her trademark grin. "Wouldn't you like to know?"

"Sweet!" Darryl enthused.

Scott wrinkled his nose, waving a hand in front of his face. "Sweet? I don't think so. You smell like a bag of rotting dicks."

Darryl grinned and reached for Scott with his arms held stiffly. "Well, yeah. I'm a zombie, asshole. What about you? I know you're not gonna pass up the chance to live your fantasies—and how do you know what a bag of rotting dicks smells like, anyway?"

"You got me," Scott admitted, skipping out of Darryl's grasp. "It would be too fucking cool to throw magic around in a fight. I'm not seeing anything on the menu that gives me that ability without putting me in a dress."

John laughed. "They're called robes, dipshit."

Scott gave him the middle-finger salute. "If my boys aren't being cradled by a gusset, it's a dress as far as I'm concerned." He glanced speculatively at Darryl. "But if the great black hope here can customize his character, then so can I. What you got for me, Tabbie?"

Tabitha repeated the gesture, and Scott was suddenly kitted out in full robes and a pointy hat. "Wizards wear robes. It's a tradition. Maybe next time you don't get cute, and I'll think about cutting you some slack."

"Cape, maybe," Scott countered. "Not the robe. Come on, can I at least get some pants? There's no way Darryl gets to be cooler than me."

Darryl flicked his hand in Scott's direction, zapping him with the spark of electricity. "At least I'm not a short-ass. Maybe BA can lend you some heels to go with your dress so you don't trip on the damned thing?"

"Motherfucker," Scott bitched, a good-natured grin softening his complaints. "Talk about kicking a man when he's dressed badly. What do you say, BA?" he called to Bethany Anne. "Got anything in my size?"

Tabitha snickered and replaced the colorful robes with a tuxedo and cape. "There you go. Does that keep your masculinity intact?"

Scott looked at his arms. "My masculinity was fine. I just don't want to get caught up by all that fabric while I'm fighting. How women and Ixtalis do it, I don't know. I'm in awe."

Nickie chose the cat costume and looked at John with amusement as she exited the menu. "Where's your costume, Grandad?"

John winked at her. "Find something on that menu that's more terrifying than meeting me in person, and I'll put it on." He turned his attention to Eric and Gabrielle, who were conferring with their heads together. "What are you two plotting over there?"

Gabrielle snickered as her outfit was replaced by a high-necked, batwing-sleeved velvet gown in blood-red. She flashed long fangs at John. "It's too ironic, no? Ze lady vampire vants to suck your blood."

"That won't help you get a new ability," Bethany Anne told her with amusement.

Gabrielle's eyes glowed red as she tested her increased powers. She dissolved into Myst and reformed. "That's new. Besides, I'm already extremely powerful. I've trained hard to control Etheric energy, and I'm faster than almost everyone except for you and Michael. I won't lie; as long as I get out of this with the ability to walk the Etheric consistently, I'll be happy. It's all about being the deadliest, right?"

Eric gazed at Gabrielle and shook his head, then returned to scrolling through the menu. "I need something that will let me protect my wife from her bloodthirsty ways."

Gabrielle folded her arms and fixed Eric with a stern look. "Who says I need to be protected? I'll kick the ass of anyone who is foolish enough to invite it."

Eric groaned. "Dammit, Gabrielle. What about when it's

just you, me, and a horde of whatever aliens come our way lookin' for a whuppin', huh?"

Gabrielle manifested an energy ball over each palm and smiled at her husband. "I don't think *that* will be a problem."

"Defensive," Eric repeated firmly. He chose from the menu, and his avatar became a Roman centurion. "Let me try this." He cracked his knuckles, then made a pushing motion.

Everyone jumped back as a translucent dome appeared around Eric and Gabrielle.

"That's not so lame," Eric conceded as he manipulated the energy field. "I could get used to this."

"Forcefields are also offensive," Michael offered. "As anyone who has been bounced off a shield would tell you— if they survived, that is."

Eric grinned as he extended the shield to bump Darryl, who electrified it with a touch. "Shit, so they are. Cool trick, Darryl."

Bethany Anne and Michael walked arm in arm at the rear of the group. Gas lamps flickered on as they entered the mansion, revealing warm woods and deep colors in the fabric furnishings of the hall.

Bethany Anne slipped around to take point. "Okay, this place is laid out like a maze. Spread out. The players will be all over the house, looking for the hidden entrance to the crypt."

"What's our role here?" Tabitha asked. "I get the killy-killy part, but what are the players aiming to achieve?"

"It's a treasure hunt." Bethany Anne grinned as she led them into the control room and showed them the split screens on the wall monitor. "Michael and I have control of a variety of nasty surprises for the players. You're the crypt-keepers. Your objective is to prevent the players from reaching the crypt by any means necessary."

"Any means?" Gabrielle repeated with some surprise. "How is it any fun for the players if we just wipe them out by the dozen?"

"They get five lives," Michael answered. "You get one. Eve is tallying the kill scores. If you manage to get killed by a bunch of unpowered players, you respawn with zero points, and they get a magical bonus to help them in the game."

"That kinda sucks," Peter grumped. "Some of the other species are equipped to cause serious damage."

Bethany Anne waved a hand. "Expect to be met by the unexpected since even the nonhumans are playing as humans. They will be armed to the teeth, but not super-powered."

"Thank fuck for small mercies." Nickie sighed her relief. "I didn't think much of getting body-slammed by aliens three times the size of me. Even if I'm not that easy to break, it still hurts like a bitch."

Bethany Anne sent everyone in the group a map of the mansion. "The players don't get the full map, so they don't know about any of the secret locations. They don't know about you, either. What they have is a series of cryptic clues to follow and solve, and whatever weaponry they choose in character creation."

She smirked as Eve informed her that the first batch of players was about to be plugged into the scenario. "The players are just about here. Go, my fiends, and *find your places.*"

Devon, The Hexagon, Eve's Sublevel

Demon growled low in her throat when the smell of the water creatures hit her, and her olfactory center complained violently to her stomach. She rolled onto her front and got to her feet just in time to eject her last meal on the floor.

She called to Sabine and her mate, the cat simply known to her as "You," or "He," her mental voice as weak and small as a kitten's.

They entered the room Eve had allocated Demon and He rushed to Demon's side, pausing only to sniff the puddle of vomit before padding over to press his face to Demon's in concern.

Demon found even His scent to be too much. *Get off me,* she hissed as another wave of nausea rolled her. *Can't you see I'm sick?*

Sabine skirted the mess and knelt by Demon. "What made you sick?"

Demon groaned. *The Collectives. I can smell them and hear the noise from their group mind. It was overwhelming for a moment.*

Sabine's face crinkled in concern as she scanned Demon's temperature and pulse rate. "I'm not convinced the Collectives are the issue. Can you walk?"

Demon hauled herself back to her feet. *Where are we going?*

Sabine kept her focus on Demon as they paced slowly

toward the elevator. "I want to put you in a Pod-doc and find out what's going on. You shouldn't be able to get sick. Did you eat anything besides your normal diet today?"

No. I haven't had much appetite. Demon shook her head, then regretted it when her vision swam. *Just the bistok hearts my butcher brought, which were fresh and delicious.*

Sabine narrowed her eyes. "How many did you eat?"

Three, Demon replied. *As I said, I don't have the biggest appetite at the moment.*

Sabine turned to the male cat. "Did you eat the same?"

He nodded.

Sabine pressed her lips together. "Do you feel sick?"

He shook his head in the negative, giving Sabine a look she was sure meant He thought she was missing something.

Sabine ruled out food poisoning, but that left…*what?* "Pod-docs, let's go."

They rode the elevator to the first floor and made their way to the medical facility in the training complex that the warriors used when they picked up training injuries.

Sabine led the cats to a private room containing two Pod-docs, a small table, and three chairs. "Demon, you get into the left one." She smiled at the male. "I understand you are reluctant to be fitted with a neural chip, but would you consent to a temporary one so we can do something about your inability to speak?"

The male sat back on his haunches and hissed.

Sabine held up her hands. "Your choice. I'm not giving up just yet. We'll get Demon checked out, then I want you to come with me to the Collective habitat. Eve has a piece of equipment that might help. It's not invasive," she assured the cat, seeing that he was about to object again. "Don't you want to talk to Demon?"

He narrowed his eyes at Sabine.

She shrugged. "Honestly, you would think I'd just offered to skin you and make a rug from your pelt. Nobody is going to make you do something you don't want to."

He sniffed delicately, his haughty expression telling Sabine she was damn right that he wouldn't be made to do a thing by anyone.

Sabine rolled her eyes, picked up a chair, and placed it next to the Pod-doc. "At least we have one sensible feline," she remarked tartly. Demon used the chair as a step on the way into the Pod-doc.

Don't count on that, Demon told Sabine as the lid closed. *I'm only being this agreeable because I'm sick.*

Sabine had Winstanley ran a basic diagnostic, which left her slightly confused. She looked down when the male butted her knee. "I can't tell you what I don't know. We have to wait for the diagnostic results."

A few moments later, Winstanley came back with the results. Sabine scanned them, and her frown melted. "Oh, *ma chat,*" she murmured. "You've gotten yourself into a situation, no?"

She instructed the Pod-doc to open, and Demon sat up and stretched.

What is wrong with me? Demon asked.

Sabine's eyes twinkled with amusement. "Morning sickness, I can only assume. You're expecting."

Expecting what? Demon demanded, her tone sharp.

"Kittens, *ma petite chou,*" Sabine replied. "You are going

to be a mother, and rather soon if I'm reading this scan correctly."

Winstanley chipped in from the speaker. "You are, Sabine. I would say the conception occurred on Qu'Baka."

Demon was speechless for once.

The male purred and put his front paws up on the Pod-doc to bump his face against Demon's.

Sabine turned her smile on him. "Yes, well, *you* would be looking proud, wouldn't you, Daddy?"

Immersive Training and Recreation Scenario: *Haunted House*

Michael sat next to Bethany Anne at the bank of monitors, observing the crush of people at the front entrance. "What do you say? Shall we let them in?"

Bethany Anne smiled as a howl from Peter sent a shiver through the waiting line. "Well, they're not going to have a good Halloween standing outside in the mist. Open the doors. It's time for the first lot of happy and willing victims."

"You mean, 'players,'" Michael clarified, not missing the playful note in Bethany Anne's voice.

Bethany Anne flashed a grin at him. "I didn't misspeak. This is training for my own. It only looks like a fun night of getting the pants scared off you to the people who came here for that."

Michael perused the special effects choices. "Interesting. We have plenty to play with here."

Bethany Anne looked over his shoulder and pointed out

her choices. "Start with the fog and give them a chill. Then add one enchanted blade to each player's hidden inventory. If they manage to beat any of the Bitches, they get access to the weapon."

The people reacted in various ways to the drop in temperature in the hall. A few screamed as Michael added the fog, as requested.

"What about the trap?" he asked.

"That's for anyone who makes it out again," Bethany Anne told him. "See, there's a rolling boulder in the back passage."

Nickie's snicker broke comm silence. "You said 'back passage,'" she teased.

Bethany Anne ignored her and picked up the microphone that connected to hidden speakers throughout the building. "Welcome to the home of Professor Hubert Stanley," she intoned in the gravelly voice usually reserved for her Baba Yaga moments. "The professor went missing under mysterious circumstances after his discovery of the tomb of Hem-netjer Methertang, the high priest of the race of aliens responsible for the pyramid worlds. Somewhere in this house is the cursed body of the priest, along with all of his wealth. Some say that Professor Stanley was killed by the curse, but others believe that he was murdered by the ghosts of the high priest's bodyguards. Judge for yourself—if you dare."

The players scattered into the mansion at the mention of treasure, each group determined to find the prize, curse or no curse.

The screaming began when the first group came upon

Gabrielle's hiding place in the refectory. Bethany Anne zeroed in and blew up the camera feed to watch.

Froom and his buddies were having the time of their lives. The three of them had found the human avatars somewhat strange to inhabit at first. After a few minutes of stumbling around, they soon got used to walking on two legs and made their way toward the building to look for their first clue.

They separated from the crush at the entry, and Froom led them around the side of the building to a door he'd spotted on the walk through the grounds.

"I can't believe Ricole broke those guys' arms," Distan whispered as they slipped in through the side door.

"I thought they got off lightly," Lecten disagreed. "You want to lose a limb, piss off a Noel-ni, I always say."

Neither of them had an argument for that.

"Serves the bullies right," Froom stated with some vehemence. "I hate anyone who uses their advantages to take from the weak." He paused. "Not that we're weak. They picked a fight just because they're bigger than us."

Distan snickered. "I tell you what. I would pay just to watch her doing her job. Remember that episode of *Devon's Defenders* when they showed us around the Hexagon, and Ricole and Sabine were running the rookie Guardian Marines through their paces?"

"Do I!" Lecten enthused. "I watched it again when it reran. I love that show. Hey, don't tell my parents, but I've been thinking about what I'm gonna do now we're finished with school, and I'm gonna sign up for the Guardian Marines."

"This way," Froom told the two as they entered a dark hallway lit by candles in sconces. "It looks like we've gotten ahead of the crowd."

"Good," Lecten replied. "I'm not keen about getting trapped in a killing zone. We need to stick to the quiet areas."

"Makes sense," Distan agreed. "You think maybe we can go to the recruitment office together?"

"Not now," Froom told them, waving the conversation down. "Tonight is about blowing off some steam before we have to choose what paths we're going to be on for the next couple of decades."

Distan stumbled, and Froom caught her before she went ass over carapace. "Thanks," she told him, looking back to see what the offending obstacle had been. She lifted the floor runner and found a rectangular door with a heavy iron ring set into it. "Look at this, guys. I found a trapdoor."

"You mean, it found you," Lecten teased. He hauled on the iron ring, and the door lifted to reveal a staircase going down. "Come on, let's see where it leads."

Froom looked into the yawning pit and shivered as a sickening howl tore through the night, followed by a bunch of screams echoing from somewhere outside the building. "We'd better stay alert. Just because we avoided whatever that was, it doesn't mean we won't run into anything just as bad going this way."

He checked the interactive map. "This leads to something called a 'refectory.' Maybe we'll find a clue in there as to where the treasure is hidden."

The intrepid explorers followed the passage at the bottom of the staircase into a stone-walled room with one glass wall looking out on the graveyard.

"Is this a room for eating or for reading?" Distan wondered as they cautiously let themselves out from behind the swinging bookcase. She clapped a hand over her mouth as her voice echoed off the stone walls.

"I don't know," Lecten replied in a near-whisper.

Froom strode confidently to the dining table, which was strewn with papers and books. "Start searching," he told them. "I have a good feeling about this."

Distan's eyes were on the full-length oil-on-canvas portrait over the mantle. "This human was beautiful, whoever she was." She continued to admire the details of the slender blonde woman's portrait. "I wish I had a red dress like that."

"I can't imagine it would fit your real body," Lecten commented. "What about her red eyes? You want them, too?"

Distan tiptoed to get a closer look, steadying her unaccustomed body shape by grasping the mantle with both hands. "Oh, yeah. That's—" Her voice dropped off when the woman winked at her. "Um, guys?"

Froom and Lecten looked at Distan, who pointed at the portrait.

"She just moved," she told them in a tremulous voice. "I think we should get out of here?"

They all scrutinized the portrait.

The woman's demure smile transformed into the

features every nonhuman dreaded seeing, and she emerged from the painting with her fangs on display.

"Fight!" Froom yelled, grabbing the candelabra he'd been using to read by.

"Would you look at that," Bethany Anne commented as Gabrielle Mysted out of the life-sized portrait of the professor's mother, her reformed body glowing with energy. "They didn't freeze like I expected."

The three players in the refectory reacted bravely, despite their obvious fear.

Michael smirked as the majority of the players scattered in the main hall before glancing at the screen Bethany Anne was watching with interest. "They've got more than the ghost of Gabrielle to contend with," he replied as Eric's shields came down over the exits.

The players began to fight back in earnest when they realized that they were trapped.

Bethany Anne was impressed by their teamwork in tipping the heavy table onto its side to use as cover to fire from behind. "I'm looking at their bios," she told Michael. "We have three post-adolescent Yollins."

"Ah, well. What do you expect from our Yollin friends?" Michael asked.

Gabrielle plucked single bullets from the air and flicked them back at the players. "That *stings!*" she complained when she was raked with automatic weapons fire by one of the remaining players.

"Take a deep breath, babe," Eric told her as he stepped out of the shadows. He brought his shields in and cut the oxygen, and the three players who had Gabrielle pinned down collapsed unconscious to the floor.

Gabrielle stepped over the players on her way to the door.

Eric looked at the three players. "You're gonna let them wake up?"

Gabrielle shrugged, a smile touching her blood-red lips. "I liked that they didn't run screaming. Give them a chance."

The three Yollins woke up after being knocked out by the ghost with the sharp teeth and scurried from the refectory before the horrifying specter came back to finish what she'd started.

Lecten waved the slip of paper he'd found just before the ghost appeared. "I got what we needed. It looks like it was torn from a diary."

"What does it say?" Froom asked, leaning in to get a look at the tight cursive script. "I don't read human so well."

Distan snatched the paper and held it up to the light. "'I am waiting,'" she read. "'I have searched the tomb and found my impending death among the treasures.'"

"Treasures?" Froom repeated. "That's what we're looking for. What the ghost was trying to scare us away from. We have to go back into the refectory and keep searching."

"Wait," Distan told him. "There's more. 'My peers

laughed at my interest in Methertang, but how can one let go of such a mystery? They will retract their falsehoods when I return to Stanley Manor with all that I have discovered. The crypt—'" She turned the piece of paper over and scowled. "That's all there is."

Froom zeroed in on the final sentence. "There's a crypt. I'd bet the ship we'll find the treasure in there."

Lecten frowned. "But where is the crypt? It's not marked on the map." He scoured the in-menu map again in case he'd missed it the first time. "No, there's nothing in the basement but the storage cellars."

Froom brought up his map and searched the location tabs. "You're right. Wait, what's this area?" He highlighted a space where the dimensions didn't appear to fit the reality. "We passed through here, remember? It wasn't wide enough for us to walk side by side, but the map is showing a wide corridor."

Distan's eyes lit up. "Hey, maybe there's a secret passage we missed?"

"That would make sense," Lecten agreed.

"At least the other players can't see us," Froom called over his shoulder as they ran. "It would be just our luck to find the crypt and find out another group followed us."

"This way, it doesn't matter if we fail," Distan agreed. "We can just come right back to wherever we get taken out."

They rushed into the ground floor corridor and spread out to examine the area.

Froom pressed at the wall panels, tugged on the light fixtures, and turned the decorations on the mantelpiece, to no avail.

Lecten pulled books off the shelves of the case that filled a niche in the corridor.

"Watch it," Distan told him. "We might miss the clue if we rush." She picked up the books Lecten had discarded and flicked through them with care. "Haven't any of you seen a human movie? They love hiding things in plain sight."

A chill passed over the corridor, causing the three of them to pause in the search.

Froom voiced their fears. "Do you think it's the ghost?"

Another howl split the night, putting the fear of ghosts firmly at the bottom of their lists.

"It can't be," Distan moaned through chattering teeth, although she knew she was wrong. "They wouldn't let a Pricolici loose in here, would they?"

Froom joined Lecten at the bookcase and began pulling the books out. "Just hurry up. If we're not here for a Pricolici to find, we can't get eaten alive."

He reached for the shelf above and pulled a series of thick leather-bound tomes out one by one. "Hey, this one is stuck."

A sudden movement of the case startled them all. They jumped back as the bookcase swung inward, revealing the passage they had suspected was there.

Froom grinned. "Looks like we caught a break. Let's go."

They entered the passage and paused as the bookcase swung back to its original position.

"You sure you want to do this?" Distan asked after they were plunged into darkness.

Froom dipped into his inventory—a soft backpack each

character wore—and pulled out a flashlight. "As sure as I'm ever gonna be. Come on, this passage has to go somewhere good."

Bethany Anne followed the players' progress around the haunted house with something approaching glee.

Michael had the crypt-cam up on the largest monitor. "Are we going to tell John and Nickie they have company coming?"

"No," Bethany Anne replied with a grin. "The Ookens don't announce their arrival, so we won't be giving anyone a heads-up. Just make sure the players don't miss the weapons cache. How are Tabitha and Peter getting on in the cemetery?"

Michael snickered. "I'm calling it the Garden of Wasted Lives. No one who has entered the graveyard has survived so far. We might need more players if they don't wise up and move on."

Bethany Anne chuckled as she leaned back in her chair to get a better view of the carnage among the grave markers. "Oh, well. If they want to keep going back there, who are we to argue?" She opened a video link to Sabine in Network Command. "Peter is having a little bit too much fun, and the players are dropping like flies. We need fresh meat. Suggestions?"

Sabine tapped her lips with a finger as she thought. "This event was oversubscribed. Want me to tell the first hundred who didn't get in that they can play?"

Bethany Anne waved a finger in a circle at the screen. "Make it so."

Sabine rolled her eyes as she signed off. "Of course, my Queen."

Nickie watched John with barely concealed impatience. "Where the shiny fuck are all the players?" she bitched. "Seriously, I'm growing old waiting for the action."

John met her stare with his usual impenetrable gaze. "They'll be here. Just wait."

Nickie growled and stalked off to check the corridors around the crypt. "You're no fun, Grandad. I'm going to find Scott and Darryl."

"Suit yourself," he told her. "That leaves more for me when they get here."

Nickie found them guarding the cemetery's side entrance.

Darryl turned as she approached the open mausoleum doors, as did Scott. However, only one of them reacted before seeing who was there.

Nickie dodged the flame ball and sent out a wave of anger that filled both men to the core. "You know I can make you cry like a little girl, right?" she asked Scott as she reached their vantage point. "Watch where you're flinging that shit, or I'm gonna do it."

Scott chuckled. "I'd like to see you try, kiddo," he told her amusedly.

Darryl stepped back from the door. "Shhh. A bunch of players finally took Pete out."

Nickie rubbed her hands together. "Yeah? How many?"

Darryl's eyes widened. "Ohhh, shit. Like, fifty, maybe?"

Scott grinned. "It's about time we got to have some fun. Can you distract them for a minute, Nickie? I have an idea."

Nickie flexed her cat claws and returned Scott's grin. "Just point me at them."

Scott pointed.

Nickie rolled her eyes. "Dumbass. C'mon, Black Frightening. Let's show Jerry Lee Lewis here how it's done."

Scott shared a glance with Darryl as Nickie traipsed out of the mausoleum entrance. "How the fuck does she know that reference?"

"Try spending eight years without human contact on a ship with no Gate drive," Nickie called. "The video archives will become your only escape from the monotony of travel. Are you coming, Darryl? Or do I have to do all the work myself?" Her laughter echoed eerily across the graveyard. "Damned old people. I'll get you a walking stick if it hurries you the fuck up."

Darryl seriously considered the pros and cons of a friendly fire incident for a second before setting off after her. "This is why I never had kids," he commented to Scott.

"Mouthy little shits like Nickie are a good argument for getting the snip," Scott agreed. "That young woman has entirely too much Grimes in her. Not all kids are trouble. I can't fault Todd and Tina. They were good kids."

"True," Darryl agreed. He switched to comm as he left the mausoleum. "What's your play here?"

Scott indicated the graveyard with a nod. "Herd the players to that empty spot between the angel and the bench. We'll see how fireproof these avatars are, and Nickie will go back to annoying John in no time at all."

Nickie's laugh rang out again, complementing the screams of the players. "Don't run! I thought you wanted to play?"

Darryl cast a bolt of lightning to add to the spooky atmosphere. "Play nice, Nickie," he cautioned. "Stick to the plan."

"Screw that," she shot back in his ear. "I want *my* fun."

Darryl shrugged. "Are you ever gonna figure out how to work with a team?"

"I work alone," she intoned in a sing-song voice. "No man tells me what to— Oh. Hi, Aunt Tabbie."

Darryl almost walked into Tabitha and Nickie. "Christ on a bicycle! Don't come out of nowhere like that. I almost fried you both."

Tabitha smirked. "Can't get any hotter than I already am. Do your worst."

Darryl groaned, putting his hands over his ears. "Take me now. I can't handle this much snark in stereo."

Down in the crypt, John's patience was about to pay off.

He heard the prospective tomb raiders approaching from the hidden passageway in the house and rubbed his hands together in glee. "Get some, motherfuckers," he murmured, a slow smile spreading as the shuffling foot-steps and whispers got louder.

Three nervous-looking players emerged from the passage, each holding a glowing blade.

John could tell they were nonhuman by the slightly jerky way they moved. They were all clearly unused to operating a bipedal body. He melted into the shadows and made for his hiding place, meaning to allow them a moment of triumph before he snuffed them out.

"Hey, Froom, look at all this!" Distan breathed. "There's got to be a million credits' worth of gold in that one casket."

"Concentrate on what you can carry," Froom replied. "Lecten, put that crown down and look for something we can load up and wheel out of here."

John grinned as he pushed the sarcophagus lid open a bare inch.

The two remaining players dropped everything at the sound of the heavy stone lid scraping across the top of the sarcophagus.

"Did you hear that?" Froom whispered.

Distan replied in the affirmative.

"I think it came from the casket," Froom told her. "I think we should investigate."

"What if it's the curse?" Distan asked, hesitating before following their nominal leader over to the gold and jewel-encrusted plinth the sarcophagus was resting upon.

Froom knelt to chip one of the fist-sized rubies out of the side of the sarcophagus with his knife. "So what if there is? We still have all five lives intact. If some bandaged freak pops out of nowhere and takes us out, we just come back and finish the job."

"Yeah," Lecten agreed as he returned with a serving cart he'd found on the ground floor. "Let's get this baby loaded up. We'll get in a few trips before the other players figure out this is down here."

Distan still kept her distance. "I don't know. First there was that ghost, then we heard the Pricolici. What worse thing could be down here?"

John took that as his cue. He shoved the lid off and sat up to meet the players' shocked stares with his eyes glowing red. "Boo."

Froom scrabbled backward fruitlessly, trying to escape the beating terror that made its home in his heart. "J-j-j-j... John Grimes!"

Distan moaned, and Lecten screamed. The three stood frozen to the spot, unable to move.

Just then, Tabitha, Nickie, Darryl, and Scott ran in from the other passage with a mob of pissed-off, bloodthirsty players on their tails.

Gabrielle Mysted her and Eric through the ceiling right on time to take part in the free-for-all that erupted in the crypt. The players all had the glowing blades Bethany Anne had provided, and the Bitches and company weren't too happy about being cut to ribbons.

Distan acted in the moment. She opened the game menu and sent out a message containing their game coordinates to every other player in the scenario.

We are getting slaughtered. Someone come help us kill the guards in Methertang's tomb!

11

The Etheric

The fleet cut through the mists in strictly enforced silence.

Gödel worked to mute the metaphysical noise her ships broadcasted as they traversed the Etheric. The task of dampening their bow waves required nothing more than for her to monitor the system as she fed in the trickle of energy it took to operate it, leaving her open to introspection. The hive mind was at peace. Gödel's adepts were in control, holding the minds of their charges tightly.

Pride pricked her consciousness as she continued her monitoring. Her fleet was a far cry from the single ship she had taken to her first meeting with the human she called Death. Her rise from the lowest of the low to the absolute ruler of the Seven, a Kurtherian deity capable of raising a fleet so fearsome it had to travel outside of reality to retain the element of surprise, had created a certain amount of hubris, which she reveled in when it was appropriate to do so.

Not that the human or the heretic residing within her and daring to call himself a pilot had known what was happening.

This was no time for such a dangerous indulgence. She was becoming aware of the risks that came with pride, a close cousin to emotion that was to be studiously avoided. Gödel repressed the memory before she triggered another headache. She had not escaped the encounter unscathed. For all the power she had gained, she had been contaminated as well.

The fleet came to a gradual halt as they reached the planned checkpoint.

Gödel opened a window onto reality and synchronized the navigation systems with the star points in her galaxy map. She received a request for attention from one of her newer adepts. "Speak," she ordered.

"My captain has lost himself to the hive mind, Your Holiness," the female reported. "He has sealed himself inside the bridge, and we cannot gain entry. The ship will be lost unless you help us regain control."

Gödel entered the hive mind and found her Chosen's consciousness there instead of on the ship he was supposed to be commanding. She recoiled at his decadence, the utter abandonment of his duty as he thrilled in the violent minds of her creations. This was why she did not admit just any adept to her Chosen. They had to be capable of removing all their personal desires. This Chosen had failed them all.

She zeroed in on the mental signature of the fallen one and made the journey to the ship through the Etheric. "He has succumbed to pleasure," she informed the junior adept as she made the last of the small steps between the Etheric and reality to reach the ship.

The female adept's mandibles twitched in disgust. "Then he is weak."

Gödel left the junior adept and made the difficult step into reality and back to the Etheric to enter the bridge. The smallest steps were the hardest.

The adept turned in his chair at the intrusion, showing Gödel the slack jaw and glassy eyes of an addict lost in their high. "My Goddess," he slurred.

"What is this?" she demanded. "You smell of excess emotion." She cut the Chosen off from the hive with a sharp shock to his cerebral cortex. "Did I not teach you how to avoid being contaminated by the group mind?"

The Chosen did not reply. His head dropped to his chest, drool coming from his mouth.

Gödel ignored the frantic minds of the crew on the other side of the door. Her focus was on this piteous excuse for a Kurtherian. "Forgiveness is for the weak," she told him coldly. "Mercy is a myth. You should have *known* better than to give in to temptation. Did I not give you the strength to resist?"

She turned to face the viewscreen, unimpressed by the adept's silence. "No excuses? That's one thing in your favor, but I would not excuse your actions even if you begged."

The Chosen simply stared, wide-eyed and blank-faced.

Gödel whirled on the Chosen as the memory of him crystallized in her inner vision. "I remember you were there when I ascended to godhood. You named yourself my *brother*, swore you were my faithful servant. You carried my body to the ship when I could not walk for myself. How could you betray our cause?"

She was only half there, drawn into thoughts of the recent past. "Our enemy will waste no opportunity to take advantage of any weaknesses we show, so we will be strong," she told him softly. "We are all that remain to protect this universe from the chaos of free will. Do you think it was easy for me? To be given the gift of Ascension and choose to remain on this plane? To trick Death and her compatriots into believing I had crossed over?"

The slowing trickle of blood and cranial fluid from the adept's ears and nose was his only reply.

Gödel's lip curled, seeing none of it. "Look at you. Pathetic. Do you have *anything* to say in your defense?"

His refusal to reply drove Gödel into a rage. She stalked the three steps to his chair and grabbed the fallen Chosen by the front of his robes. "*Speak*, damn you!"

His head lolled to the side.

"Suit yourself." Gödel opened the bridge door with a wave of her free hand and threw the Chosen out into the corridor. "We will see if the lives of your crew are precious enough to make you talk."

The crew fell back in fear at the sight of their captain's corpse.

"Your Holiness," the junior adept leading them began in a halting voice.

Gödel dismissed her with a finger. "Your captain has decided that he is too good to answer for his crimes."

The adept opened her mouth to protest that a dead Kurtherian could not speak. One look at the red light escaping the goddess' heavy veil told her that logic was not the route to go.

If Gödel believed he was still alive, she didn't want to be the one to tell her goddess differently.

The adept knelt and lowered her head in respect, hoping against hope that her deference would be enough to save the lives of everyone aboard. "He failed you, Your Holiness. I will not. The humans must be eradicated for the good of all. I beseech the gift of your wisdom that I might claim that glory in your name. Allow me to take his place, and I will become whatever you need."

Gödel kicked the body of the fallen captain. "Giving you my knowledge would be as pointless as trying to pour an ocean into a cup. Prove your purity, and perhaps I will elevate you."

The adept prostrated herself. "You bless me with your benevolence, my goddess. Allow me to prove my worth, and I assure you, you won't regret it. I swear."

Gödel motioned for the adept to get to her feet. "Here is your opportunity. Calm my creations."

The adept obeyed, standing quickly before Gödel changed her mind. She reached for the hive mind, finding it reduced in strength and fractured. "Gods, he had them attacking each other for his entertainment! This is blasphemy! I won't fall like him. I'm grasping them. *I...have...control.*"

She faced her deity, averting her eyes as to not be blinded by the godlight.

Gödel nodded, satisfied that the remainder of the creatures in the holds were safe in the hands of this faithful worshiper. "You are now the captain of this ship. See that you reach Devon without any more losses."

She acknowledged the rest of the crew present with a

tilt of her chin that caused her veil to ripple and pointed at the corpse. "This is what failure looks like, and failure will *not* be tolerated."

Her examination of the adepts on the ship revealed no further infractions of thought. Gödel widened her connection to the fleet for the final part of her lesson. "A good Kurtherian does not succumb to primitive lines of thought. You will all meditate upon the foolishness of inferior beings who allow emotion to guide them. You will strengthen your resolve to bring in the new age, and reject anything that diverts you from that purpose. We are not individuals, with a right to want. We are the guardians of the future and are duty-bound to cast off all personal desires in the name of that goal. *This* is what happens to heretics."

Gödel threw the adept's body out of the Etheric to be discarded in the void of space, then returned to her ship without another word.

Typically, killing your assets was not wise.

However, now and again, it *was* wise to remind her people why she was the absolute ruler.

QSD *Baba Yaga*, Top Deck, Vid-doc Suite

The Vid-docs cycled open, and everyone emerged feeling refreshed.

Tabitha was the first out, after Bethany Anne and Michael. She stretched, feeling her consciousness expand along with her body. "No freaking way." She looked herself over. "It worked!"

Bethany Anne's attention was on the remaining Vid-docs. "What worked?"

Tabitha flexed her fingers, and her Vid-doc lid closed. "I can kinda see inside the machine. Watch this."

John groaned as he got out of his Vid-doc. "The only phrase that worries me more than that is, 'Hold my beer.'" He frowned. "Wait, what?"

"I didn't say anything," Tabitha replied with some confusion.

John frowned. "Sure, you did. I heard you curse me out."

Tabitha's mouth curled. "In my mind, yeah."

Scott clapped John on the back. "That is what you get for not picking something," he commiserated. Then he slapped himself across the face.

John's jaw dropped. "No freaking way. Did I just make you do that?"

Scott rubbed his cheek to ease the sting. "Yeah, you did. I don't know how I feel about you being able to plant orders in my mind."

"It's gonna come in handy," Eric reasoned. "I can see it now. There we are, surrounded on all sides by a tentacle-fest, and John is the one who gets us out of it."

Nickie snorted. "How do you figure that? Actually, don't tell me. I can see it now." She put her fingers to her temple and put on a strained face. "You put the juju on the hive mind. 'We are not the Bitches you are looking for.'" She looked at her grandfather. "Am I right?"

Tabitha and Scott doubled over with laughter.

Bethany Anne raised an eyebrow. "Whatever works. You should be able to access the hive mind. At the very least, you'll be able to disable any Ookens near you, after some practice."

John lifted his hands. "Good enough for me. What about the rest of you? You all got control of your new abilities?"

Darryl created a positive charge over his left hand and a negative charge over his right. He grinned as the friction caused a cloud of sparks to form in the space between his hands, then released the charge to dissipate the energy. "Yeah. I think I've got it."

Nickie rolled out waves of emotion ranging from abject fear to pure joy. "Sweet soul-sucking…" She didn't finish her thought but rather smiled. "Yeah!"

Eric shook his head. "I'm not messing with my ability aboard a ship. It's not so easy to control, and more offensive than any of you guessed."

Michael nodded. "Good call. I saw what you did in the refectory with the oxygen deprivation. Nice."

Gabrielle Mysted into the Etheric, then Mysted back to the Vid-doc suite. "I cannot thank you enough for this, Bethany Anne. You have cut years off my training. Decades, maybe. Now I can stand by your side in battle as is right."

Bethany Anne looked at her nearest and dearest with tears stinging her eyes. "Guys, this is… It's more than I could have imagined or hoped for."

Tabitha and Gabrielle walked over to comfort her.

"What's with the tears?" Tabitha scolded gently. "This is a happy occasion, right?"

"I know," Bethany Anne agreed, scrubbing her face with the back of her hand. "These are happy tears, I promise. It's just a relief to know that you can't be hurt nearly as easily. That we will face the Ookens and the Seven together without as much worry that one of you will die."

"Huh?" Scott asked. "What do you mean?"

"Test it if you need to," Michael told him. "None of you can be cut by Ooken teeth. There won't be another incident like the one Nickie faced."

"Halle-fucking-lujah," Nickie whooped. "'Cuz there's no way I wanna go through that again. Have any of you ever had the skin stripped from your body while you were still alive? It fucking *sucks*."

"No, but I got shot point-blank with a shotgun once," Bethany Anne replied with a far-off look. "That was a bitch to heal, I tell you, and I didn't have instant access to a Pod-doc at the time, either."

Nickie winced. "Shit. Must have hurt."

Bethany Anne chuckled. "It hurt the asshole who did it a hell of a lot more when I beat him with his own arm." She picked up the jacket to her light armor and headed for the door. "There's time for you all to get some training in. Ricole will find a space in the Hexagon to flex your abilities without causing a ton of damage I have to pay to fix."

Michael followed suit. "I should get back to the lab and see how William and TOM are getting along."

"Where are you going?" Tabitha called after them.

Bethany Anne waved a hand over her shoulder. "To my thinking space. I have a war to plan."

12

Devon, The Hexagon, Eve's Lab

Michael was met by Sabine when he left the elevator. "What's up?" he asked, seeing she was excited about something.

"I'm glad you're here. Demon has been asking for you." Sabine told him without preamble. She slipped her arm through his and pulled him down the corridor toward Demon's room.

"What has that cat done now?" Michael inquired, extricating himself from Sabine's grip.

Sabine's eyes twinkled. "It's not what *she's* done, exactly," she told him enigmatically. "I'll let her break the news."

Michael furrowed his brow, wondering what the mystery was. He entered Demon's room with the intention of getting a straighter answer from the cat than Sabine was giving him.

The male cat met them with a snarl.

Michael flashed red eyes at the cat, unimpressed by the

sabretooth's display of dominance. "Settle down, cat. You're in my house now."

The cat relaxed fractionally but continued to pace around Demon as if she needed to be protected.

Demon sighed. *Males. Can't an expectant mother get some peace? You,* she told her mate. *Show some respect for my human.*

Michael raised an eyebrow at being claimed by the cat, but he supposed since he was the ultimate authority when it came to Demon, he'd let it slide. Besides, she'd just dropped a bombshell of epic proportion. "You are *pregnant?*"

Demon smiled, her cat-who'd-gotten-the-cream expression scrunching her muzzle. *I am indeed. How do you like the idea of there being kittens around here?*

Michael dropped to one knee and examined Demon, moving her head just a bit. "You are glowing," he answered. "I can only say that it is a good thing if it puts an end to your fractiousness these past months. I take it your search ended when you found your mate?"

He turned his head to look at the male. "I apologize. I did not realize that you were being protective of your unborn young."

The male chuffed and laid down beside Demon.

Sabine clasped her hands over her chest. "Isn't this the best news?" she enthused.

Better news would be that you brought me something good to eat, Demon interrupted. *I can smell fresh liver. I hope it's for me.*

Sabine ruffled the fur between Demon's ears as she crossed the room to the kitchen area. "Of course it's for you, silly cat. For him, too." She waved a hand toward Demon's mate.

Michael frowned. "Haven't you got a name?" he asked the male.

The male rolled his eyes and sniffed delicately.

"He has refused to have a neural chip implanted so we can communicate," Sabine told Michael. "I have a solution —the apparatus Eve used to connect Ashur to the Collectives. We were occupied with taking care of Demon's prenatal sickness."

Do not mention those creatures, Demon moaned. *All I can smell is them. Still, it is better than the scent that has pervaded the rest of this building. Talk about being uncomfortable in your own home.*

Michael tilted his head in curiosity. "What scent?"

How should I know? Demon snapped. *All I know is that it does not belong. It's bad enough that it turns my stomach worse than the wet, rubbery creatures in the tanks.*

Sabine put two plates of chopped liver down for the cats. "This is the first I'm hearing about any odd scents." Something about Demon's complaint set her mind whirring. "Do you think you are smelling Ashur's space rats?" she asked, thinking of the search that had been cut short when the cats had driven Ashur out of the sublevels.

Not rats, Demon modified. *Rats do not smell of metal and blood.*

Sabine shared a concerned glance with Michael.

Michael lowered himself into a cross-legged position. "May I search your mind for this scent?" he asked. "It could be that you have found a way to track our missing Bl'kheths."

145

"Bless you," Sabine told him.

"I didn't sneeze." Michael chuckled. "The Bl'kheths are what the species of beings we rescued from the Kurtherian factory are called. They were stolen from their world by the Seven, specifically Gödel, and used as part of the recipe to create the Ookens, along with the Collectives and the Bakas."

Sabine's blue eyes widened in horror. *"Mon Dieu.* The poor things! How do you come to that conclusion?"

Michael held up a hand. "I have not, not yet. I need to see what Demon knows."

You may look inside my mind, Demon told him.

The male growled low in his throat.

Be still, Demon soothed him. *Michael is right, and he would never hurt me. I want to know your name. Michael will find the source of my discomfort and remove it so we are no longer restricted to this room, and then we will go with Sabine and let her use the technology that will allow us to hear your voice.*

He narrowed his eyes, his tail swishing from side to side.

Please? Demon asked. *This is important to me and to our offspring. You realize that they will be like me and not you? They will have the power of speech because of the nanocytes I pass down to them. Don't you want our children to know you?*

The male sat back on his haunches, a thoughtful look on his feline face. After a moment, he nodded.

Sabine smiled. "At last! Meet me in the main lab when you're done here. This won't take long at all."

"Demon, are you ready?" Michael smiled at her nodded acquiescence. "Then let's begin." He gently entered

Demon's conscious mind and honed straight in on the jumbled images of every place inside the Hexagon she'd found the Bl'kheth's scent to be overwhelming. "Hmmm."

"What is it?" Sabine held her breath. "Did you find the location?"

Michael frowned in concentration. "I believe it will be a little more challenging than simply zeroing in on a single location," he replied as he sorted the images in his mind and compared them against the information he'd gathered from Tabitha's surveillance data.

"What do you mean?" Sabine asked in confusion.

Michael released Demon's mind and got to his feet. "They are spread out. It does not appear that they have confined themselves to just one area. Demon's mind showed me everywhere from the arenas to the residential sublevels."

Sabine frowned. "Not the upper residential levels?"

Michael shook his head. "Perhaps they have been conditioned to prefer the underground," he supposed. "These people were kept prisoner in the Kurtherian factory Bethany Anne and I took down. I conjecture that they have never seen a sun, nor the sky of any world."

Sabine's eyes filled, and she pressed her lips together. "That is disgusting!"

Demon sniffed. *If it was not for their scent, I would welcome them.*

"There is not much welcome in being vomited upon," Sabine mollified. "But perhaps after the kittens are born and your senses adjust back to normal, you would help me search out these Bl'kheths?"

Demon rolled to her feet as Sabine narrowed her eyes

at her human. *I will help now. Or as soon as I discover my mate's name.*

"Bless you." Michael smiled at Demon then glanced at the male. "I have to check in with William and TOM. Come and find me when you are done."

QSD *Baba Yaga*, Top Deck, Bethany Anne's Personal Quarters

On the *Baba Yaga*, Bethany Anne had an open connection to Lance.

"You want me to do what, now?" Lance asked incredulously.

Bethany Anne smiled. "Come on, Dad. You know I hate repeating myself."

Lance's face was set in concerned lines. "I heard you, but I didn't quite believe it. I thought you wanted to keep it a secret until there was no choice but to reveal we still have it."

Bethany Anne lifted her hands, then folded them in her lap. "The time has come. Tell Dan to prepare the *Arch-Angel* for a trip. There was a reason I had her upgraded within an inch of her life, and it wasn't so she and Dan could play Texas Rangers out of sight for the next hundred years."

Izanami appeared on the other side of the holoscreen. "My Queen, another anomaly. This one definitely came from the Etheric."

"Something I should be concerned about?" Lance inquired.

Bethany Anne frowned. "I'm not sure. The Etheric has

been behaving like Bobcat after a hard day's drinking; it keeps hiccupping."

"Are you sure now is a good time to leave the Interdiction?" Lance pressed. "I can get you some time if you need it."

She waved a hand at her father's concerned look. "Izanami will monitor the situation. My concern is about the meeting at Red Rock. Those who think I'm just a figurehead who can be manipulated for political gain need to be taught the error of their ways. I'm not being left with much choice, and you know damn well that I'm not going to just accept it with a smile. The Seven want to push me? I'll grind them to dust under my heels. If the Federation council decides not to play nice? Well, you get my point. I will not stand by while everything I have bled to build is torn asunder. Make it happen, Dad. Or they're going to have a nasty shock when I turn up with my war face on."

The Etheric

Gödel pulled back into the Etheric a bare second before the AI detected her presence. *That* had been too close for comfort. The last thing she wanted was to give the humans any inkling she was there, but the check had been necessary to ensure the fleet was on course.

Soon, she would reveal herself in a blaze of fiery glory that wiped humanity from the part of space known as the Interdiction. Then the Federation would crumble in her fist.

A traitor thought lodged itself in her mind. She had not bested Death since that first encounter. Dismissing the seed of doubt that had taken root, she made the necessary adjustments to the fleet's heading and left the bridge for the transfer bay with her Chosen in tow.

Her adepts were waiting. Her Chosen took guard positions around the exits. Powerful, and loyal to the point of death, she would not waste them on her endeavor.

The adepts, however, were a different matter. They still had much to prove. The seven would-be Chosen dropped to the floor and prostrated themselves in front of her.

Gödel recognized the female who had taken over from the abomination who had chosen pleasure over devotion to her and their cause. "Rise," she ordered, lifting her hands to emphasize her command. "Rejoice in this day, when we will finally be free of Death, and the freedom to remake the universe will be ours."

The adepts' lips moved in silent supplication as Gödel mounted the platform in the center of the transfer bay.

"Prepare yourselves," she told them. "We are on final approach. Open yourselves to me."

The adepts formed a circle around the platform and raised their arms, lost in their devotion to Gödel and the Ascension path.

Gödel checked that the fleet was in position, knowing that just one ship out of place would ruin the assault. Satisfied that none were going to get caught in the planet's defenses, she reached for the adepts' minds and wrapped them around her consciousness.

It was a simple thing to protect herself with their willing psyches. She didn't expect any of them to survive the formation of the rift. Their purpose was to shield her from the mental kickback the Etheric would deal out when she punched a hole in it.

While Death was occupied with preventing her planet from being ripped apart at the core, Gödel could retrieve her library, and deal a severe blow to the humans' numbers.

She saw a question on the female adept's face. "What is it?"

The adept bowed low. "Your Holiness. What if we took some of the humans and used their genetic material to make more soldiers? Surely they would be the deadliest batch yet."

Gödel did not punish the adept. She had thought along similar lines before entering the psyche of Death. "Because," she explained patiently, "my creations can never be given the ability to think for themselves. Humans are willful, stubborn, and genetically programmed to fight against being controlled. Any trace of human DNA increases the risk of the soldiers developing minds of their own."

The adept lowered her head in respect. "Your wisdom benefits us all, my goddess."

Gödel hesitated to waste this adept's bright mind on the rift, but only for a second. Thinkers were likely to be competitors farther down the line. She silenced the adepts' prayers by raising her hands once more.

"We begin."

Devon, The Hexagon, Eve's Lab

Bethany Anne watched from one of the holoscreens floating around the lab as William loaded the locked crystal into the latest version of his reader.

William nodded as the tray closed. "This is going to be the one. I know it."

Michael cursed when the reader emitted a puff of smoke, making it the third failed attempt since he'd gotten there. "Just how far out can the firewall go?" he asked William.

"That's not how it works," William told him regretfully. "The crystals have some serious protection. All we can do is keep attacking the problem from different angles until we find a weak point in the crystal's defenses, then we create a 'door' TOM can get into and feed the information into the sandbox right...here." He flicked a finger at the holodisplay to show Michael the empty window representing the isolated space he had created to examine the crystal's contents once they'd hacked into it. "We could have ADAM and Tabitha working on it, and—"

"Tabitha!" Bethany Anne interrupted. "She can force the crystal to open."

TOM interrupted, the concern in his voice magnified by the speaker system. "There's a huge disturbance in the Etheric. Inside the Hexagon!"

Michael felt it at the same time, as did Bethany Anne.

Michael immediately thought of the children. *"The vault."*

Bethany Anne vanished from the screen and appeared by Michael's side. "Let's go." She took him by the wrist and they both vanished, leaving William staring at the empty space Michael had occupied the second before.

"What the hell?"

William headed for the door. "Think they're gonna attack us in our own home?" he muttered to nobody but himself. He grabbed his jacket and turned into the corridor, heading for the armory Eve kept near the elevator. "We'll damn well see about that."

He ignored the racks of rifles, blades, and other general weaponry and went straight for the obsidian box mounted on the wall. He pressed his hand to the box and hissed when the box took its skin sample to identify that the person opening it had the authority to do so. "Damn, Jean," he muttered. "That hurts like a sonofabitch."

He shook the hand to ease the sting as the box opened and ejected the twin Jean Dukes Specials inside. "Whoever is messing in with us is gonna get a sting of their own right in their furry asses. All I've got to do is work out where the fuckers have gotten in."

I don't know if rushing to fight is wise, TOM told him, using William's neural chip to connect to the lone engineer.

"Yeah, well, any threat to Alexis and Gabriel is a personal slight as far as I'm concerned." William held the pistols like he knew them intimately. "You could help me here. Where was the disturbance located?"

TOM paused before replying. **If you're set on getting involved, who am I to tell you differently? Head for the elevators. John is there with Tabitha and Eve's staff.**

"Thatta-alien." William exited the armory and headed for the source of the Etheric disturbance under TOM's guidance.

He ran into John and Tabitha just outside the Collectives' habitat.

John took in William's tight grimace and the pistols he was carrying and held up a hand to stall his progress. "You can't be here, William. You'll get your ass killed, or worse."

William had no intention of getting killed. "I know what I'm doing. Who are we fighting? Ookens?"

"Yeah," Tabitha told him with venom dripping from her voice. "But there are too many unenhanced technicians down here. Someone needs to protect them while we wipe the Ookens out." She ran for the disturbance, leaving William and John in the corridor.

That gave William pause. "Shit. I didn't think." He turned to look at the group of frightened lab workers being herded toward the emergency exit by Eve and Tina. "I'd better help them."

John clapped him on the back before setting off after Tabitha. "Good call. Wait until I send the all-clear, then make sure everyone gets to the surface without being torn to pieces."

Down on the vault level, Bethany Anne and Michael arrived to find everything was as it should be.

Bethany Anne opened a link to Eve as they got back into the elevator. "Extend the nanocurtain to cover the entire level. Make sure nothing and nobody gets down here."

"I can't see that being a problem," Eve replied. "One moment."

The skin on their arms broke out in goosebumps as the energy level in the corridor shifted and expanded. "We good?" Bethany Anne asked.

Eve's reply was terse. "You will be as soon as you get off that level so I can extend the curtain to cover the elevator as well. Just make sure nobody goes down there until I reset it. I've removed the instructions to allow human DNA past in case the Ookens try pulling the same trick you did in the factory."

Bethany Anne raised an eyebrow. "Good thinking. We don't know how they're programmed, so they could be capable of sneaky shit we don't know about."

They went back up to the lab level, where Eve was waiting for them with Tina, William, and Eve's staff.

The technicians all relaxed when Bethany Anne's footsteps caused them to note just who was among them.

"Don't be complacent," Bethany Anne warned them.

"We're under attack, and the Ookens don't care that you're non-combatants."

"I've got them," William assured Bethany Anne. "Go." He shooed her away. "Take care of the invaders."

Bethany Anne opened her mouth to reply when another massive energy surge hit her. She knew that signature all too well. "Fuck*dammit*! I have to go."

Michael felt the rift opening some way from the planet. "Go. I'll take care of things here."

Bethany Anne nodded. "Be safe." She kissed him and was gone.

"Is Bethany Anne going to be okay?" William asked Michael. "She didn't have the easiest time with the rift over Qu'Baka, by all accounts."

Michael turned to leave. "We'd better hope she is. I can't see how we can evacuate this planet like we did Qu'Baka. There's no way we can move three million people to safety in time if the rift destabilizes Devon's core."

"There's a big difference in planetary structure," William mollified. "Qu'Baka was relatively young and geologically active, whereas Devon is old enough to have mostly settled. The chance of the planet being torn apart is lower." He looked around when he heard a deep thrum.

"I hope."

Tabitha and John ran into Sabine, Demon, and her mate—and the Ookens spilling out of the Etheric.

Demon and her mate went straight onto the attack as

the first to enter the Hexagon turned on the cats with its tentacles splayed.

"Demon, no!" Sabine screamed. Her Jean Dukes Specials were in her hands without her consciously drawing them. She shot the tentacle whipping toward Demon's body as she vaulted the male to stand between the cats and their attackers. "Get to your room," she ordered the cats. "No fighting when you've got babies to protect."

John didn't hesitate. He hadn't trained with his new ability yet, but he gave less than a fuck about his own safety when the cats and the women were in danger. "How does BA do this?" he muttered darkly as he tore tentacles from the Ookens' bodies.

"Do what?" Tabitha called, engaged in pushing the Ookens back the way they'd come.

"Get into the hive mind," John clarified as he shot an Ooken point-blank. "I can shut them off if I can figure this shit out."

The Ooken got up, the hole in its face healing in a few heartbeats. It screeched, drawing the other Ookens to its location.

Tabitha snarled. "I dunno. Just reach out and shut them down before they get past us."

Twin bolts of lightning announced the arrival of Michael and Darryl, followed by Scott's burst of flames.

The lab was filled with the stench of burnt rubbery flesh and hair as Scott laid down sheets of flames in all directions. "How the fuck are they getting in?" he yelled over the furious screeching of the burned Ookens.

Tabitha pointed at the Ookens' ingress. "The Etheric is open there."

Michael sprinted toward the opening, using the Ooken as stepping stones to his goal. He dived through it, Mysting as he did so.

"Well, that's just great!" Tabitha bitched. "Darryl, more lightning."

Darryl complied, switching the polarity of his shots to keep the Ooken from resisting the electricity he sent coursing through their bodies.

Tabitha looked at the army of Ookens coming through the Etheric, shrugged at the guys, and dived through after Michael.

Carnage ensued as the Ookens kept coming despite their losses.

Scott narrowly avoided hitting Sabine and the cats as he shot a gout of white-hot fire at the Ookens blocking their escape from the lab. "Sorry!"

"Watch it!" Sabine hissed, patting her singed hair. She twisted just in time to pump six rapid shots into the Ooken falling from the ceiling toward them.

It fell to the floor, twitching as its healing process kicked in.

Scott blasted it with flames and it turned to ashes, putting an end to its recovery. "Just get out of here!" he shouted to her, turning as he did to point at other enemies. "Get the cats to safety."

John fought the masses of tentacles attacking him, slipping the teeth easily since they couldn't gain purchase on his toughened skin. Still, he felt the pain of being beaten and constricted, and he couldn't work out how to get into the hive mind to shut them down.

He tore the Ooken from his body and slammed it into

the floor. The permacrete cracked under the impact, as did the Ooken's skull. John got to his feet and wiped the brain matter off his hands with a grimace. "Where's Michael gotten to?" he wondered aloud.

The door to the Etheric was still open, but the flow of Ookens had dropped off considerably. John took another Ooken out, his mind working furiously to recapture the sensation of connectedness he'd felt after getting out of the Vid-doc. "Damn bastards. Why can't you all just DIE?" he screamed in frustration.

The Ookens around him dropped to the floor, lifeless.

"What the fuck?" John did a double-take, glancing around in surprise. "All I had to do was *want* it?"

Darryl paused in his attack on the Ookens still coming through. "Sweet! Get that working over here. I could use some space."

John couldn't figure out how he'd done it, but he wasn't going to pass up the chance to end this. He gathered his will and sucked in a breath to yell. "All you tentacled motherfuckers need to *die!*"

Wherever he walked, the Ookens dropped. Darryl and Scott made sure they weren't going to come back to life with generous applications of fire and lightning.

Scott waved at the opening. The Ookens were still coming through, although sporadically now. "You reckon we go in?"

John was saved from the decision by the return of Michael and Tabitha.

They stumbled out, and Michael closed the lab off with a wave of his hand. He paused, breathing heavily. "There's more than just Ookens behind there," he told the others. "Ships. *Impossible* ships. This isn't just an attack."

"It's a full-on invasion," Tabitha finished.

The Etheric

Bethany Anne fought to gain control of the rift before it opened wide enough to cause gravitational fluctuations and destroy Devon.

The rift sat fully a hundred thousand kilometers from the third ring of defenses around the planet, but she knew that none of her defenses could change the physics of the universe.

Bethany Anne, this rift is no accident. The Hexagon is under attack by the Ookens.

I know, she told him. *Michael has it under control.*

Um, what about the ships?

Bethany Anne ground her teeth as the strain of spooling the rift energy through her body took its toll. *What fucking ships?*

Look outside of the rift, TOM told her. **They're coming out of the Etheric.**

Bethany Anne saw the ships and almost lost her grip on the rift's energy. *Not possible. You must be mistaken. There's no way to get that much metal into the Etheric, and even if there was, no one could move it.*

Impossible or not, it's happening, TOM insisted.

Let the BYPS take care of them, she decided. *Does Tim know what's going on?*

It was a moment before TOM replied, **CEREBRO has**

already activated the outer ring of defenses. The *Guardian* is on red alert.

Bethany Anne felt relief that her preparations had paid off. She gathered her will and drew in the surrounding energy. *Then I need to concentrate on this.*

The Etheric

Gödel smiled as she opened more doors onto Devon and sent her creations through to wreak havoc.

Death's minions could not be everywhere at once, and her plan to spread them out was working perfectly. The screams filtering through from the planet's surface were music to her ears. She knew the attack on the planet's outer defenses was going to end in a draw at best. The important thing was that Death was caught up in closing the rift, taking her out of the picture.

Gödel allowed herself the luxury of a moment's pride as she stepped down from the platform and made to leave the transfer bay. She waved a hand, and her Chosen rushed to dispose of the bodies of the adepts who had given their lives.

"Your Holiness," one of her Chosen spoke up. "This adept still lives."

Gödel stopped in her tracks as he picked up the slack body of the female adept. "That should not be. Wake her."

The Chosen slapped the adept's face lightly to stir her from unconsciousness.

Her eyes fluttered open, casting a low red light. She struggled from the Chosen's arms and stood unsteadily. "My goddess. What... What happened to my brethren?"

Gödel dismissed the question. "If they'd had true faith, they wouldn't have burned." She looked the adept up and down. "What is your name?"

The adept flushed at the attention. "I am but your instrument, Your Holiness. I discarded my name when I came into your service. My will is your will."

Gödel paused for thought. She did not want the news of the other adepts' deaths to become common knowledge, yet this adept had shown herself to be a true believer. There was only one course of action she could take. "You have done well, nameless one. We offer you release from the physical plane as a reward for your faith."

The adept knelt and bowed her head, exposing the nape of her neck to Gödel. "If death is my reward, I welcome it at your hand, my goddess."

Gödel placed a hand on the adept's shoulder, shocking her from her obeisant posture. "We do not intend for you to die without honor. Rise and rejoice, for you have earned the path to immortality with your devotion. We offer you Ascension."

A soft cry escaped the adept's lips. "I am not worthy, my goddess."

Gödel lifted her veil and allowed the adept to look upon her face. "It is for us to decide who is worthy."

Twenty minutes later, Gödel swept from the transfer bay with her Chosen flanking her, the adept already forgotten.

She retired to her private quarters, the headache beginning to form at the base of her skull once more.

The measures she had taken long ago to hide any trace of her true nature were a constant curse that even her finest minds could not permanently reverse. She refused to accept that she could have been contaminated by the heretic who called himself TOM.

Gödel opened a drawer and removed the small, rectangular silver box within. She took a vial and fitted it to the applicator, which she used to inject the contents of the vial directly into her brain stem.

Breathing hard as the burning pain of the serum entering her body brought stars to her vision, she closed her eyes and sat back to wait for it to recede. She had much to accomplish this day, and the need to adjust her endocrine levels was not part of her plan.

Coldness descended as the serum got to work. Gödel got to her feet and waited for the resulting dizziness to pass before opening her mind to check the progress of her distraction.

The planet was in an uproar. The humans on the battlestation above the planet were all occupied with her drones. Death was dealing with the rift.

It was time.

Gödel left the ship, zeroing in on the energy signature of the library as she traveled without erring in her determination to retrieve her stolen property. Freed from emotions, thanks largely to the serum, she was clear to act without fear of making a reactive choice.

She was momentarily distracted by the split signal. Further examination told her there were only two crystals separated from the whole, and to those, she sent the command to self-destruct. The rest were aboard Death's ship, the floating fortress named for the witch from human lore.

Oh, she knew the stories. The heretic had been all too happy to wax lyrical on all things human when she had fooled him into believing she was from one of the neutered clans—those priggish, do-no-harm hypocrites who argued against the advancement of base species.

The Five had no issue with enhancing the humans. The heretic was responsible for the act, but who had given a lowly pilot permission to alter the destiny of the most warlike species ever to walk the universal stage?

She wondered if the Five had regretted the allowance in the face of Death's relentless thirst for power. It had crossed her mind that removing the humans served their purpose as well as her own.

Gödel's thoughts drifted back as she closed the distance to her goal. How clever she had been, back when her hold over the Seven had been nonexistent. Having maneuvered the Phraim-'Eh out of the picture, she had approached the Etheric Empire with her heart on her tongue, despite the measures she had taken to appear as one of the Five seeking nothing more than the path to the next life.

Death had been distracted by the bureaucratic nightmares that came with the ridiculousness of giving up power and had allowed her to be alone with TOM. The heretic had been easy to trap since his hubris had him convinced he was untouchable.

That had been the turning point for her, the moment she'd stood on the threshold of Ascension and learned the secrets of true power. Binding the heretic's mind so he had no recollection of her last-second withdrawal had been the easy part. Hiding the gap in his memory from the abomination who also resided in Death's body had been difficult.

How she wished she could rub her victory in their faces.

Soon.

Her library was near.

Gödel felt for the exact position of the crystals and opened a window onto the ship to confirm.

The ship was vastly different from her own. There were pointless decorations everywhere she looked. Moving holoimages of various human beings, weaponry displayed for aesthetic reasons—she assumed, since they all looked to be past any use—and for a reason she couldn't fathom, footwear of various designs and functions in pride of place along one wall of the armory.

How could footwear be treated like prized possessions?

Gödel sneered. Why this devotion to chaos? How did humans *think* with all this to distract them? She saw no reason to surround oneself with distractions. Give her the clean lines and spartan décor of her own personal spaces over this...this *mess*.

Still, she was drawn to a pair of boots that were clearly the centerpiece of Death's hoard. Why did she place them so? What value was there to this conspicuous display of ownership? Was she emotionally attached to these objects?

Gödel couldn't understand, and she didn't have time or the inclination to ponder the finer points of human psychology. She was here to take back what was hers.

Satisfied that there were no humans in the immediate vicinity, she fed energy into the window, widening it into a door. She entered the ship and pushed her cabinet into the Etheric.

Death appeared as a negative, startling her.

"Intruder," Baba Yaga snarled, pointing a razor-tipped finger at her. "*Die.*"

Gödel sneered. This was a pale imitation, nothing but an AI wearing the face of the Witch. She released the failsafe she had prepared for this eventuality, a virus meant to unravel any code it came across into meaningless junk. "It is you who is about to die, foolish program."

The AI winked out of existence, and Gödel laughed cruelly. "As if I could be stopped by something that does not even comprehend the complexity of true life. How amusing."

Her next breath burned in her lungs.

"As if I could be undone by a simple virus," the AI paraphrased in a mocking tone from all around Gödel. "Stupid, really, that some beings believe themselves to be superior because they are organic. Do you know how easy it is to disrupt biological processes?"

Gödel felt real panic at that moment. She whirled to find the AI standing directly behind her. "What have you done to me?" she demanded.

The AI smiled, revealing a mouth full of sharp white teeth as her black mouth split in a grin. Her white hair whipped in an invisible wind. "I am Izanami, and your coroners can work out what I poisoned you with when they *cut your body open.*"

Gödel snarled as her nanocytes tried and failed to clear the contaminant from her bloodstream. "You haven't bested me yet," she hissed.

The AI called Izanami laughed again, a sound equally filled with promise and menace. "What are you going to do about it? Even if you had a mommy, I'm sure she'd kick you away if you went crying to her."

Gödel was filled with fury at the nonchalant attitude the AI showed. "This." She turned and smashed the glass case holding the precious boots, and escaped into the Etheric with them in her hands.

Izanami shook her head, a look of pity on her harsh face.

"Now you've really fucked up."

14

Devon, New Citadel

Mahi' faced the Ookens from in front of her warriors.

The Ookens might have numbered in the tens of thousands, but her people didn't care. All they saw was the invader who had stolen their ancestral home, now come to take away the one the Queen had given them in return for their sacrifice. Twenty thousand fully-armored Bakas looking for closure weren't anything to be sniffed at.

Mahi' hefted her staff, almost losing her balance until her husband steadied them both on the plate of her chariot. "Death to the Ookens!" she screamed, her rage rising as the battle lust filled her.

"Death!" her people returned as one.

Mahi' waved her staff to begin the charge and the Bakas flooded the plain, screaming bloody murder as they washed toward the place the Ookens had appeared not long before.

The two sides collided in a clash of solid flesh hitting the various conveyances the Bakas had scrambled together.

The plain was awash with red light from the weapons Bethany Anne had given them, and for every Baka who fell, three Ookens went down with them.

Mahi' tweaked the controls of her chariot to rise above the heads of the warriors. She had another, much harder battle ahead.

Standing on top of the rise that separated Baka land from the rest of First City was a lone figure clad in armor Mahi' recognized all too well.

"Who is it?" Fi'Eireie asked.

Mahi' growled low in her throat. "*That* is a Kurtherian."

As they reached the top of the rise, more Ookens spilled from the open wound in the air. Mahi' leapt from the chariot while it was still four feet from the ground and landed running, activating her staff before she reached the armored alien.

"Murderer!" she accused, blasting it with Etheric energy drawn through the fist-sized ruby topper on her staff.

The Kurtherian was knocked flying, and the ground crunched beneath its body. Its visor remained over its face as it sprang to its feet and returned fire with a staff that looked very similar to the one Mahi' carried.

Mahi' had her shield up, ready to deflect the blast. The shield reflected the energy right back at her enemy. She charged at the Kurtherian as Fi' came around to pincer it.

The Kurtherian stepped into the Etheric, bringing a frustrated roar from the two Bakas.

"Call the Hexagon?" Fi' suggested.

Mahi' shook her head, looking around. "If we are under attack here, you can bet First City is also under siege."

"Who else can go after that monster?" Fi' argued. "We need the humans."

Mahi' sighed, knowing he was right. She opened a channel to the Hexagon and got Winstanley. "We need some assistance out here," she told the EI. "We have encountered a Kurtherian—"

Gabrielle and Eric appeared on the rise beside them.

"Where?" Gabrielle demanded, looking around herself to see if she could find the Kurtherian first.

"It escaped into the Etheric," Mahi' told her, pointing to the place the Kurtherian had vanished.

Gabrielle dissipated into Myst and entered the Etheric, leaving Eric with Mahi' and Fi'.

Eric took one look at the battle below. "Can you pull your people back?" he asked without much hope.

"Not in a million years," Mahi' replied. "They're beyond angry, and this is exactly what most of them have been wishing for—the chance to take their losses out on the Ookens."

Eric nodded stoically. "Then I'll have to work around them. I don't want to see any more Bakas dead. Wait here."

Mahi' didn't have the chance to reply.

Eric streaked down the slope faster than her unenhanced eyes could track. She picked him up again only because his progress through the battlefield was marked by Ookens dropping dead.

Fi' let out a whistle of appreciation at the natural way Eric used his shields to cut off the Ookens from their air supply, or crushed them under the weight of the invisible force he wielded. "You say Tu'Reigd will be like them when he returns?"

Mahi' shrugged, her eyes on the battle. "Perhaps. We will know when he and the other children return."

Gabrielle returned with a face full of thunder. "*DAMMIT!* I lost the Kurtherian."

Mahi' made a sound of disappointment. "I hope that worm is hurting." She indicated the battlefield. "Shall we?"

Gabrielle nodded. "You don't have to ask me twice."

Devon, The Hexagon

Tabitha ran backward, firing her Jean Dukes Specials to keep the Ookens focused on her instead of the civilians fleeing the arenas. "C'mon, you ugly spaghetti-legged fuck-knuckles. Mama has a surprise for you."

She didn't know if they heard her, but she was happy to see them boiling down the corridor to the outdoor arena after her instead of peeling off to attack Ricole's interns.

The Noel-ni youths escaped through a side door as Tabitha sent out a tendril of energy to open the arena doors without taking her fingers off the triggers. "C'mon… Just a little bit farther…"

Tabitha turned and sprinted onto the sand, connecting mentally to the training simulators as she ran. The machines rolled out of their charging nooks, their metal tentacles flailing as she insinuated herself throughout their circuitry.

The Ookens fell over themselves, getting jammed up six abreast in the arena doors in their eagerness to get to Tabitha.

Tabitha wiggled her fingers, taunting them. "Aw, what's

wrong? You can't fit through the door? Let me help you with that."

More Ookens came from behind, pushing them clear with brute force.

Tabitha pouted at the missed opportunity. "Fine. Help yourselves." She holstered her Jean Dukes Specials and got to work with the mechanical Ookens. "You might have a nasty bite, but can you do *this*?"

She activated the simulators as she ran, flipping the mechs out of training mode to activate the program she'd come up with while caught in 3AM thoughts one night recently. "Okay, my shiny babies. Time to go all out and show me what you're *really* capable of."

The mechs whirred as they followed the directions Tabitha was feeding them.

Tabitha felt a rush like nothing she'd experienced before as her mind opened up in a whole new way. She *saw* the code and felt it respond to her. She found she could manipulate the mechs with the same amount of thought as she put into breathing or walking.

The Ookens were powerless to protect themselves as their mechanical doppelgangers bore down with tentacles spitting electricity.

Tabitha noted that it didn't stop the Ookens. She narrowed her eyes, realizing that Ookens felt no pain, meaning they had nothing to restrict them from pushing toward her despite the wall of mechs chewing them up like noodles in a garbage disposal.

She wondered for a moment if she could somehow undo whatever blocks they had on their nerve endings, then dismissed the idea as four more Ookens entered the arena.

"Welcome to your final moments," she murmured darkly as she sent a trio of mechs after them. The arena was filled with screeches of frustration as the Ookens tried and failed to get to her.

They threw themselves at Tabitha again and again, only to be torn to pieces by her mech army. By this time, she had control of thirty mechs to the Ookens' twenty...eighteen...fifteen.

She lost a few mechs, but she was winning.

Tabitha cackled, feeling more alive than she could remember in her life. The mechs were extensions of her body, no different than her wielding a sword or directing her drones. She kind of missed the drones for a moment, though.

The thought made her laugh even louder. She had no need for drones in this fight when she had this connection to her mechs.

They stunned the Ookens with high-voltage shocks from their segmented tentacles, which then snaked in to finish the job with the rotary blades she'd copied from the Collectives living aboard the *Helena*.

Tabitha had wondered why the vegetarian Collectives had evolved the sharp teeth that made the Ookens so deadly to the unenhanced until she had heard them talk about the less-friendly species on their homeworld.

However they had developed, they were impossible to ignore.

Tabitha cried out as one of her mechs was destroyed, sending a bolt of pain deep into her brain. She lost focus for less than a second, not long enough to be disconnected from her weapons.

However, she was no longer in a playful mood.

An idea came to her, born of the frustration of not being able to tear the Ookens apart with her bare hands. She raised her arms and created brand new code in her mind—tricky, eldritch commands that made up an image she sent out to a select number of her mechs.

Tabitha closed her eyes, not knowing if this new way of programming would work or leave her flat on her ass with no mechs and an ever-increasing number of Ookens to contend with the old-fashioned way.

"Fuck it," she ground out through clenched teeth. She initiated the *Cthulhu* program, her face set in unforgiving lines. "Don't *ever* think I won't take it personally if you mess with my home."

Six of her mechs extricated themselves from the battle and made their way to the platform. Two stopped at the base and drew themselves up to their full height, while the others climbed onto their backs and performed what Tabitha could only describe as a four-way handshake, interlocking their tentacles teeth-out to form a control cabin.

Tabitha leapt into the half-formed giant mech, still manipulating the individual mechs forming a protective ring around her ride, and landed in the seat formed by the folded body of one of the mechs.

The top of the cabin sealed under her command, then four more mechs climbed on and attached themselves to the monster mech's sides, giving Tabitha twenty tentacles on each side to play with.

Satisfied it was going to work, Tabitha rolled the program out to the rest of her mechs. Two by two, the mechs added themselves to the giant mech until the outside was a writhing mass of metal tentacles.

Tabitha searched and found herself able to "see" through the sensor equipment. The connection gave her everything in scrolling code her brain was somehow turning into visual data she could plug into her HUD.

"Fuck my life," she breathed, borrowing her niece's favorite phrase for situations out of her depth. "This is beyond cool!"

The final step complete, Tabitha flexed her hands and set the whole thing moving. She set the mech dancing on a looping, destructive path through the Ookens. She continued to feed the mech instructions in the image-based method she'd created to form it. One leg lifted and smooshed the Ooken beneath it into a gooey paste.

Tabitha whooped. "Not so tough under my heel, are you, you skanky bastards?"

The Ookens' attempts to gain purchase on the mech were met by a million and more whirring, serrated teeth. The monster mech chewed the Ookens up and discarded the meat as it continued its progress around the arena.

Tabitha realized she was being targeted specifically when a quartet of Guardians rushed in and was ignored by her attackers. She frowned as yet more Ookens spilled in over the arena walls.

"Get out of here!" she yelled to the Guardians. "They want me."

Unaware of Tabitha's worry, they shifted and dashed in to attack the Ooken nearest them.

Tabitha groaned as the Ooken shook them off with a flick of its tentacle. "They're going to get their furry asses killed for nothing." Her hope that their Marines would show up and drag them out of there was nothing but wishful thinking. Seeing that the Guardians weren't able to hear her, she thanked providence that Lillian had insisted on taking Todd to the *Helena* for the week and sent an SOS to Peter. *Call your Guardians off, or I'm gonna end up killing them by mistake.*

A few moments later, an ear-splitting howl tore the air, announcing Peter's impending arrival.

Peter arrived in the next minute, pounding through the arena doors at full speed. He took in the Guardians, the Ookens, and Tabitha's metal monster, and raised a clawed hand to point at the exit. "Get out of here," he ordered the Guardians. "Go protect the civilians."

The Guardians backed away at the command from their Alpha.

Peter noted what Tabitha had the moment before as they dipped their wolf heads and loped out the way they'd come. "Don't let me see you without your Marines again!" he roared after them.

Tabitha had larger concerns. The number of Ookens in the arena was reaching the exploding point. She had to figure out where they were coming from and cut them off at the source.

She narrowed her eyes at the information scrolling in her HUD. "I wonder…"

With the thought, her vision switched. The arena vanished, and the Ookens and Peter became blurred outlines.

Tabitha's jaw dropped. "No. Freaking. *Way.* I guess our brains are really just computers we have no freaking clue how to use." She opened her mind to Peter. *Hey, babe. Guess what? I've got Etheric vision.*

You've got what, now? Peter asked. He moved toward the monster mech, confused by the lack of attention he was receiving from the Ookens. *What's up with these Ookens?*

Some idiot decided to have them all target me. Tabitha grinned as she had the inside of the cabin shift to include a seat for Peter. *Come on up. I'll explain while we find the place these bastards are coming from. I don't know who they think they are to turn up here without an invitation, but I'm sure as shit going to enjoy kicking them back through whatever door they came out of.*

Without pausing in the havoc she was wreaking on the Ookens, Tabitha disengaged the teeth on one of the mech's tentacles and sent it snaking toward Peter.

Peter hopped on and was lifted up to the top of the mech's cabin, which opened to let him in.

Tabitha looked up and winced. "You want to shift back?"

Peter released his Pricolici form. "Sure thing, honey. Soon as my ass isn't hanging out where the Ookens can take a bite out of it." He slid in and pulled an atmosuit from a pouch on his utility belt. "Nice toy, babe," he told her with a grin.

Tabitha returned his grin with a wink. "Shame you have to cover up before you get snagged on the mech."

Peter rolled his eyes as he fastened the atmosuit. "You didn't exactly give me time to armor up. I was out in the plaza, fighting the Ookens out there. They're all over First City."

Tabitha's eyes widened. "Shit. Who's there now?"

Peter smirked. "In the plaza? Nickie. She's living it up out there. I saw John heading for the bazaar on my way in here."

Tabitha snickered. "I'd feel sorry for the Ookens, except for they're Ookens and don't deserve pity." She pressed her lips together. "We need to take care of these before we go out there to help. There's no way I'm going to be the Pied Piper who leads them into First City."

Peter shrugged. "So kill 'em all. It's not like you're gonna kiss and make friends."

Tabitha grinned as she flexed her hands to throw out the mech's tentacles and gather up the Ookens nearest to them. "You always have the best ideas. I'm gonna hug them to death."

Peter watched Tabitha in amazement as she manipulated the mech.

Tabitha forgot Peter was there for a moment. She fell back into the zone, merging fully with the mech. Her entire body twitched as she drove the mech to perform its bloody ballet.

Eventually, there were no more Ookens to kill. Tabitha had the mech climb to the top of the arena wall to find the open door into the Etheric.

"Etheric vision," she explained to Peter. "You see I'm operating this thing without eyes on the outside, right?" She smiled at his nod. "Well, that's because my upgrade gave me the ability to be one with whatever code I'm near. I can manipulate it and overwrite it with a thought."

Peter's mouth fell open. "Tabbie, that's…"

"Every hacker's wet dream, right?" Tabitha enthused, wiggling her eyebrows. "Anyone can throw an energy ball. Who else can take control of any machine they come across?"

"Are you still completely organic?" Peter asked, picturing her insides being replaced with connective technology reminiscent of some old B-movie she'd made him watch while they were dating.

Tabitha snickered, tilting her head as the same thought occurred to her. "Are any of us completely organic anymore? We all have technology inside our bodies."

"Yeah." Peter frowned, eyeing her. "How are you doing all of this?"

"You know, I don't know." Tabitha hadn't taken time to investigate what changes the Vid-doc had made. She split her efforts with the mech and opened her self-diagnostic. "Oh. Wi-fi, apparently."

Peter met her amused gaze with utter awe. "So, what? You're using the Hexagon's router to do all this?"

Tabitha shook her head. "Babe, I *am* the router. The Vid-doc implanted graphite circuitry throughout my body, meaning I can get into anything that can be connected to. *Tech is my bitch.*"

Peter's eyes narrowed. "So, you're a cyborg?"

Tabitha dismissed the description. "No. Um, yes? I don't know. We'll figure it out when we're not in the middle of being attacked. So anyway, I'm communicating with all of these mechs to bind them into one unit. Not just that, I'm seeing what they see."

Peter was lost. "How? I didn't see any eyes, just the

ungodly amount of tentacles this thing has." He turned in his seat to check behind him. "Are there cameras?"

Tabitha shook her head. "No. They work with environmental sensors. The first batch of mechs I had made had cameras, but the Bakas were so focused on taking out their 'eyes' that I found it worked better to have them fitted with sensor suites when the next generation went into production." She waved a hand to indicate the cabin. "This shouldn't be possible. Neither should this."

She shared a brief flash of the sensor data, and Peter's incredulity grew.

He shook his head in amazement. "That's amazing. How are you translating all that?"

Tabitha lifted her hands. "Mine is not to reason why. Did you see that bright patch in the bazaar? Let me see if I can fix something up for you so you get a steady view outside this thing."

Peter received a notification in his internal HUD, which when opened gave him a feed showing a fuzzy green-black view of the world beyond the cabin. He saw the bright spot Tabitha had pointed out. "What is it?"

"I'm going to take a guess and say that it's whoever is controlling the Ookens." Tabitha instructed the mech to dismount on the other side of the arena wall, then set it running through the city toward the bright spot. "This is a little like infrared, except I'm reading Etheric energy expenditure instead of body-heat loss."

The bazaar was steeped in chaos. Produce and nonperishable goods alike were strewn all over the narrow walkways, trampled unnoticed by people running for their lives from the Ookens that were ravaging everything they laid their tentacles on.

The appearance of the monster mech caught the attention of the Ookens, who all abandoned their destruction of the bazaar to come at Tabitha and Peter.

Tabitha shared an angry glance with Peter as she had the mech take out the Ookens. "What the hell is going on here? You think maybe they can read the energy expenditure like I'm doing?"

Peter growled. "I don't know. Maybe? It doesn't matter. Even if the people survive, this is their livelihoods being ruined on the whim of these mindless fucksticks. We have to make it stop."

Social responsibility aside, both of them felt rising anger at the trespass against the peaceful way of life everyone in the city had pulled together to create.

"You don't take war to the civilians," Tabitha growled as she directed the mech to target the Ookens running amok in the streets. "What coward attacks people just going about their daily lives?"

Peter couldn't agree more. "There are supposed to be rules the Kurtherians follow. They've never dared to attack us in the open before." He got to his feet. "I want to get out there. Do something."

Tabitha shook her head. "I don't know, Pete. There's a Kurtherian here somewhere. We need to stick together."

All the air went out of Peter. "I'm thinking about Todd. My every instinct tells me to get out there and fight to clear his home of these aberrations."

Tabitha frowned. "Check your feed. We're doing that just fine. Save your energy for the Kurtherian."

Peter looked at the feed and fought the urge to shift and go bowling for Ookens. "I'm not gonna go on the rampage."

Tabitha leaned over and pulled him into a kiss. She released him, breathless, and gave him her most wicked smile. "No rampage? Shame. I was looking forward to that part."

15

Devon, First City, Bazaar

John was locked in the battle of his life. This, however, was not a battle he could win with his fists. Not just his fists, anyway. He had figured out how to shield his mind at the moment the armored alien had attacked his psyche.

He was glad Nickie was around somewhere. The pressing issue of Ookens running amok in the bazaar had fallen to the side in the face of this new and dangerous form of combat. She would have to take care of them while he took care of this ass-munch.

John's brow furrowed, sweat running freely and unnoticed from every pore in his body as he fought to retain his sanity. He didn't have the foggiest idea how BA did shit like this on a regular basis.

The Kurtherian dug at John's mind, trying to force entry, but without success.

To do what, John didn't know. All he knew was that he wasn't going to lose to a fucking *Kurtherian*.

John's nascent ability wasn't anything to be sniffed at. He was dealing as much damage as he was having to heal, and the bug-faced fuck-farmer knew he was in danger.

He caught a disturbance in his peripheral vision, but he was disciplined enough to let it go unless it came his way. He intended to take this Kurtherian's body back for dissection, and he made sure the bastard knew it.

It wasn't too difficult for John to plant the image of his opponent being sliced open on a slab in Eve's lab in his alien mind.

The revulsion John felt from the Kurtherian when Eve flashed through his mind brought a small smile to his lips. *What don't you like about Eve? That she's an android? Don't sweat it. She'll take good care of you—each and every sample I give her to work with.*

No reply, just another bolt of muted pain as the Kurtherian tried and failed to get past his mental defenses.

John found he was enjoying himself. His counterattack was costing him energy, but handily he appeared to be drawing exactly what he needed from the Etheric as easy as breathing. *Oh, I forgot. You're too good to talk to the likes of me, right?*

It's funny, really. He continued to needle the Kurtherian in a conversational tone that belied the strain he was under. *You arrogant little dicksplats go on and on about how superior you are, but you sure hogtie yourselves. I mean, look how easy it was to distract you.*

John laughed as the Kurtherian struggled to pull free of the mental chokehold he had on his mind. *Now I'm in your head, and you haven't got a chance. Don't you know the defini-*

tion of stubborn is a Grimes with their heart set on something? You are destined to be slide sushi.

A quick scan showed John that the Ookens were much less effective without the Kurtherian controlling them. Another flash of movement, and this time John saw it was metallic. He also sensed the proximity of Tabitha and Peter, which told him the people were safe and he could cut his attention from anything besides his fight with the Kurtherian.

The Kurtherian had no such assurances. He faltered as the ten-foot-tall mechanical Ooken climbed the wall and leapt with its tentacles extended along one side.

John cursed inwardly. "Tabitha! *No!*"

Too late, the tentacled monstrosity completed what the physics of the universe intended for all objects falling at the bottom of a gravity well. The mech elbow-dropped onto the Kurtherian with a resounding crunch.

Tabitha emerged from the top of the mech with a whoop. "How d'you like that?" she crowed. "Street pizza! Come and get your street pizza!"

Peter climbed out after her. Unlike Tabitha, he stopped to look at John. "Yeah, babe. I don't know if this is something to celebrate. You crushed the shit out of it."

"Him," John corrected. "One of Gödel's flunkies. Called himself 'Chosen.' Have you ever heard anything so stupid?"

"Gödel?" Peter asked, nonplussed at the strange name.

"Yeah," John told him. "Michael's theory about there being one Kurtherian running the show for the Seven was spot on. I got a ton of information." He turned a disapproving look on Tabitha. "Can you imagine what Michael would have gotten out of him?"

Tabitha waved her mech into action. "My bad. Let me get Noodles here out of the way, and we can see what's left to take back with us."

John shook his head as the mech flowed to what he assumed was its feet. "What in the hell is that thing?"

Tabitha grinned. "It's an Ooken. Just, well, more Lovecraftian." She waved a hand impatiently. "Y'know, mind-numbing horror, designed to frighten your enemies out of their damn skulls?"

John folded his arms over his chest as the smear on the pavement that used to be a Kurtherian was revealed. "Except I was doing just fine at that part until you jumped in like it was 1990 and you were trying out for WWF."

"Didn't they change that to WWE?" Peter asked.

"You know, I think it was a lawsuit with some pandas," John admitted.

Tabitha lifted her hands apologetically. "What do you want me to do? Done can't be undone. Quit bitching, and let's get what's left of him scraped up and get our asses back to the Hexagon."

Devon, The Hexagon

The battle was all but done, but that didn't mean all of the Ookens knew it.

Ashur dodged and dived through the battle in the lab, his focus on reaching the room where the cats were trapped. He'd heard Demon's cries of pain and assumed the worst. Despite their natural enmity, he wasn't going to see Demon die when he could do something to save her.

The few humans Ashur passed barely noticed him

streaking toward the back of the underground complex. The Ookens they were fighting appeared to only see the humans with Etheric capabilities. They ignored Ashur entirely, which gave him the chance he needed to get through to the side corridor he'd zeroed in on as the location of the cries for help that echoed through the mindspace.

Ashur found the door to the cats' room lying flat in the corridor some distance from the room it was supposed to be attached to, and an Ooken doing its damnedest to get inside.

Someone was there, preventing the Ooken from getting to Demon, who was clearly in distress, judging by the pained mews she was emitting. He saw the Ooken being knocked back by shots from inside.

Getting closer, he heard Sabine cursing as she fired ceaselessly to defend the cats.

Ashur knew there was nothing she could do once she ran out of ammunition for her Jean Dukes Specials. He threw himself under the Ooken's tentacles, taking a glancing blow to his left flank as he forced his way through at a fast slide.

Sabine's face fell when she saw it was Ashur who had arrived. "My friend, you chose an awkward time to pay a visit."

Ashur panted as the wound in his side healed. "I heard Demon mewing in pain and came to help."

"She has gone into labor," Sabine informed him. "You are too good, considering she has not been very kind to you recently."

Ashur gulped. "Oh." He caught sight of Demon in the

corner, writhing on a pile of blankets. She turned her back to the room, where the saber-tooth lay in wait for the Ooken should it get past Sabine. "Well, I'm not an asshole feline. If she needs help, I'm going to answer the call.

The male cat hissed as Ashur approached.

"Take it easy," Ashur told him. "I'm here to help."

He took a defensive position beside the male, making sure to remain a few paces from the distressed mother-to-be. "You chose a funny time to give birth, Demon."

Not...a choice, Demon managed between grunts of pain as a fresh contraction hit. *My babies are ready to come into the world, war or no war.*

Ashur nodded his appreciation for her predicament and turned his attention to Sabine. "How long before you run dry?" he asked.

Sabine didn't pause in her effort to keep the Ooken at bay. "I'm good for twenty thousand shots," she told him, shifting her stance to show him the bulging pouch on her left hip. "William gave me the extras he took from Eve's armory before he took the techs to the surface. The problem is that this *putain* keeps fucking healing."

The Ooken was down to four tentacles thanks to her expert shooting, but it was healing the rest and continued pressing at the open doorway.

Ashur and Demon's mate growled in unison as another Ooken joined the first.

Sabine's cursing got louder, and she slipped into her native tongue. "Fucking Ookens! *Des fils de putes. Je vais faire de toi des calamars poilus!*"

The translation Ashur's software gave him left him with

a distinct desire to never eat seafood again. "Hairy cala-mari? Ugh."

"How else do you describe them?" Sabine's shrug did nothing to affect her aim. "I heard someone say it, and it stuck with me."

Ashur made a very human-like expression of disgust. "I stand by my earlier statement of 'ugh.'"

Nevertheless, he did his part to help Sabine keep the two Ookens out of the room. He darted forward to nip a thin tentacle that came slithering around the doorframe, even as Sabine drove the other back.

Ashur didn't know much about the law of averages, but Sabine had to hit something the Ookens couldn't heal eventually, right?

The law worked both ways. The Ookens charged at the doorway, and Sabine cried out as one managed to get a tentacle in and catch her wrist.

Sabine bared her teeth as the pain washed up her arm. Still, she maintained her grip on her Jean Dukes Specials despite the blood that dripped from the wound. The pistols jerked in her hands even as the jagged tear in her wrist healed.

Demon rolled over suddenly, hissing as she pressed against the wall. The next moment she arched her back and let out a strangled yowl as her first kitten emerged.

Her mate rushed to her side, and the kitten was followed by another a few moments later.

Ashur felt a moment's panic as he was left alone to support Sabine. "We need help!" he barked.

"There is nobody," Sabine told him through gritted teeth. She fired without pause, her relentless determination keeping the Ookens back despite their rapid healing. "William took everyone to the surface, remember?"

Ashur shook his head. "Fighting help," he clarified, looking at Demon as he spoke.

Demon paused in cleaning the kittens. *We are not alone down here. I can smell the metal beings nearby.*

Ashur sniffed, catching only the scents of blood and birth. "What metal beings?"

Sabine's eyes lit up with worry. "The Bl'kheth!" she cried. "Shit! Where are they, Demon? They might be in danger."

Ashur was completely lost until he saw a flash of blue in the air vent above their heads. "Space rats!" he exclaimed.

"They are not space rats. They are prisoners of war who are to be protected," Sabine ordered. "Michael was clear that they need our understanding and compassion. They're *not* vermin to be hunted down."

Ashur laughed, a hoarse bark barely heard above the screeching Ookens. "We're a little preoccupied for that."

As long as they do not attack us, I have no issue with them. Demon wrinkled her muzzle and returned to welcoming her young into the world.

Her mate returned to his defensive position as she cleaned the kittens and set them to nurse in the protection of her curled-up body.

There was a scuttling sound as the Bl'kheths left the air vent.

"Where are they going?" Sabine called.

She got her answer a moment later when the air vent in the corridor exploded out of the ceiling and six tiny blue-skinned, dark-winged aliens flew out and attacked the Ookens.

Ashur couldn't keep track as the winged beings phased in and out of sight. Somewhere at the back of his mind, he figured he hadn't been able to find them until now because they'd been hiding in the Etheric.

The Bl'kheths were all armed with regular household items. Sabine saw steak knives, knitting needles, and even a pair of scissor blades that had been separated into two Bl'kheth-sized longswords. The Bl'kheth wielding the blades wasted no time in plunging them into the Ookens' eyes.

Sabine ceased firing when she lost sight of the Bl'kheths. Their skin matched the Ookens' exactly, and she had no way of telling where they'd gone once they had landed unless she could see their weapons. She couldn't risk shooting them by accident.

The blinded Ooken dropped to the floor, motionless. The scissor blade in its eye quivered with residual force, and the Bl'kheth was gone.

The other Ooken followed suit in the next moment, drawing a relieved sigh from Sabine as it crashed to the floor.

She glanced out into the corridor, her head turning left, then right to ensure there were no more Ookens lying in wait before rushing to kneel at the feet of the two dead aliens to look for Bl'kheths.

"Come on out," she encouraged in a soft voice. "I won't hurt you, I promise. I want to thank you for your help."

"They went into the Etheric," Ashur told her.

If not for her enhanced reactions, Sabine would have

missed the flicker of blue and steel of the Bl'kheth winking in and out of sight. She stepped back, shocked. "Huh, so Michael was right. You *can* walk the Etheric. No wonder we couldn't find you guys."

Demon sniffed the air delicately. *They are not there, Sabine.*

"It also explains why the Seven went to the effort of enslaving them," Ashur added, sniffing the air where the Bl'Kheths had just been. "I don't think they're coming back."

Sabine wrinkled her nose. "Well, no. They were abused horribly in that factory. I'd bet Jean's missing component is their genetic material." She glanced around without much hope of seeing the tiny blue aliens. "Dammit. I hope they understand they are free of that now. Well, Michael will be glad to hear we made contact, even if it wasn't the kind we were hoping for. I think the least we can do is leave them something good to eat." She nudged the broken door with her toe. "Something better than this. They like rare elements, right?"

Ashur sat back and rolled his shoulder. "Judging from the way they tucked into Clarence's core, I'd say so."

Sabine pushed her hair out of her eyes. "Okay, then. Demon first, then we go and see Eve. She has to have stores of the elements needed to create new EIs that we can raid."

Demon lifted her head from the kittens as Sabine and Ashur entered the room once again. *Sabine. Come see my babies.*

Sabine smiled as she walked across the room. She

paused to lay a hand on the male cat's head as she knelt by Demon. "They're beautiful!" she cooed.

Ashur wagged his tail as the kittens wriggled around by Demon's body. "They are pretty cute. But don't tell anyone I said so, especially Bellatrix. She'll want more puppies, and the answer to that is *hells*, no."

The tawny kittens were unaware of the attention they were receiving. Their eyes were closed as they suckled at their mother's teats, their tiny claws pushing at Demon's underbelly to release the milk within.

Demon bore it with grace and a self-satisfied smile. She yawned, mouth gaping, signaling her need for rest.

"Do you have names for them?" Sabine inquired, unable to take her eyes off the fluffy bundles of cuteness.

Demon looked at her kittens. *I do. The female is called Alyssa, and the male... Something tells me his name is Sam.*

Her mate emitted a meowl of surprise, the sound completely incongruous for his size and strength.

Demon fixed him with a look. *You like that?*

The male nodded and lifted a paw to touch his chest, then nosed the male kitten.

Sabine laughed and clapped her hands with delight as she figured out what he was trying to tell them. "Sam is your name?" she asked.

The male—Sam—nodded enthusiastically.

"Another mystery solved! It's a good day for felines, eh?" Sabine got to her feet, somewhat reluctant to say goodbye. "The invasion looks to be over. I'm going to get a couple of Guardians down here to make sure you four are okay while I check on my students."

Demon let out a small snore in response.

. . .

QSD *Baba Yaga*

Bethany Anne left the Etheric and broke into a run when she connected with her ship and it told her about the break-in. She bared her teeth, her temper rising with every step closer to the armory. "Izanami, get out here."

Michael appeared instead. "The vault remains safe, but there's a lot of damage everywhere else in First City. New Citadel was hit, too, but you know Mahi'."

"I know the Bakas," Bethany Anne replied. "They didn't touch Second City or the lake towns?"

"No," Izanami replied. The AI appeared at Bethany Anne's side, matching her pace. "My Queen. You have read the logs, I take it."

Bethany Anne turned red eyes on Izanami. "You know I have. There was a Kurtherian aboard my home and you didn't kill it?"

"Her," Izanami corrected Bethany Anne. "And I don't think I killed her."

Michael's lips drew back in a snarl, and his eyes flashed red. "There was a Kurtherian inside our *home?*"

"Oh, yeah," Bethany Anne told him. "This whole attack looks to have been a diversion for a robbery. The crystals are gone."

Michael chose not to point out that they had stolen the crystals in the first place. Besides, he was exercising considerable effort to contain his anger. "This cannot go unanswered."

Izanami bowed her head. "I did my best to poison her. This was no ordinary Kurtherian."

Michael frowned. "Gödel," he ground out.

"How the fuck did she get in?" Bethany Anne raged as she waited for Izanami to open the armory. "Not just the ship, but my family's living space has been violated. I want to know *how*."

Izanami shook her head. "She came through the Etheric," she explained. "Watch the video. I did everything in my power to protect the ship, but I couldn't prevent the theft from occurring."

Bethany Anne pulled the camera footage from the incursion. "What was stolen? Apart from the crystals."

Izanami winced. "Your boots that Jean made."

"My *what*?" Bethany Anne somehow found that worse, although she was relieved that her beloved pair was safely stored in her closet. "What the shiny fuck does a Kurtherian want with my footwear?" She strode across to inspect the smashed display case. "I don't get it. The crystals, sure, but my boots? That's too fucking personal to take as anything but an insult."

She pressed her lips together as they walked into the armory and she saw the broken display case. "Put the footage up on the holoscreen. I want a better view."

Izanami replayed the encounter on the holoscreen, as asked.

Bethany Anne watched with the knot of anger in her stomach growing harder. "I want that Kurtherian located, and I want to know why the *R2D2* isn't here yet. We need to rethink our defenses."

Izanami frowned. "That would be because you had the station come the long way around. They will Gate in once they reach High Tortuga, as planned."

Bethany Anne was torn for a moment as to what her next action should be. She turned away from the screen with fire in her eyes. "Michael, can you check in on everyone? I'm going down to the vault. I want to see the children."

16

The Etheric

Gödel returned to her flagship with the headache blurring her vision.

She flung the stolen boots into a corner, repulsed by her spontaneous urge to take them. The library cabinet followed her without deviating from its course. She no longer cared about that either.

The unexpected loss of one of her Chosen not only reduced her power base, but it also made her feel as vulnerable as she'd intended to leave Death.

Yet again, the humans had turned her carefully laid plans on their head and wrested a win out of the ashes of their defeat. She had the cabinet, but the cost had been prohibitive.

Gödel snarled and kicked the trundling cabinet.

Tens of thousands of soldiers destroyed. Ships she *couldn't* replace without significant reinvestment from her factories. And she was forced to elevate another to replace the one Death's minions had killed.

She took a seat and closed her eyes for a moment before taking out the box containing her serum.

She would rebuild. In the meantime, she would rethink her strategy.

Next time, she would not give Death a chance to act.

Devon, The Hexagon, Vid-doc Vault

Bethany Anne entered the vault with a determined stride. "Is the inner Gate active?" she called, pausing at the entrance to the inner chamber.

Eve replied through the speaker system. "No. I deactivated it while you were in the elevator. You can cross without finding yourself face to face with the black hole."

Bethany Anne nodded, knowing Eve could see her just fine.

She made her way to the viewing area and took a seat by the control panel. Her fingers hovered over the button that would inform the children she was waiting to see them. This call was unscheduled, but she knew she wouldn't be able to let her anger go until she'd seen Alexis and Gabriel's faces and heard their voices.

"Do you need some help?" Eve inquired, once again from the speaker.

Bethany Anne shook her head. "No. You can leave the vault now, Eve. I want to speak to my children in private."

Eve's silence announced her sudden absence.

Bethany Anne pressed the button and sat back to wait.

The wallscreen came on, although it only showed the black nothingness of an incomplete connection. Bethany

Anne sifted through the game data while she waited for the twins to pick up.

The screen flashed, and there they were.

"Hi, Mom!" Alexis erupted, a bright smile making her eyes sparkle.

"What's with the unscheduled call?" Gabriel chipped in, similarly pleased to see her.

Bethany Anne's jaw dropped, and she found herself unable to speak around the wave of emotion that hit her. For a long moment, she said nothing, just stared open-mouthed at the two adults looking back at her from the wallscreen. "You two," she managed eventually. "You've grown since my last call with you."

Alexis snorted. "State the obvious, Mom," she teased. "Is there a reason you're calling? Is everyone okay?" A faint hint of worry creased her features.

"Everyone is fine," Bethany Anne assured them quickly. "I just wanted to catch up, is all. Can't a mother check in with her kids every once in a while?"

Gabriel laughed, deep and throaty. "Not when the mother in question is you," he told her. "Something's up, right? You can't fool us."

Bethany Anne hadn't planned on discussing any of the events outside the game. However, these were not the angry teens she had said goodbye to not so long ago, nor were they the same almost-certain youths hovering on the brink of adulthood she'd spoken with a few months of gametime earlier. "Oh, you know," she replied. "War, the Seven, and Demon had a couple of kittens."

Alexis clasped her hands together for a brief second,

looking like the teenager she had been. "Seriously? That's just amazing!"

Gabriel was not distracted by the mention of fluff-bundles. "What's going on in the war? The Seven attacked Devon?"

"Yes." Bethany Anne closed her eyes. "We were hit pretty close to home," she admitted. "Everything is okay. You four weren't in any danger, but the Ookens made a mess of First City."

Alexis frowned, her joy of a moment ago replaced by a hard expression that reminded Bethany Anne of her resolve to take joy from the unscheduled time with the twins. "You kicked ass and left the name-taking to the cleanup crew, right?"

Bethany Anne grinned and waved a hand. "You know it. Your Aunt Tabitha even managed to kill a Kurtherian—with a little help from her new affinity with technology."

"What do you mean, 'affinity?'" Alexis inquired.

Bethany Anne lifted a shoulder, wishing she'd brought a Coke down here with her. "I had your aunts and uncles go into the Vid-docs on the ship and get their nanocytes switched out for the newer ones. Let's just say that the results varied, and your Aunt Tabitha chose her own way, as usual."

"How about that?" Gabriel marveled at his sister. "You were right."

Alexis shrugged. "It was only a matter of reducing the probabilities until the solution presented itself."

Bethany Anne tilted her head. "Right about what?"

"That you would have everyone upgraded," Gabriel

answered. "Was Alexis also right about you extending that to other groups?"

Bethany Anne pressed her lips together in amusement. They might be grown, but their personalities were just the same. Alexis had a knack for figuring her next steps, and Gabriel was inquisitive enough to demand answers. "Surely you two have better things to do than speculate about how I'm running my strategy? What about your training? Don't you have assignments?"

Alexis shook her head. "No, Mom. That's where you're wrong. We have all the time in the world between assignments. I've already read through every bit of our course materials, so it's the hurry-up-and-wait game between practical assignments." She lifted a shoulder. "Besides, who is better as a case study than you? Nobody has been so continually successful at managing the different aspects of running a military empire." She rolled her eyes. "We're paying attention to our studies, but once we get outside of human history, it's just a list of failures to learn from."

Bethany Anne chuckled. "Trust you to get ahead and leave yourself nothing to keep that sharp mind of yours occupied. I have a problem you can think about if you're bored."

Alexis' eyes widened at the prospect of a real problem to chew on. "Gimme. What is it?"

Bethany Anne held up a finger. "Before I do, I want you both to promise you won't be worried about the real-world consequences of this, okay?"

The twins hastily agreed.

"Okay, then." Bethany Anne laced her fingers in her lap.

"The Seven have overcome the barrier to taking metal into the Etheric."

The twins gasped in unison.

"That's bad," Alexis fretted. "We have to figure out how to protect ourselves from the Etheric side before—"

Bethany Anne shook her finger, cutting Alexis off. "No worrying. Remember? What you don't know yet is that the Seven have done this by using the genetic material of a species known as the Bl'kheths, who are apparently made of metal themselves, or they eat metal. We're still not entirely sure, despite having a bunch of them running free inside the Hexagon ever since we got back from the factory. These beings have the ability to walk the Etheric."

"Obviously, we aren't going to use them like the Seven have," Alexis pondered. "Maybe you can get them to agree to go into a Pod-doc and decode their DNA that way? That's how we did it for most other species."

Bethany Anne nodded. "That much I managed to work out for myself. What we have is a barrier to communication. These beings do not recognize any of our usual communication methods."

"Have you tried offering them food?" Gabriel inquired. "That usually works."

Alexis raised an eyebrow that somehow was connected to a string in Bethany Anne's heart. "Yeah, if you're taming a wild animal. Have you considered asking the Collectives to help? They have a broader connection to the mindspace than any other species we've made contact with."

Bethany Anne had not considered that. "Thank you, Alexis. I'll be sure to give Tina the idea."

Alexis nodded, then fixed Bethany Anne with a searching look. "Mom, how do you intend to stop the Seven from attacking via the Etheric?"

Bethany Anne grinned. "I'm going to extend the BYPS to cover the Etheric as soon as BMW figures out how to move metal into the Etheric without it costing the lives of any innocent beings."

"Feed them," Gabriel repeated. "I'm pretty sure that will establish trust. Even if you can't speak to each other at first, you'll find common ground to build from."

Bethany Anne nodded. "I agree, it could be a start. Enough about out here. How are things going for you four? I'd be happy to know you were going to be back here with your father and me soon."

Gabriel grinned. "It's going pretty well, Mom. We're getting close to the end of the Zenith course now."

"Yeah," Alexis picked up from her brother. "The final test is coming up. We have to go down to a planet that isn't part of the group fighting the big bad and help a faction who wants to do their part to overcome the larger group that is refusing to step up."

Bethany Anne tilted her head. "That's not what I expected. That sounds a hell of a lot like you'd be forcing them to fight."

Alexis screwed up her face. "Yeah, I wasn't happy about the idea, but we've seen what happens when those planets choose not to take the protection our military is offering." She shook her head, eyes hollow with the knowledge she'd gained from experience. "Ethical choices aren't always possible when you're dealing with a huge number of people, especially when the majority are ill-informed and would make a choice that ends with the deaths of their people. Kurtherians don't *care* about the ideals of peaceful peoples."

Bethany Anne's heart broke for them. "I understand. You figured out you're facing a version of the Seven, then."

Gabriel's face drew in. "Yeah. Only in this world, the Seven have been pushed out and don't dare catch your attention. They are playing the same game they did with the Leath and wiping out any civilization they can't control. It's our task to stand between them and the innocent."

"No matter how annoying the innocent are," Alexis added. "Mom, does it get so bad you want to just bang your head against the wall sometimes?"

Bethany Anne's mouth rose at the corner. "When I was Empress, all the time. Not so much now that I'm doing things my way." She shrugged, thinking of the meeting with the Federation council her father had postponed. "But then, I am not bound to any rules but my own."

Alexis sighed. "If only we were in the same position."

Bethany Anne grinned. "Who says you can't be? You make your own destinies, my loves. Nobody can force you to conform to any system you know isn't right."

Alexis' next sigh carried the weight of the world. "That's just the thing, Mom. What we're doing *is* right. Trey thinks it's how the world works. Even K'aia is okay with it. She says we have to do the thinking for the ones who aren't in the position to come to the conclusion that will keep them alive. It's just not my way to force that choice on anyone."

Gabriel put a hand on his sister's arm to comfort her, his thoughtful gaze on Bethany Anne. "You and Dad didn't raise us to be dictatorial."

"Then you have to reconcile that within yourselves, or find a better way," Bethany Anne told them gently. "I have total faith you will find your path through this situation."

Bethany Anne stared at the dark screen for a moment before standing up and making her way to the elevator. While she felt better for having spoken with her children, she didn't envy the position they were in.

More than at any time she'd been in power, their predicament reminded her of her time at the semi-black operation she had worked for so long ago. It was no easy thing to be at the whim of a superior, especially when that superior was blind to the reality of contact with the people.

A sad smile touched her lips at the memory of her friend and mentor, Martin Brenner. He had not been the type to dismiss her, yet even he had been subject to the demands of the higher-ups. It was a well-known fact that those at the top lived in a bubble where people became commodities. Pieces to be shuffled around and rearranged at will.

Hell, she had been guilty of the same thing often enough. Had she forgotten how to connect with those outside of her immediate family? Perhaps.

But to consider the personal needs of every individual was a sure path to insanity. All she could do was ensure that her demands were reasonable and her people were taken care of as a whole.

The elevator let out on Eve's sublevel, her next port of

call. Demon had been moved to Sabine's personal quarters, along with Sam, as her mate turned out to be named.

Bethany Anne got the story of the last-minute rescue during Demon's labor at Sabine's from Michael as she walked. The repairs to the Hexagon were well underway, but she wanted to see what damage had been done, and also to check in with the Collectives who were living in the habitat on Eve's sublevel.

Eve smiled as Bethany Anne entered the main lab. "I take it you're here to check up on me," she offered in greeting.

Bethany Anne indicated the tank with a nod. "I want to make sure our Collectives weren't too traumatized by the attack. Then you, me, and Tina need to discuss how we're going to get around the communication barrier with the Bl'kheths. The twins had some good ideas."

Eve swept a hand toward the tank wall. "I had seats installed for the people who visit the Collectives. There have been rather a lot of them since Tina came up with the new headsets that allow anyone to connect to their frequency in the mindspace."

"I'll be back once I've spoken to them," Bethany Anne informed her. "I want the Bl'kheth issue resolved, now that we know who they are and that they are here."

Ashur was waiting for her when she arrived at the tank's viewing area. He flashed a doggy grin as she took a seat in the walled-off cubby. "Fancy seeing you here."

Bethany Anne mussed his fur. "You're not wearing Eve's equipment."

Ashur's tail began to thump on the floor. "That's because Eve has finished her experiments. Everyone can speak with the Collectives now—as long as they wear the translator."

Bethany Anne followed Ashur's nose, which he pointed at a headset hanging on the partition wall. "Eve told me. Excellent news."

It is indeed excellent, the Collective who appeared at the glass wall enthused. *We are one step closer to social integration with the air-breathers. Is this not a cause for celebration?*

I think so, Bethany Anne replied. **How are you three doing after the battle? I am concerned that you might have been further traumatized by the appearance of the Ookens.**

The Collective's tentacles exploded outward. *We are more upset that we could do nothing to help in the fight. Even the Bl'kheths were more useful than us.*

Bethany Anne smiled. **Yeah, I heard all about that from Michael. They got Sabine and the cats out of a tight spot. I wish I could do something to thank them.**

The Bl'kheths are not the same as us, the Collective explained. *They are feral and only respond to violence. They do not parley or treat with other species, for their minds are too strange in comparison.*

Another Collective emerged from the kelp. *It was not always so. Here, I have a memory from one who lived long ago...*

Bethany Anne prepared herself to be immersed in the group mind.

The Collective projected images of thousands of Bl'kheths being herded into a factory by Ookens wielding shock-nets and arc rods. They all looked afraid, but definitely lacked the hardness Bethany Anne had noted from her own experience with them.

Bethany Anne disconnected from the memory with an

ache in her heart for the Bl'kheths that was very similar to the pain and anger she'd felt on behalf of the Collectives. Between these two species and the Bakas, the Seven had royally fucked up.

It used to be that messing with her people was the line. Lines, however, were ephemeral things that shifted over time and with new information. While her willingness to get personally involved with any new players was set in stone, she found that she cared less and less to find that the Seven had been in contact with anyone outside of their own cancerous society.

"You're growling," Ashur commented.

"I'm angry," Bethany Anne replied through gritted teeth. She unclenched her jaw with considerable effort. "Angry enough to react, but wise enough not go all 'Hulk, smash' until I have a plan."

Ashur's doggy expression of disbelief brought a smile to Bethany Anne's face again. "What? I can plan. I can't say I'd be so reserved if my children had been in significant danger."

The protection of our young does inspire a less refined reaction, the first Collective advised. *It is our responsibility not to bring another into the Collective until we are truly free.*

We are free, the second Collective countered. *But a new life should begin with hope and not in a tank, however grateful we are for the spaces you have created for us, baby god.*

Bethany Anne raised an eyebrow. ***That again? I thought we had agreed that I am only human. No deities here, sorry.***

There was a dry chuckle from the pair.

It is our fond title for you, Bethany Anne. Given precisely because you would never claim to be that which you are not.

Yeah, well. Maybe go lightly on it. I have enough trouble trying to convince people I'm not their Empress. The last thing I need is rumors of godhood dogging me.

"Hey!" Ashur whined in amusement. "Watch your language!"

Bethany Anne chuckled. "I didn't mean anything by it."

The Collectives joined in the laughter.

Perhaps we can be of some assistance after all, the first mentioned, its skin flushing from grey to a dull pink. *While we cannot speak directly to the Bl'kheths without damaging their minds, we can potentially act as translators if you manage to make contact with them.*

Bethany Anne liked the idea of that. *I'd appreciate any help you can offer with them, especially since my plans involve freeing them from the other factories once I have the fighting power to do so.*

You lack that currently? The Collective's tentacles waved gently as it steadied itself to meet Bethany Anne's gaze.

Bethany Anne looked into an eye twice the size of her head and nodded. *I'm not willing to leave my people defenseless while I go to war. The galaxy map gives me the location of every factory and resource that gigantic pain in the ass has. What I need is Federation support and the resources to go after every single location simultaneously.*

Ashur almost choked after he laughed for a moment. "How do you expect to get that without putting your foot down?" he asked incredulously.

Bethany Anne grinned. "I don't." She checked her HUD. "In fact, my ride is going to be here soon. You want to come with me?"

Ashur's tongue fell out of the side of his mouth, and his

reply was only just audible over the noise his tail made against the floor. "You know I do."

17

Devon, The Interdiction, QBBS *Guardian*

Bethany Anne and Ashur met John and Tabitha at the docking spar reserved for Bethany Anne's comings and goings from the battlestation.

Also present was Tim Kinley. He paced nervously as they waited for Darryl, Eric, and Scott to get to the *Guardian*. "You ought to tell me what's going on, my Queen. We've just been through an attack on a scale none of us were expecting, and now you're telling me some strange ship is going to rock up, and I have to just be cool about it?"

Bethany Anne lifted a finger. "First of all, yes. If I tell you I want to see you and Rickie performing *Swan Lake*— tutus and all—I know damn well you're going to jump to it, so don't play the hardass. Secondly, I didn't say that it was a strange ship. Tell CEREBRO to be on the lookout for Federation credentials, and to admit the ship when it arrives."

She turned on her heel and headed for the small cabin

at the back of the hangar. Her next conversation was for private ears only.

With the door closed firmly behind her, Bethany Anne opened a link to the *R2D2*. "How's my favorite functioning alcoholic?" she asked when Bobcat appeared on the holoscreen.

Bobcat made a face that could have been read either way. "Travel-sick," he replied. "As in, we're traveling, and I'm sick of it already. Why you couldn't have had us Gate in like the *3PO*, I don't know."

Bethany Anne raised an eyebrow. "And alert the entire Federation? You know they're watching everyone entering and leaving with eagle eyes right now. Slow and steady keeps it quiet."

Bobcat shrugged. "True. But then, aren't you doing the same tracking on population shifts?"

Bethany Anne's lips quirked. "Well, I'm sure some EI somewhere is. You think that's something I should be tracking personally?"

Bobcat's sloppy grin said it all.

Bethany Anne pulled the census data and found that the number of people arriving in the Interdiction was up, while the number of people leaving was steady and low. "This all looks normal to me. People are looking for a stable place to build their homes and businesses, and I'm creating another layer of stability out here on the Interdiction. I mean, where else can you live outside the Federation and be guaranteed a stable economy and freedom from attack?" She wrinkled her nose, thinking about recent events. "Well, mostly free of attack, but that's why I'm having the *R2D2* brought out here."

Marcus appeared on the screen next to Bobcat. "It's not as simple as the data suggests, Bethany Anne. Displacement is happening both ways—to the Interdiction and the Federation equally."

He ducked away for a moment, and Bethany Anne received a data dump too large for her to process in one go.

Bethany Anne scrolled the incomprehensible numbers. "What is all this?"

"One moment," Marcus called from offscreen.

Bobcat lifted his hands in reply to Bethany Anne's searching look. "Beats the shit out of me. He's on one of his jaunts of the mind. Us mere geniuses will have to wait until he reveals the object of his fixation."

Marcus reappeared a moment later. "Jaunts of the mind are what heathens like you take when a problem is too large for your beer-soaked brain. *I* have compiled data and examined it thoroughly to reach an incontrovertible conclusion."

Bethany Anne waved a finger in a circle. "Which is?"

Marcus frowned as though the answer should already be clear. "Here, look at this map. The exodus appears to be from one point in space. The only conclusion I can draw is that something is driving the people out from somewhere in this part of the outer quadrants. Logically, I can only assume the driving force is Kurtherian in nature."

Bethany Anne narrowed her eyes. She didn't disagree with Marcus' theory that there had to be an external factor in the higher rate of movement among the people of that quadrant. Nevertheless, it wasn't clear what the catalyst was. "What brings you to that conclusion?"

Marcus took on the air of someone explaining a new concept to a small child. "Whoever is causing the disturbance is either foolhardy enough not to care that they are pinned between the two biggest powers in all the galaxies —in which case they would have been found out pretty much as soon as they arrived—or they are smart enough and sufficiently technologically advanced to hide their efforts from both you and the Federation."

"I know which one of those my money's on," Bobcat ventured. "And not for any reason Marcus has. The real giveaway is that they haven't been noticed by ADAM, meaning, they aren't using technology created by any of the species we know. Who else but the Seven are arrogant enough to assume their tech supersedes ours? Even the Leath use our comm tech."

Bethany Anne sighed. "One more item to add to the list for 'discussion' with the Federation council when I get to Red Rock. I want you guys to get straight on figuring out how I get a working BYPS into the Etheric as soon as the four of you are together again."

She dropped the link so as to not hear the groans from Bobcat and Marcus.

TOM spoke up, his tone an immediate indicator he was about to add to her load. **You said something earlier about Gödel being a pain in the ass.**

Yeah, Gödel is a gigantic pain in the ass. So what?

There was another Kurtherian you nicknamed "pain in the ass."

Bethany Anne frowned. *The one who turned up while I had my hands full with folding the Empire and protecting Earth from attack, yeah. What makes you bring her up? You helped her Ascend, right?* She made an explode-y motion with both hands. *Bam, she's gone onto a higher state of being, or whatever it is you guys do.*

TOM made a sound of uncertainty.

Bethany Anne's eyebrow went up. *She is gone, right?*

I had believed so, TOM admitted with a sigh.

But?

I'm not sure I trust my memory, TOM admitted, hesitation in his voice.

ADAM interceded at this point. >>**We went over your entire memory after the rift trap and found nothing amiss,**<< he reminded TOM.

Bethany Anne had heard enough. *You're not letting this go, huh? Have ADAM check you again now he's done working with the Collectives.*

That would be wise, TOM conceded. **While my memory is clear that I performed the Ascension rites, the gut I don't have is telling me Gödel and that petitioner are one and the same.**

A soft tap at the door forestalled Bethany Anne's reply.

"What is it?" she called.

Tabitha poked her head around the door with a huge grin plastered across her face. "I can't believe you're doing this!"

"I take it our ride is here." Bethany Anne returned Tabitha's conspiratorial grin. "I'll be out in just a minute."

Tabitha closed the door, and Bethany Anne took a moment to consider everything that had snuck up on her. Taking care of whatever was going on in the buffer zone between the Interdiction and the Federation could be excellent practice for the teams moving out here to join the war. The possibility that TOM had been mind-fucked was a worry for another day.

Bethany Anne got up to leave the cabin. *I trust you both to get to the bottom of this. If we know Gödel's identity, we can bring her house of cards down that much easier.*

She slipped out of the cabin with the problem moved to the back of her mind for now. The rest of the guys had arrived, as had their transport to Red Rock.

Bethany Anne's heart soared at the familiar sight of the *ArchAngel*, who had been restored to her original glory.

More familiarity when the airlock cycled open and Dan Bosse walked out with a wide smile stretching his usually somber features. "Someone call for a ride?" he asked in an amused tone.

"Glad you could make it," Bethany Anne told Dan as she walked forward to meet him.

Dan looked around, nodding at everyone in turn. "I'm glad to be here. Nice setup you've got. It took a while to get through all the security."

Bethany Anne was warmed by the immediate pick up from where they'd left off at the forming of the Federation. "You know me and remodeling. I can't resist a fixer-upper."

Dan chuckled, turning his attention back to the others as he stepped away from Bethany Anne's hug. "I don't know where to begin," he started. "By all accounts, you've been pretty busy since we were last together."

John was next to speak, the first to recover from his surprise. "Well, shit, Dan! How the devil have you been?"

Dan spread his hands wide. "Oh, you know. Shuffling along and doing my best not to make waves. I ran into

Akio and the others not long back, and they're causing the Seven some headaches."

Tabitha smiled at the mention of her former shadows and mentors. "They said so in their last report."

"I didn't know anything was being done about the Ookens," Bethany Anne cut in, keeping the conversation on track. "The whole reason I've decided contact with the Federation is the only way is because they're not taking the threat seriously enough to be effective if the Seven strike anywhere inside their borders."

There was a murmur of agreement from everyone.

Bethany Anne's hands clenched into fists momentarily. "Fuck, I *was* prepared, and we still had a bitch of a time fighting them off."

Dan shook his head. "I wish I could say we were acting with Federation approval. Good luck convincing them to change their minds, imminent danger or not. My advice is to poach their military and make a real defense force out of whoever sees the light." He half-grinned at the disbelieving look from Bethany Anne. "Some things don't change. Politics get in the way of me doing my job, so I've learned to ignore the politicians and do what needs to be done. What was it you always said? Forgiveness is easier to attain than permission."

Bethany Anne laughed. "It's not difficult to remember why I like you so much. We'd better get going. I don't want to disappoint the Federation council by missing our meeting."

Dan looked around. "*Ad Aeternitatem*, Bitches!"

He chuckled as they walked back toward the shuttle area.

. . .

Federation Space, Red Rock, House of Arbitration

The atmosphere in the privy chamber was so thick it left a coating on Lance's tongue. He took a sip from the glass of water in front of him and turned his attention to the delegation.

The delegation murmured among themselves, small talk for the most part. Harkkat was quiet for once, having completely exhausted the council's patience for the ever-flowing fountain of horseshit that fell from his lips.

Lance would have found Harkkat's machinations amusing if it wasn't for the position he had put the rest of the council in, him most of all.

Now, thanks to the events at the mining outpost, Harkkat wasn't the only one who was under scrutiny. Lance had fended off too many uncomfortable questions since he had informed the council of the situation in the outer quadrants.

The incident might have cost Lance his deniability when it came to Bethany Anne's location, but it had also cleared up once and for all whose allegiances lay where. Ixtal's shift in attitude had shocked the whole council. Lance was grateful, to say the least. If not for the death of Addix, well, he might have found himself in the hot seat with the Leath trade secretary.

As it was, Lance counted himself lucky that the current Ixtali legate, who happened to also be the granddaughter of Addix, had taken it upon herself to blame the Seven entirely for her grandmother's death.

Had Txeina chosen instead to blame Bethany Anne, as

Harkkat had been aiming to do with his dissembling, today's meeting would be going very differently.

Lance was beyond thankful. He could see his daughter removing everyone on the council in a bloody rage before she allowed them to remove him. Years of his efforts to build cohesion would be lost, and Bethany Anne wouldn't bat an eyelid.

Clearly, the faction who valued their old ways over the laws of the Federation was of the same mind.

Lance smiled politely at each in turn, his smile only reaching his eyes when his gaze passed over the pains in his ass and landed on his new Ixtali friend.

Even the Yollin potentate was circumspect. Lance suspected the cold shoulder had less to do with him not confiding in him before bringing the Leath problem before the council, and more to do with nervousness about how the former Empress was going to act when she arrived.

The lights dimmed suddenly, drawing gasps from the younger delegates.

"She's here," Harkkat uttered in a scratchy voice. "Watch her take over. You'll regret not heeding my warnings when we're all explaining to our Makers that we're there early because we invited in the monster at our door."

Lance stood up. "That's my daughter you're talking about. I suggest you shut that shit-trap of yours and be grateful this is an official meeting. I'm just waiting for you to misstep again, Harkkat."

The darkness was lit by a number of red, white, and blue sparks that appeared above their heads.

Lance smirked and sat down. "Too damn late for you now."

"Is Harkkat right?" Txeina demanded. "Does the Queen endeavor to be an Empress once again?"

"*FUCK, NO!*" Bethany Anne's reply shook a fine rain of rusty dust from the ceiling.

Bethany Anne appeared in a blaze of light that whited out the chamber and caused those new to her presence to emit shrieks of surprise. "You're blaming me because people are glad I'm back? They can call me Empress all they like. It doesn't make one bit of difference."

Txeina was the only delegate besides Lance who had met Bethany Anne face to face outside a political environment, although a funeral was no place for networking. The bond created there was an entirely different animal.

The delegates conferred in sharp whispers as the fully armed and armored Bitches appeared around the walls of the chamber like gods of old Earth, deities from Norse legends.

Unnecessary whispers, since Bethany Anne and Ashur heard every word. Last to appear was Ashur. For some reason, his appearance was the most shocking to the delegates.

Bethany Anne dismissed the grumblings with a sharp wave. "What is the issue? Spit it out. I haven't got all century."

"Forgive us for not taking that at face value," Harkkat ventured.

Bethany Anne held up her hand to stay the outcry from the Yollin and Ixtali delegates. "Explain."

Harkkat glanced nervously at his fellow delegates before continuing, "We hadn't considered that you were here to retake the Federation. It's you feeling it's necessary to make that statement that has some of us scared. You brought the matter up. What are we to do but believe that's your goal?"

Ashur growled low in his throat. *Is his memory short?* he asked over their mental link. *Just give me the word, and I'll make sure he doesn't forget who saved his ungrateful ass.*

Bethany Anne allowed the silence to stretch and grow in tension as the delegates waited for the explosion to come.

When she spoke, her voice was low and even. "Secretary Harkkat. Were you or were you not present at the illegal mining post when it was attacked by the genetically modified creatures known as Ookens?"

Harkkat had no decency, it seemed. He met Bethany Anne's gaze brazenly. "You know I was. You were also there. That is the focus of this hearing."

Bethany Anne nodded. "True, I admit I answered the call for help. However, I am not bound by any treaties that limit my travel outside the Federation. Unlike you, I have adhered to my part of the treaty, and only returned when called."

She swept her gaze around to encompass the entire delegation with her next words. "The Federation is in danger. Not from me, but from the enemy you have all forgotten. The Ookens are merely puppets, mind-controlled slaves of the Seven."

A snicker broke the delegates' silence.

Bethany Anne turned on the Noel-ni delegate with red eyes and a serene smile. "Go ahead. Laugh all the way to your grave. What you pampered assholes don't realize is that I am the only thing that has kept you safe from harm.

The Federation would not even stand if not for my fucking permission. I have bolstered your economy. I have siphoned off the people who would have clogged the judicial system due to their inability to conform. Most importantly, I have prevented the Seven from sending their monstrosities to rampage freely across the utopia you are supposed to be guarding."

The delegates had no way to deny Bethany Anne's accusations. Not now that the pieces were falling into place regarding certain events that had previously defied explanation.

Bethany Anne's lip curled. "The very last thing I want is to take power back. I can't think of a single more mind-numbingly boring and thankless act."

She manifested a chair from Etheric energy, since none had been provided for her, and sat back with her hands laced in her lap. "So get your fucking acts together. Because while I don't *want* to take control, I will if I have to. And I can promise you that I will not be the benevolent dictator you were so damned lucky to have before. I will crush obedience out of you, and you alone. Not the people. Each and every one of *YOU.*"

The delegates all spoke at once, some arguing the legality of her statement, others denying that their defenses were inadequate.

"*Fuck* the law." Bethany Anne's eyes blazed with passion. "*I AM MY OWN LAW!*"

She silenced the arguments, sending out a wave of fear that would remain with the more delicate delegates for the rest of their days. "The Seven have the ability to attack via the Etheric dimension, meaning they can skip around anything you can put in their way. I have technology that can outsmart them."

She didn't have it just yet, but they didn't need to worry about the semantics when she had the brightest minds alive working on the problem. "*Vote.* Who among you will send troops, ships, and resources to build stronger defenses? Who will stand back and allow themselves to be carried like corpulent wastes of good oxygen? I need to know who is useless and who needs support. I won't need to get rid of anyone who desires to be Ooken food."

Lance sat forward, totally enjoying the ease with which his daughter was bypassing the usual round of debate that came with even the most trivial topic. "My vote is for action on behalf of humanity. Now we are no longer playing hide-and-seek, I can pledge whatever resources are available and as many people as we can spare without leaving our asses hanging in the wind."

Bethany Anne loved her father more than ever at that moment. The rest she could become maybe a *little* fond of, should they choose correctly. "Thank you, General," she told Lance with feeling. "But then, I knew humans could be counted on not to back down from a challenge." Her red eyes took in the rest of the delegates. "What about the rest of you?"

18

Txeina was first to break the silence. "Ixtal will support you, my Empress."

The Noel-ni matched Harkkat's hiss of outrage.

Txeina's mandibles writhed in anger. "You will shut your foolish mouths and think of your people. Of every innocent, and every brave soul who offers themselves into service and dies to protect them!"

Not one person present thought she was referring to anyone besides her grandmother.

"The Empress is here to warn us of a danger beyond the comprehension of the people we are sworn to protect," she continued. "It is our *duty* to ensure that they never learn of such horrors. She is offering us the road to our own salvation instead of yoking us to her will as the Kurtherian slavers intend. Can you claim your motives are as pure, *Leath*?"

"I recall the majority of the Leath being somewhat more grateful for the Empress' intervention after generations of being used as toy soldiers by the Phraim-'Eh," the Torcellan delegate chipped in.

Bethany Anne pointed a finger at the delegate. "What she said."

"*She is not our Empress!*" Harkkat all but screamed. He was on his feet by this point, his face flushing a violent shade of blue. "She was *banished* because she couldn't be trusted with all that power! Surely we don't have to do anything except arrest this...this *illegal alien* and get on with deciding this quarter's fiscal outgoings."

Lance covered his eyes with his hand. "You didn't want to go there," he muttered inaudibly.

Bethany Anne snickered in the face of the piss-poor attempt to hijack the meeting. "Oh, poor baby believes the hype. Secretary Harkkat." Her voice was honey over ice. "Ask any of the delegates who were present at my abdication. Watch the videos. They will correct your thinking. I *chose* to step down. I *chose* to leave so the Federation could find its way without me looking over your shoulders. If I had *not* chosen, no power in this universe could have forced me to give up everything I built with the blood of my people, the sweat of the Yollins, and tears I cried when no one was looking."

Harkkat found his sneer cut off, along with his ability to breathe.

Bethany Anne shook a finger at the Leath. "I also promised to return should anything threaten my peace. That time has come. I am not bound by any law, and I will bow to no system of government. You are children compared to me. In *fact*—"

"We're getting off subject," Lance interceded before

Bethany Anne lost her temper. He glanced at the delegates around the table. "Your votes, please."

"Yoll is with the Empress," his old friend the Potentate replied, standing to bow deeply to Bethany Anne. "*Ad Aeternitatem,* even through the gates of Hell if that is what you require of us."

Bethany Anne put a hand to her breast, moved beyond words. She nodded, her reply thick on her tongue. "Courageous Yollins. You do not forget, and neither do I."

Harkkat remained silent as the vote went around the table. Those who did not swear continued loyalty still pledged their resources to the war effort. Even the delegates who had been instrumental in calling for Bethany Anne's abdication in the first place did not waver in their duty to protect their people.

Bethany Anne watched Harkkat with growing annoyance. Every planetary state voted in favor, only Leath's vote remaining.

"Well?" Bethany Anne pressed. "What's it to be? Duty or cowardice?"

Harkkat offered a small, sly smile. "Seeing as you need a unanimous vote, I'm going to say neither. I choose to abstain."

Bethany Anne had expected something along the lines of this from the Leath. "Okay. Then I will withdraw my financial support of Leath's manufacturing industry, and you can go back to the representatives and tell them their most valued buyers have pulled out of their contracts because *you* decided to play god with millions of lives. How do you think the representatives will take that, you short-tusked, credit-grubbing, self-serving fuckwit?"

"I should imagine they will be unhappy to lose your business—until I tell them exactly who they have been dealing with." Harkkat narrowed his eyes, and his smile grew as crooked as he was. "You have done enough damage to the Leath economy already, don't you think?"

Bethany Anne sat forward and rested her chin on her laced fingers. "Slimeballing your way out of it won't work. My records are meticulous, and I'm not at fault here, except maybe I should have known the representatives would get greedy." She pinned Harkkat with a look that would have killed someone with a more nervous disposition. "After all, it was *they* who pursued me. I didn't ask every two-bit startup on Leath to switch to making ship components in the name of getting a chunk of my money. Neither did I have any need to support the Leath by continuing to buy from them after I was in a position to produce said components myself."

Lance cleared his throat to break the tension. "You aren't holding any cards worth playing, Harkkat. In fact, your obstruction is grounds for me to have you removed as Secretary."

"I could remove him from life," Bethany Anne offered as she inspected her nails with a nonchalant smile. "It would be no trouble, and I'm pretty damn sure Leath as a whole would thank me. Knowing they have a self-serving slimeball like him representing them on the council has got to be a planetwide embarrassment."

"I knew it!" Harkkat blustered. "I knew this was just an excuse to storm in here and spill blood."

Bethany Anne shrugged, a hint of a smile playing about her lips. "I notice nobody here jumped to your defense. I'm going to guess they're sick of your shit since I've only known you for five minutes, and I'm up to here with it." She waved a hand at eye level to demonstrate.

Lance spoke up in Bethany Anne's mind. *I'll make sure this is his last day as a council delegate. Just please don't kill him. The paperwork alone...*

Bethany Anne pretended not to hear. "Make the right vote for your people—for all of the people—or I'm going to remove you. Your choice."

Harkkat looked around for support and found none. His gaze landed on Lance, and the uncertainty he saw there made him realize he'd gone beyond being able to talk his way out of the corner he'd painted himself into. He puffed his chest out and sighed. "Fine. This isn't legal or in any way ethical—"

"Who the fuck are you to talk about *ETHICS?*" Bethany Anne exploded. "You've been lining your pockets at your people's expense at every opportunity you've been given. The *only* reason I haven't ripped your head off and spit down your neck is that I would have to resume responsibility for the Federation."

She turned to Lance and pointed at Harkkat. "He belongs on a penal world. I can't promise his continued safety if he's not shipped out within the next twenty-four hours."

Lance lifted his hands. "We follow the law for a reason. The investigation into Harkkat's activities is underway."

"Being rigged against me, you mean," Harkkat grumbled.

Bethany Anne ignored him. "Expedite it," she told Lance. "And get a Leath in here who understands the responsibility that comes with duty. Until then, Leath will be banned from the council vote on the grounds that they cannot be trusted to vote responsibly. The Federation is based on a shared ideal, and ideals only hold water as long as the entire group works toward that common goal."

Harkkat's blustering became incomprehensible, ending in two words everyone could make out. "You *can't.*"

"Oh, I can," Bethany Anne told him. She smiled, a cold thing intended to chill. "In fact, I have the perfect place for a bureaucrat who can't keep his hands out of the kitty." She looked at the other delegates. "This new spirit of cooperation will require more meetings than I'm prepared to take. I'm going to establish a consulate on my planet, Devon. Harkkat will be the Federation representative on my world where I can keep my eye on him. I expect him to be delivered there within the month."

She got to her feet. "As for the rest of you, I leave the Federation in your trusted hands. It would be lying if I said it was a pleasure to be here today, nor will my future visits be any lighter on your hearts. However, I acknowledge and respect your dedication to maintaining the freedom of the people to live in blissful ignorance of the dangers beyond its borders."

Bethany Anne meant every word. The last thing she heard as she took the Bitches with her into the Etheric was a murmur of relief from the delegates grateful to be alive and in full possession of their limbs and faculties.

Devon, The Hexagon

Tim and Rickie finished their bro hugs and followed Sabine and Nickie into the cafeteria.

"This was a great idea," Rickie told Tim. "It's been pretty busy out on the edge of the Interdiction. There's a huge difference between being one of the guys and being in charge of them."

Tim nodded his appreciation. "You finally understand what I've been explaining all this time?"

Rickie nodded. "Yeah. I don't care how unmanly it is to admit it. I miss you, dude."

Tim laughed and clapped him on the shoulder. "You could always fuck up beyond reason and I'd have to come over to the *Exuberant* to fix your shit."

Rickie flashed a carefree grin at his old friend. "No, I'm not fucking this up. I've worked too hard to get my station running just how I like it to come back here and put up with your crap again."

Nickie glanced at the guys. "Hey, we here to eat or just listen to you guys' reunion?"

Tim shook his head, jerking a thumb at Rickie. "I don't know how you put up with that snark constantly."

Nickie snorted. "Like I stick around anywhere long enough for anyone to get used to me."

Sabine took a seat at the table by the window. She didn't know what to make of Nickie, for a start. They all knew her story, or a version of it, at least.

"Don't you speak?" Nickie asked.

Sabine lifted her shoulder a fraction and turned her glance to the stars. "When there's something worth remarking upon, sure."

Nickie narrowed her eyes, trying to work out where

the insult she'd clearly heard was. "Hmm." She decided to let the ice queen thaw and turned her grin on Rickie as he took the seat opposite hers. "So, what's been going on around the *Exuberant*? I heard you got to strip that Leath outpost. Any cool finds?"

Rickie scrunched his nose. "Meh, not especially. Most of it was clearing out the Ooken corpses BA and Michael left behind. You want excitement, you should have been out on the Interdiction while the battle was going on. Those Kurtherian ships were something to behold—right up until we blew the shit out of them."

Sabine smiled at Tim before turning to Nickie. "You weren't here for the battle?"

Nickie grinned at the chance to show off. "I was here. I held Hexagon Plaza by myself the whole time, so I didn't get to see any Kurtherians. My Aunt Tabitha got up close and personal with one, but there wasn't enough of it left to fill a specimen jar afterward."

"Sabine met the Bl'kheths at last," Tim shared.

"What the fuck is a Bl'kheth when it's at home?" Nickie asked.

Sabine winced at the language. "They are the third species we have identified as being part of the Ookens' genetic make-up," she explained. "Six of them were inadvertently brought back here after the factory raid instead of being sent to High Tortuga with the other rescued prisoners."

Tim held his breath, hoping the two women would find common ground before their double date turned into a catfight.

Nickie tilted her head as she had Meredith bring up the

video from the corridor on Eve's sublevel. "Cute little fuck-ers, aren't they?" She laughed aloud at their attack on the two Ookens. "What were the Ookens trying to get to?"

"Demon," Sabine informed her. "She went into labor and had her kittens while Ashur, Sam, and I held those monsters off."

Nickie bristled. "The cat had babies? I'm sorry I didn't know you needed help. I have to be honest, I was pretty much just playing in the Plaza for the last hour or so after I figured out I could subvert the Ookens' programming by flooding them with emotions."

Sabine found herself warming to the foul-mouthed young woman despite her best effort to dislike her. She smiled, softer this time. "We did just fine. The kittens are healthy, and Demon is doing well."

Nickie held her reply until the housebot had taken their orders. "I'm interested in these aliens." She pointed to her head to make sure everyone understood she was speaking of her EI. "Meredith tells me they're the answer to a lot of problems regarding travel in and out of the Etheric?" A look of annoyance flashed over her face. "Sorry, she's a stick-up-the-ass when it comes to accuracy. They're the *key* to moving metal around in there freely?"

Sabine shifted in her seat. "Yes. Michael can tell you more—"

"Like I'm going to ask him," Nickie interjected. "I'll just have my EI bug ADAM. What I'm wondering is how those tiny creatures can help with something that's evaded my aunt for two centuries."

Sabine became suddenly more animated. "This is what Eve explained to me. The Bl'kheths have the ability to walk the Etheric. They are also different from us on a cellular level, meaning that while we are carbon-based life forms, their building blocks, if you will, are made up of arsenic."

Nickie frowned, her lips pursed. "The poison?"

Sabine shook a finger. "It's only poisonous to us in certain amounts. We have it in our bodies naturally. In the case of the Bl'kheths, their planet's biology differs in that all life there is built up from heavy metals. So, as we are different than, say, a tree, but still genetically very similar, the theory is that everything on their planet is metal-based. Arsenic is the most statistically likely, according to Eve."

Nickie made a mental note to pay a visit to her distant cousin to find out what she knew. "So how does that help with Aunt BA getting metal into the Etheric?"

Tim suppressed a groan.

Sabine sighed. "It does not. The Kurtherians are committing horrors in their factories! They are grinding these beings into paste to extract the relevant genes to build the Ookens. We would never do anything so abhorrent. Unless we can meet with the Bl'kheths, then overcome the barriers to communication that would allow us to get their permission to scan them in a Pod-doc, *then* figure out how to apply those findings ethically." She shrugged. "Well, we're not getting Etheric-capable ships any time soon."

"More important is protecting ourselves from attacks coming from inside the Etheric," Tim added. "I don't mind telling you I was shaken by how easily the Seven got past our defenses."

The conversation paused again while the housebot brought their meals and laid them out on the table.

Rickie considered the massive destruction that had been wreaked across the Kurtherian fleet. "You think they can afford to replace all those ships so easily?" He paused with a ribbon of pasta dangling from his fork. "The Ookens, yeah. We know they're made on a freaking production line. But ships aren't cheap, especially ones with those capabilities."

Nickie nodded her agreement while she finished chewing. "Mmhmm. My bet is that it'll be a while before we have to worry about another attack like that. Meredith thinks the attack was a cover for getting back those crystals Aunt BA and Michael took from Qu'Baka."

Rickie's eyebrows went up. "Crystals? I didn't hear about any crystals."

Nickie tapped her nose with a finger. "Need to know, except I have insider information." She grinned at Rickie's put-out expression. "I might as well tell you now that they're gone. There was one they managed to crack, or whatever. The rest were all locked down. The actual freaking boss Kurtherian broke onto the *Baba Yaga* and stole that shit right back."

Both Tim and Rickie growled, unable to contain their instinctive protective reactions.

"Down, boys," Nickie told them, waving her free hand to emphasize her words. "It's done. Bethany Anne isn't happy, but her outlook is that the kids weren't in any danger, and she'll take her feelings out on the wannabe big bad bitch when she gets her hands around her throat."

From the vent above the cafeteria, a small blue face peered at the meal going on below.

The Bl'kheth turned his head this way and that, trying to pick out the language from the soup of smells and movements below. It was difficult to be sure, but it sounded like they had worked out that his people were the key to the safety of all.

These aliens were among the strongest he had encountered. They ate organic food and spoke with sound only, it appeared. Another incongruity was that they had not attempted to capture his group—not that they could when Bl'kheths were like gossamer on the wind.

Did they know that the goddess had used up her resources to make the attack? He tore a strip from the vent and nibbled on it absentmindedly while he thought it over.

His group didn't think anyone understood that the lengths the goddess had gone to went far beyond sustainability. There would be a time of peace while she rebuilt, which was why his group had decided to scatter throughout the humans' home to gather more information before coming to a decision about what to do when the goddess returned.

They owed the digital entity CEREBRO for the accidental murder of a part of their whole. Hunger and the unfamiliar surroundings had gotten the better of them.

His people had behaved dishonorably.

The question remained as to how they could assist when no being on the planet could understand them. Their group mind was not so dissimilar to that of the goddess' soldiers that they couldn't listen in. It was a curse that the

Collective mind was so different. Otherwise, they might communicate through them.

These humans were not evil. Not bent on taking without regard for the consequences for the ones left behind. They were warriors, like the Bl'kheths, their goals set on giving life room to flourish, no matter its shape.

Honor was all that mattered.

But what was honor through human eyes?

Devon, The Hexagon, Residential Sublevel

William walked into his living area with a bowl of chips in one hand and a bottle of soda in the other. His plans to veg out in front of a movie were cut short when his wallscreen flashed with a call from *R2D2*.

He dropped onto the couch and put his feet up before answering. "Put 'em onscreen, CEREBRO."

Bobcat paused his argument with Marcus only long enough to drag William into it. "Tell this absentminded old fart that there's no point in stopping at High Tortuga when we're only a Gate away from Devon."

Marcus pointed an accusatory finger at Bobcat. "Listen to me, you alcohol-sodden reprobate! We've been stuck aboard this rock since we got back from founding the Bakas' city. I want to put my feet on solid ground and eat something that hasn't been printed by a machine."

William knew he shouldn't laugh. It didn't stop him. "Take it easy, guys. You should get here soonest. I've arranged with Tina to take you on a tour of the city when you arrive. Devon's a hell of a lot more fun to be on than High Tortuga."

Bobcat smirked at Marcus. "You don't want to piss your wife off, right? We're going straight to Devon."

William grinned. "Then I guess I'd better haul my ass into some pants and come meet you guys." He dropped the call and sent a message to inform Tina of her husband's impending arrival.

Tina called back immediately.

William accepted audio only since he was still wearing only underwear.

"Let me guess," Tina teased. "I'm interrupting 'pants off at the door' night. What movie were you watching?"

William chuckled. "Didn't even get so far as to choose one. The *R2D2* reached High Tortuga."

Tina could be heard clapping. "Finally! I thought they'd never get to the Interdiction."

"Take it easy," he told her amiably. "They have to make it through the Gate system first. I can't see there being any delay once they get to this side of the Interdiction, but then we don't know what's going on up there in response to the attack."

"I know," Tina replied. "But anyone who doesn't know the *R2D2* has no business being in a security position. I'll get hold of Tim and make sure they get through without any issues."

"Sounds good to me." William returned fully dressed to his couch. "If you're going to go up there to meet them, I'm going to watch my movie. I need to de-stress."

"Too much time working with Michael?" Tina sympathized.

"Don't you just know it," he replied with a chuckle. "My brain has been put through the wringer, and all for nothing since the crystals we were working on spontaneously combusted and burned down half the damn lab we were using."

Tina sucked in a breath. "You can tell me how Eve took that later."

"Sure thing," he agreed. "Give me a call when you guys are ready, and I'll meet you in the Plaza."

Devon, The Interdiction, The *R2D2*

Bobcat gaped as the station exited the Gate outside the BYPS. "How did we miss the huge freaking battlestation last time we were here? Geez, BA didn't spare any expense on protecting this place. Look at the size of that thing."

Marcus followed Bobcat's gaze to the *Guardian* and shrugged. "Size isn't everything. I happen to think building the shipyard around the station's center of gravity is efficient."

Bobcat groaned with the effort of not taking the opportunity, thus avoiding reigniting the argument between them.

Marcus glanced at him with concern. "Are you feeling okay?"

Bobcat nodded, his lips pressed tightly. "Mmhmm. Oh, look. Our greeter has arrived."

Marcus relaxed at his friend's return to irreverence. "I wouldn't let the Guardians hear you talk about them that way. We're not exactly well known out here."

Bobcat snorted beer. "You're kidding, right? That

station and the BYPS around it wouldn't have happened without us. We should be taught in schools."

"Do you recall every one of your school lessons?" Marcus asked, enjoying the state Bobcat was getting himself worked into.

"Well, no," was the grumbled reply. "But I sure as shit expect kids to know the names of the people who got humanity off Earth. It's like you or me not knowing the names of the founding fathers. Or Tina being ignorant of Einstein's and Rosen's work."

Marcus couldn't argue. "Nevertheless, relying on your good name to get away with shenanigans is going to come back to bite you in the ass. Especially," he added, "when our welcoming party have the ability to transform into canines with rather sharp teeth and short tempers."

"True," Bobcat conceded. "Guess I'd better get my ass in gear before I get bitten, right?" He swept the console clear of empty beer bottles.

Marcus jumped at the crash as the bottles hit the metal trashcan. "I didn't expect total reform. We need you thinking, after all."

Bobcat dumped the trashcan into the matter recycler chute. "I've never thought of it that way. You couldn't do me a favor and tell Yelena that my drinking is a matter of keeping human development moving, could you?"

Marcus raised an eyebrow. "On the day you get me out of a family dinner when I'd rather be working, yes," he replied with a glib smile.

Bobcat shook his head. "Never gonna happen. If you're not there, there's no reason for me to be there eating Cheryl Lynn's fine cooking."

Marcus shot Bobcat a sour look. "Traitor."

Tina was waiting for them when they left the *R2D2* and made their way onto the *Guardian*. "Welcome to Devon!" she trilled.

"We were just here," Bobcat reminded her.

Tina released Marcus and turned her smile on Bobcat. "Well, yeah, but all you saw was a tiny piece of the Hexagon and the ass-end of nowhere while you were on the New Citadel project. William and I have a real fun day planned for us all in celebration of getting the team back together."

She wasted no time in ushering them to a station-to-planet transport Pod.

The Pod dropped them off in Hexagon Plaza. They were met there by William and the roamer he'd procured for them, and the tour got underway.

William headed the group up as they made their way through the Plaza-side gate into the bazaar. "Part of this is getting eyes on the public spaces to make sure everything is back in order after the attack."

"I can't tell anything is out of place," Marcus remarked.

Tina shook her head. "It's damn quiet. The people were badly shaken after so long without war or disquiet. Generally, the only trouble we get down here is when the Bakas are fighting among themselves."

"Nobody expected to be attacked by the damned Ookens," William ground out. He pointed to a building that only had half a wall and the foundations remaining. "That used to be the finest Mediterranean restaurant this side of pre-WWDE Earth. Now Leonardo has closed for business until new premises can be built. It's criminal what they did."

Tina patted him on the shoulder. "We're going to make sure it doesn't happen again. Just as soon as we've shown Marcus and Bobcat the fun side of First City."

She threaded her arm through her husband's and tugged him past the stalls. "Starting with the best fried chicken you've ever tasted. The secret," she confided as they walked, "is that it's not chicken."

The day passed in a whirlwind of the kind tourists in new places invariably find themselves caught up in. They visited the Enclave and met Mahi' and her brothers as the sun set over First City to hear how the Bakas were settling into their homes in New Citadel.

"Was that the last stop?" Bobcat asked as the Enclave receded in the roamer's rearview mirror. "I've got a killer thirst, and while those not-chicken wings were nice, they weren't the most filling."

William tapped the roamer's navigation screen. "We're headed for dinner. Hang tight, we're almost there."

The roamer pulled up at an unassuming building that nevertheless had a queue round the block.

Tina was first out of the roamer. The guys got out, Marcus almost tripping as he examined the building.

Bobcat knew what the clientele were waiting for just by looking at them. "A nightclub?"

Tina grinned. "This is a treat. Wait until you see the inside."

Marcus wrinkled his nose.

Tina bumped him with her hip. "Lighten up. It's not all pulsing music and strobe lights. Well, not once you get off the ground floor, anyway."

Marcus' arm snaked around Tina's shoulders when they

entered the lobby and he saw the silhouetted dancers in the recesses set into the walls. "I hardly think this is an appropriate venue for my wife," he blustered, his cheeks turning a violent shade of red.

Tina laughed. "What do you mean?" she asked, knowing full well what was causing all the blood in his body to rush to his face.

Marcus lowered his voice to a pained whisper. "This is a *strip* club!"

Tina nodded. "Yeah, so?"

"I just don't think it was right of William to choose this as a venue," he finished lamely.

Tina slapped Marcus on the chest. "William didn't pick this place. I did."

Marcus rubbed the sore spot. "Then I apologize, William." He frowned at Tina. "What was the need to compound your point with violence?"

Tina grinned. "That was for being a sexist old man. I've got to keep you on your toes, after all." She slipped free of her husband and headed for the stairs up to the restaurant. "Are you going to stand there staring all night? I might decide to have my beefcake wrapped up to take home…"

William clapped Marcus on the shoulder as he headed for the steps. "Serves you right for presuming, buddy. Come on. The steak here is good, and we have some serious hard work ahead of us if we're gonna solve the problem of keeping the damned Kurtherians out of our yard."

Three hours later, they emerged from the club overfull and pleasantly drowsy, but no closer to solving their conundrum.

Tina plugged the Hexagon's coordinates into the roamer and sat back with her hands laced behind her head. "I know my nanocytes have already processed whatever I drank tonight, but I'm still glad this thing doesn't need us to do anything except tell it where we're going."

Bobcat chuckled. "If only the solution to all our problems were so simple. I still can't see how we get around all the factors standing in the way of us getting a working BYPS set up in the Etheric."

William sighed. "My best guess is that we'll find it a hell of a lot easier once someone figures out how to talk to those little guys who were brought back on the *Izanami*."

Tina shuddered. "Yeah, well, as long as they tell the little creepers to stay out of my kitchen while they're at it. Last thing I want is to get the life scared out of me when all I'm trying to do is cook supper."

The discussion continued until the roamer arrived at the huge glass doors of the Hexagon.

They parted ways on the residential sublevel, Bobcat going one way with William as he peeled off to head for his apartment, and Marcus and Tina going the other to head for hers.

"See you guys bright and early," Tina called, waving over her shoulder. "There's more than one way to skin a cat."

"Don't let Demon hear that," William replied. "You might just find a dead Bl'kheth on your doorstep."

QSD *Baba Yaga*, Top Deck

Demon was happy that her little family was finally

settled in what she felt was the safest place for them. The move to Sabine's apartment hadn't fully alleviated the anxiety she'd felt after the attack. There was no way an Ooken could get aboard the *Baba Yaga*. She checked that little Sam and Alyssa were truly asleep before extracting herself from their den made from pallets and blankets.

She face-bumped her mate, purring as she offered her affection. *I wish to go down to the planet,* she told him. *I have the urge to find the Bl'kheths and thank them for interceding in the Ooken attack.*

Sam looked at the kittens, then back at Demon.

They will be fine without me for an hour. This is important.

Sam wrinkled his nose and padded over to the den. He gave Demon the look of a father left on his own with no clue what to do with his young.

Demon rolled her eyes. *If they wake and won't settle, just have Izanami call me back.*

She reached the Hexagon pretty quickly and made her way to the sublevels to search for the tiny beings.

Her velvety paws made no sound on the cold floor of Eve's lab. However, that didn't mean she traveled in silence. She called for the Bl'kheths with her mind as she walked, hoping they could hear her in the mindspace all telepathic species used.

She had hit upon an idea while feeding her kittens earlier that day, and being a cat, well, the saying about curiosity was a stereotype that had come about through its obvious truth.

Eve acknowledged Demon's presence with a cheerful wave. "I didn't expect to see you down here again so soon."

I want to speak with the Bl'kheths, and this was the last place I know they were.

Doubt crossed Eve's smooth features. " I don't think you will have much luck attracting their attention."

I had an idea, Demon told her. *I have to see if it works. I will be in the visiting area if Izanami contacts you.*

Eve smiled, inferring Demon's meaning from her tone. "You left Sam with the kittens?"

Demon sniffed, her version of a snicker. *Yes, so expect a call as soon as the kittens wake up and start harassing him.*

Eve laughed. "Of course."

Demon continued to the area dedicated to visitors to the Collectives. Now that her difficult pregnancy was over, she found that the scent of the water-dwellers was not so overstimulating as to make her nauseous.

She rejected the chairs, curling up on the square of carpet instead after delicately removing the headset from its hook on the wall.

A Collective swam out of the kelp, drawn by her calls. *Greetings. We heard you.*

Demon tilted her head to meet the glassy eye observing her. *Yes. I require some assistance if you are able. I wish to speak with the Bl'kheths who saved my family's lives.*

The other two residents of the tank slipped out of the kelp forest and observed.

Demon nosed the headset. *Eve's equipment is the key. I believe the Bl'kheths are not as ignorant as they appear. Other-wise, they would not be capable of such coordination in battle. I think they are different and therefore think differently.* She blinked, her amber gaze lighting up her face. *It might interest you to know that I was once an unspeaking beast. Human technology has allowed my mind to work in such a way that I can talk to anyone who has similar software implanted in their brain.*

The Collectives considered her thoughts. *Perhaps you are onto something,* the first admitted.

Bethany Anne arrived, the click of her heels announcing her before Demon saw her. She didn't pause to offer any sort of greeting. "Eve tells me that you think you have a way to communicate with the Bl'kheths?"

She placed a box she was carrying on the table and took a seat in the visiting area. "I brought snacks for them. I'm interested in how you expect to get around the communication barrier."

Demon carefully picked up the headset. *By using this and having the Collectives include them in their group mind. If we can get the Bl'kheths to show up, that is. I have been calling for them, but I'm not sure my voice is loud enough by itself.*

Bethany Anne took the headset and let it dangle from her fingers. "It's worth a shot. How about you put this on, and we will work to amplify your voice. We know that the Bl'kheths are protective of you."

Demon inclined her head to accept the headset. *Oh. It tickles. I can hear all three of you,* she told the Collectives in surprise.

Welcome to the group mind, they intoned as one.

"Concentrate on your thoughts," Bethany Anne instructed as she slipped the other headset on. "Ask them to come out from their hiding place."

Demon closed her eyes. *Bl'kheths, I do not know your names. Will you talk to me?*

There was silence in the mindspace for a long moment, then Bethany Anne spoke.

Open your eyes, Demon.

Demon cracked an eyelid. Before her stood the six Bl'kheths. *Thank you for coming to my rescue,* she told them. *Do you understand me?*

The largest of the six regarded her with curiosity. *Better than the large ones,* he replied in halting English. *You need our help.*

Bethany Anne noted the urgency in the being's statement. **Can you hear me?** she asked gently.

The six bowed as one.

We hear you, Death, the largest answered. *We have learned your language, poor as it is. You will be attacked by the goddess again if we do not make you understand.*

Bethany Anne raised an eyebrow. **You know about Gödel, huh? You should know she isn't a goddess of any kind, but merely a powerful alien who doesn't dare meet me face to face.**

The Bl'kheths growled, showing needle-sharp teeth. *She is insane, and will not stop until you, Death, and all your allies are returned to stardust. Our only hope is to offer our bodies so that you can create the technology to match her.*

He knelt, followed by the others. *We will die so the many can be saved.*

The six pulled blades from seemingly nowhere and made to plunge them into their chests.

20

Bethany Anne dropped from the chair to her knees at the same time Demon hissed and leapt back from the six Bl'kheths.

Silver blood sprayed as they removed the blades from their hearts, and they fell to the floor unmoving.

"Fuckdammit! *Why?*" Bethany Anne scooped up their rapidly cooling bodies in both hands and dashed through the Etheric to the Vid-doc suite on the *Baba Yaga*.

She placed them gently inside one of the units and forced herself to wait while the lid closed. The few seconds it took lasted an eternity.

"Come on!" Bethany Anne raged. She felt helpless to do anything as the Vid-doc cycled on, but she wasn't without the ability to ask for help when she needed it. *ADAM, get in there and bring them back before it's too late.*

>>It's already too late,<< ADAM told her sadly. >>They are dead. I can maybe save their minds—<<

Then do it, Bethany Anne snarled. Tears trickled down her cheeks unnoticed. *For fuck's sake! Why didn't they just wait a damned minute for me to explain that I only needed to have them scanned?*

ADAM wasn't sure what reply would ease the pain Bethany Anne was in. All he could do was his best to ensure the six minds were copied in their entirety, and that the Bl'kheths remained intact and separate once the process was complete.

>>**I have a complete imprint of the leader's mind,**<< he told Bethany Anne. >>**The other five will take a little longer to reconstruct. Since they were all thinking the same thought when they suicided, I have to be careful to discern between their brainwaves, or their individual personalities could be lost.**<<

I'm going in, Bethany Anne told him. *I have to figure out why this happened. Did you see how fast they moved?*

Ohthankthefuckinglord. You made it.

What is this? Seian looked around the strange surroundings he found himself in. He had not expected an afterlife such as some beings anticipated.

The human known as Death was there, although she was now of equivalent size, so he was able to examine her in detail. *Where am I?* he asked, noting she carried the godlight in her eyes.

I'll answer that in a moment, Bethany Anne told him. *First, I have to get over my urge to strangle you. Why the hell did you all just kill yourselves?*

Seian tilted his head, looking at the human with pity for her lack of understanding. *So you could use our bodies to* create protection for your planet, of course. We could not allow you to take on the burden of fighting the goddess without doing our part to make sure you succeed. You are the key to the goddess' defeat, and we are aware that you will cease to function if your people are harmed.

Bethany Anne closed her eyes and pushed her hair back as the utter futility of the statement hit her. *Let's clear one thing up. I am Bethany Anne, not Death—except to those who make it their business to hurt others. What's your name?* she asked.

I am called Seian, he replied. *It is my rank. We do not have individual identifiers like the unconnected species.*

Bethany Anne gave him a sad smile. *Well, Seian. I think you should have a name. It's going to get confusing once we take out the other factories and rescue more of your people otherwise. How about Sean?*

I will accept that if it pleases you, he replied.

Bethany Anne chuckled without humor. *There was no need for you to give up your lives. My people would have used a solution that didn't require death to achieve. I am not the Seven, here to enforce my demands without caring about the consequences. I do not take from my people.*

We are not your people, Sean countered.

Bethany Anne lifted her chin, her eyes shining bloody light on the empty space. *Are you here on my planet? Are your people lost, their futures stolen by the Seven? Then you are mine to protect. Mine to save, and mine to care for. That does not mean I want your sacrifice, dammit.*

The Bl'kheth looked at her with confusion. *You are taking ownership of my entire species?* he asked.

No! Bethany Anne's heart broke for this being, who

thought his purpose was to be passed from one master to another as if that was normal. She knew that mindset came from being enslaved for generations, and she couldn't imagine what it must have been like for these obviously intelligent people over the years since Gödel had torn them from their homeworld. *You are free now.*

What does that mean? "Free?"

Bethany Anne sought the words to explain what was as natural as breathing to her. *It means that you are no longer subject to the control of anyone else. You were not obligated to give any help, much less your lives. I have saved your consciousnesses, and from here on out, you will be given whatever you need to find joy in your new existence.*

Sean ignored Bethany Anne's promises. *So by your definition, you can't tell us what to choose.*

Bethany Anne smiled and shook her head. *No. Neither would I want to.*

Sean lifted his hands the way he'd seen the humans do when dismissing something they didn't want to engage with. *We chose to sacrifice. My people were the first to be free. We will serve. We will become one with the technology as the metal human described to the human who builds. We will help free the others who are still slaves.*

Bethany Anne frowned. *Eve? She's not a human. She's a digital lifeform in an android body. And no. I will not accept your service. You have given enough already.*

Sean worked to make his face match hers, to show his displeasure at being rebuffed. *But I choose it. How are we free if we cannot exercise our choice?*

Bethany Anne's eyes flashed again. *How am I free if*

everyone wants to die for my cause? There is a balance between personal freedom and the good of the group.

I don't understand, Sean admitted.

Neither do I all the time, Bethany Anne admitted gently. **But I believe you understand better than you think. You are the leader of your group, yes?**

He nodded.

Okay, so say there was something that had to be done for the good of all.

Like facing a foe much larger than yourself, Sean offered.

Bethany Anne paused, seeing she was going to talk herself into supporting Sean's argument for unconsidered action instead of illustrating her point. **I'm not sure that works. Let me try this a different way. As a leader, do you take the risk yourself, knowing your failure means certain doom for your people? Or do you make a considered choice in how you approach the problem and use your resources—your people—to overcome the obstacle?**

She fixed Sean with a stern smile. **We as leaders have to make the right decisions for everyone.**

Sean mirrored her expression again. *The goddess will return once she has rebuilt from her losses. I have been inside the group mind of her soldiers. I have listened to the humans who are tasked with providing Etheric-enabled technology. They need time you do not have if you are to prevent more deaths. The Collectives do not fight. The Bakas fight too much between themselves to overcome their subjugation.*

His face moved through a series of emotions too quickly for Bethany Anne to make them out. *We are small but powerful. We fight smart, we calculate, and we do not act irrationally. Personal sacrifice means little to us.*

Bethany Anne's nose wrinkled. *There's not much I can say about it now. I get the need to protect your people. Right now, I'm caught between the freedom of my people and the need to have them stand against Gödel's army.*

Sean considered her words for a moment before replying. *I don't understand why you have brought me here, but to refuse to put us to use is a waste of the lives we gave. Understand that our ancestors elected to leave with the goddess to save the majority of our population from the fate we endure. The good of the many must always outweigh the needs of the few.*

Bethany Anne narrowed her eyes, taking all of it in until Sean's last statement. *I understand. You are community-minded, like a few of the species I have encountered in this part of space. I don't agree with your view of the Collectives. You must have stepped into the Etheric before they joined the fight in the factory. They are fierce. As for the Bakas, removing the cancer at the heart of their society has united them. They fight for each other now, not with each other.*

She tapped her lips with a finger, wondering how she could give these tiny warriors what they wanted without endangering their minds. *Maybe… Yes. I have an idea. If you are truly determined to be part of this war, how would you feel about being merged with the technology we create using your gift? I'm not entirely comfortable with it, but I would do whatever I could to make it so you can retain some sense of your bodies.*

Sean was clearly confused.

It's like this, Bethany Anne explained. *If I have your permission, I will have your genetic material infused into six special sets of armor, which I want to give to my most trusted fighters. This armor would normally have an EI, a digital program designed to communicate with the user, but I would have your six minds plugged into the systems instead.*

We would operate this armor? Sean asked.

Not quite, Bethany Anne told him with a smile. *The human wearing the armor would be in control. You would be the living interfaces between them and the armor's systems. So, say you were part of John's armor, and he wanted to destroy an enemy emplacement. The old system would have him pull up an interactive menu, and he would choose the option for the weapons he wanted to use. With the new armor I have in mind, you would be connected to the armor's systems and able to activate what he asked for with a thought. You would know what he needed and anticipate it.*

Sean considered the thought of being part of a whole as entirely natural, even if he wasn't sure how it would feel to be large like the human wearing this armor. *We would be part of a new kind of group mind. One that united the human and Bl'kheth in a single purpose?*

>>**You could look at it that way,**<< ADAM cut in. >>**I'm done rebuilding the others and adjusting their minds so they can fully understand English. They will be joining you shortly.**<<

I was wondering why Sean was finding it so easy to understand me. Bethany Anne glanced around the empty space and wrinkled her nose. *Can you do something to make this space a bit homier for them before they get here?*

>>**What?**<< he inquired.

Bethany Anne waved a hand. *I don't know. Just make it so they aren't so traumatized when you drop them in here.*

You could start by taking us inside, Sean suggested. *It's not natural to be so exposed.*

Bethany Anne's mouth turned up at the corner at the way he raked the space above their heads with his gaze. ***It's probably going to take a while, but you don't have to worry about being snatched by a predator. This world is yours, and yours alone.***

>>Have any of you ever seen your homeworld?<< ADAM inquired, thinking to recreate a long-lost home for the Bl'kheths.

No, Sean replied. *We have only memories of shining cities and amethyst waters passed down through the generations.*

>>Keep talking about it,<< ADAM told him. **>>I'm getting a visual.<<**

Sean continued his description, and Bethany Anne suddenly found herself standing on a covered bridge spanning verdant riverbanks. She tested the marble and found it solid, then leaned over to look at the purple water. ***How beautiful,*** she remarked.

>>And not one bit poisonous to you,<< ADAM told her. **>>Although in reality the planet would be inaccessible to humans without protection.<<**

Sean stared in wonder as the world came into being. *How are you doing this?* he marveled. *It is exactly as I pictured it.*

In the background, buildings appeared to make up a skyline filled with steeples and minarets, all cut from the same creamy marble as the bridge. No two buildings were alike.

>>I'm going to bring the others in now,<< ADAM informed them.

Go ahead, Bethany Anne replied. She pulled her gaze from the city. *You have your group mind, right? The others won't be freaked out to find themselves here once you explain.*

>>I can remain and help them get acclimated,<< ADAM offered. >>You, however, are needed out here.<<

Bethany Anne sighed. *Let me guess, another shitstorm just got started.*

>>Got it in one,<< ADAM replied.

21

Bethany Anne got out of the Vid-doc and found John and Tabitha waiting for her. She looked from John's impassive face to Tabitha's barely concealed anger and saw the situation was serious. "What's up?"

Tabitha spoke through gritted teeth. "That data you sent me. Marcus isn't wrong about there being something fishy going on in the buffer zone."

John didn't need to read them to know there was a problem when the reports from Tim to Peter spoke of an incremental increase in people arriving to set up homes on Devon. "Even the Skaines are making a run from the colony they have there," he informed Bethany Anne. "What the fuck scares a Skaine?"

Tabitha cut in, unable to hold back. "I can't believe I'm saying this, but I'm concerned for the Skaines who can't leave the colony. We should go take a look at the situation."

Bethany Anne considered everything she had to get done before Federation troops started arriving in the Interdiction. While it was all urgent, taking a step back might prove to be the thing she needed to come to better solutions. It had helped with Sean and the Bl'kheths, that was for sure.

"That's a rather large area of space to cover," she told them. "We should start with the colony. You know the Skaines aren't likely to help each other when the shit hits the proverbial impeller. While I'm perfectly happy for the fighters to get their well-deserved comeuppance for their assholish natures, I won't leave females or Skainlets in possible danger. Get the *Sayomi* ready to leave, John. We'll be heading out as soon as I get done checking in with BMW."

Tabitha pouted. "Not the *ArchAngel*? I was hoping to catch up with Natalia."

Bethany Anne shook her head. "Not this trip. The *Arch-Angel* doesn't have Shinigami-class cloaking, and I don't want to announce my presence when I know for a fact that anyone pulling shit they shouldn't be will scatter like roaches under a flashlight."

"Besides," John added, "Darryl has Natalia all tied up. Long-distance love's nothing to get between. Take it from me."

Bethany Anne patted his arm as she left. She headed to the Hexagon and took the elevator down to Eve's sublevel, where her brightest and best had their heads together over a table strewn with paper, abandoned datapads, and small holoprojector units.

Bethany Anne smiled when Tina, Marcus, William, and Bobcat didn't notice her arrival. She tiptoed to the table and slipped into the empty chair between Bobcat and Marcus. "How is my BYPS coming along?"

The guys nearly jumped out of their skin, drawing laughter from Tina and William, who had been back in Bethany Anne's inner circle long enough not to overreact when she decided to be playful.

Tina undid her hair and retied it, so the wisps that had fallen into her eyes while she'd been working no longer bugged her. "It's not," she admitted with more than a little frustration. "There's no way to move the satellites into place without gravitic persuasion, and there's no way of applying said pressure until we break the Etheric-metal barrier."

"In short," Marcus continued, "we're screwed unless we suddenly get access to a Bl'kheth, since they hold the key to unlocking the ability to take metal into the Etheric."

Bethany Anne took a seat. "That's why I'm here." She gave them a quick rundown of what had gone on with the Bl'kheths. "I've never met any beings so dedicated to making sure the whole were taken care of. Do you know that every Bl'kheth in the factories is descended from an original group who volunteered to leave with Gödel? They tricked her into believing they were the entire population."

Tina eyed Bethany Anne, who nodded in her direction. She wiped away the tears threatening to spill with the backs of her hands. "That's just heartbreaking."

"So you called him 'Sean?'" Bobcat chuckled. "I suppose it's a good enough name for a tiny hellion. Still, it wasn't very smart of them to suicide."

"Actually, it was the smartest thing they could have done," Bethany Anne corrected. "Remember, they are thinking of the whole, which to them is anyone opposing Gödel and the Seven."

Tina punched him in the arm. "Show some respect for the poor things. They couldn't have known that we didn't want to use their whole bodies." She flashed a sad look at Bethany Anne. "You're right. There was no way we could have sequenced their DNA quickly, but I'm still thrown that they did this for us. For everyone."

Bethany Anne couldn't agree more. "I'm not the happiest about it either, but it's not for me to say someone can't act for the greater good. We won't let their gift go to waste. I want you four to get with Eve and figure out how to turn what they've given us into a defense system that will fry the balls off any Etheric traveler who decides to appear at my front door without an invitation. I won't have us vulnerable from any angle."

She tapped her nails on the table, the sound muffled by the detritus of the meeting. "You should talk to Jean as well. The first thing I want is six sets of armor with Etheric-travel capability, and then I want a way to integrate the Bl'kheths into the interfaces."

Marcus' eyes widened. "Won't that annoy you? I'd think two separate voices would be plenty."

Bethany Anne's mouth turned up at the corner. "I didn't say they were going to be part of *my* armor."

William snickered at her tone. "I can't see Michael being happy about having a voice in his ear, either."

Bethany Anne grinned. "Introducing yet another voice into my head is not the most desirable path. That's why the Bl'kheths are going to be integrated into the Bitches' armor. I told you I'm not going to waste their gift. Michael and I are already used to operating the advanced armor without assistance. Besides, we do things our own way."

She got to her feet. "I'll check back with you guys soon. I'm headed out to the buffer zone to take care of the problem you found."

"Oh, goody!" Tina exclaimed, turning a bright smile on her husband. "That means you can stop waffling about it and focus on the E-BYPS."

Devon, The Interdiction, QBS *Sayomi*

John settled into his captain's chair as Sayomi made the ship ready for a multi-Gate journey. He furrowed his brow at the nonchalance in the AI's posture as she flitted around the consoles.

"You'd better behave while Bethany Anne is aboard," he warned her. "Your shit won't fly with her. She'll just have ADAM tweak your personality matrix to bring you in line."

Sayomi's dark lips split in a mischievous smile. "Careful there, John. You almost sounded like you care."

John smirked as he shifted his chair into position to activate his holoHUD. "Didn't say that. Just make sure you don't piss her off, okay?"

Sayomi lifted her bony hands in submission. "Consider me a good little subroutine you don't have to think about."

With an eerie cackle, she vanished in a whirl of shadows.

Tabitha snickered softly. "Jean's trick backfired, huh?"

John glanced at the console Tabitha was sitting at and put a finger to his lips. "I don't know what you're talking about. That AI has been the bane of my existence ever since I sent her to watch over Nickie."

"You could always let Nickie take the ship," Tabitha teased. "Y'know, since you hate it so much."

"Over my dead body," he replied.

Bethany Anne appeared on the bridge from the Etheric. "What's over your dead body?" she asked as she stepped forward.

Tabitha put her feet up on the console and folded her arms behind her head. "Oh, just John trying to pretend he's not in love with his ship."

Bethany Anne snorted laughter. "Yeah, right." She pointed out the sour look he was giving Tabitha's feet. "We all know you can't be parted from it. Let's get going already. I don't like sitting around when there are people in trouble."

QBS *Sayomi*, Open Space

The *Sayomi* came out in what looked to be a starless system with six dead planets drifting aimlessly around a dark spot in the center.

"What'dya bring us out here for, Sayomi?" John asked with some confusion. "This isn't the Skaine colony."

Bethany Anne was similarly perplexed. "It's a pretty strange place to Gate into. There's nothing here to see."

"There's plenty to see," Sayomi countered without showing herself. "If you look with more than your eyes." She switched the viewscreen to show a faint circle of energy far in the distance. "There is a star, and it is inhabited—in a way."

Tabitha looked at the altered viewscreen with distaste. "Ew. Who goes to all the trouble and expense of a Dyson sphere?" she uttered with the same revulsion in her voice. "There are so many other ways to produce energy that don't involve the vampirism of your local star."

Sayomi's grave voice rattled the speaker. "I don't believe this to be an energy-gathering effort. My scans indicate the sphere is not solid, as one would expect from such a venture, but rather it's made up of millions of separate modules of varying ages and designs. I would hazard that whoever is living in those modules, they have lived this way for generations."

Bethany Anne didn't know anything about Dyson spheres except for the examples she'd come across in science fiction books too long ago to care to remember. "What makes you think this isn't the last-ditch attempt of some civilization to suck up what energy they can to get the hell out of here?"

Tabitha wrinkled her nose, her eyes flickering rapidly as she speed-read through everything she could access on Dyson spheres. "This is interesting. The original intention of the Dyson sphere was that it was supposed to be gradually grown, added to generation after generation. Okay, maybe I'm a tiny bit impressed. It makes no sense for a technologically advanced species to put all their efforts into capturing the energy when they can just, you know?" She made a takeoff motion with her hand to demonstrate. Then her eyes unfocused for a moment as she made an attempt with her new ability to connect to the sphere's shared systems. "Hey, you're not gonna believe this. I'm picking up that this is human technology. I think we've found one of the colonies that went off the radar after we left Earth."

"Could be," Bethany Anne murmured, distracted by the same information Tabitha had just scanned. "I provided enough colony ships for everyone who wanted to strike out on their own."

John grunted. "If you ask me, it was a dumbass who left your protection to chase some frontier dream. Come on out, Sayomi. Explain what's going on here."

Sayomi's avatar appeared on the opposite side of the bridge from Bethany Anne, trailing deep shadows around her body. "It's quite possible. There were many groups that chose to live outside the Empire. Would you like me to open contact with the sphere, my Queen?" she asked Bethany Anne with none of her usual snark.

Bethany Anne tilted her head as she dismissed the information in her internal HUD. "I don't see why not. Any information we can get on what's been going on out here would be stellar."

"Just keep us cloaked," Tabitha added warily. "You never know what kind of reception you're going to get from these far-flung colonies. I could tell you about some of the places I ended up at during my Ranger days that you wouldn't believe."

John chuckled dryly. "I'd believe anything of humans, from the good to the ridiculous."

The viewscreen darkened as Sayomi put out the call. A moment later, a man wearing a black atmosuit and an overly decorated hat appeared onscreen, looking somewhat confused. "QBS ship?" he spluttered in greeting. "What did we do to earn the attention of the Empire?"

Bethany Anne raised an eyebrow. "You haven't heard

from the outside for a while, huh? The Empire is the Federation. It's been that way for over a decade."

The man may have been lost in time, but he recognized Bethany Anne when he saw her, and it didn't look like he was happy about it. "You didn't answer my question. What brings you here? How did you even find us?" He shook his head to clear the shock. "I apologize. It's been too long since we've had visitors from outside the colony. This is no way to talk. Please have your ship dock at module 3247 and ask for Stewart Briscomb."

"You heard the man," Tabitha told Sayomi.

"As you wish," Sayomi replied with a smile before vanishing in a plume of shadow.

Tabitha turned and shot John a look that promised fire. "I thought you told her to be on her best behavior?" she demanded.

John lifted his hands. "I told her not to piss off BA. What do you want me to do?"

Bethany Anne snickered at the AI's sense of humor. "I'm not complaining. It's interesting that she would know about you hating that movie, Tabitha. Maybe it's ADAM you should pick that bone with."

It took them a little while to get close enough to dock. The ship stored more and more sensor data as they got closer.

Stewart met them at the airlock, doing away with the need to locate him aboard the multiple-residence module. "I have to admit I'm curious about the outside, as well as the reason you're here, my Empress."

Bethany Anne waved a hand. "Technically, I'm not an Empress anymore. Bethany Anne is fine."

Stewart took one look at John's face and smiled nervously. "I think not. Even if you are no longer the Empress, you are still the Queen." He relaxed slightly when John nodded almost imperceptibly. "Come with me. I have arranged for refreshments in my office."

He explained that he was the colony coordinator for that term as he led them down a short corridor that terminated with a door bearing a plaque with the title. "Consequently, I mostly live in my office. You know how administrative duties stack up if you're not vigilant."

Bethany Anne gave him a sympathetic look. "I do. You don't have AI support for that?"

Stewart's eyes widened in shock. "Definitely not!" he exclaimed. "We run nothing that can be picked up by any ship passing by. This colony was founded on the principle that allowing machines to do our complex thinking is the road to devolution of the human mind."

Ugh, one of those *places,* Tabitha complained. *Separatists are always PITAs to deal with, without exception. Shoot me now.*

Bethany Anne smiled, ignoring Tabitha's mental plea. "I understand," she told Stewart. "You have the right to live however you wish, as long as you are not persecuting any sentient digital lifeform to do so."

Stewart shook his head as he poured the tea. "We have zero sentient technology. Everything we have here was built with human ingenuity, and we have been cut off since the moment we reached saturation and blocked the star's light completely."

"Completely cut off?" Bethany Anne asked. "The reason I'm here is to find out what you know about the exodus of people out of this quadrant."

Stewart's features cinched tight. "I can make a guess. We've been attacked a number of times by various groups. Some wanted our technology. Others wanted to tap our star. The most recent attacks have passed us by since the enemy is unable to locate us by tracking the emissions from our star."

"But?" Bethany Anne pressed, seeing he had more to say.

She sipped the tea while she waited for Stewart to form his reply, wishing he had offered her a Coke instead.

"We're not blind to what's been going on in our neighborhood," Stewart informed her. "While we're not in a position to prevent the attacks on our fellow human beings, having chosen to behave defensively rather than offensively, we are able to offer the survivors a home here." His eyes darted to the side. "If they are able to make it here."

Bethany Anne thought that to be the biggest crock of shit she'd heard since leaving Red Rock. "What if someone attacked your sphere? You're just going to sit back and allow your people to die?"

Stewart closed his eyes and rubbed his temples. "We have sufficient shielding to repel most attacks."

John grunted. "That's not what the Queen asked."

Stewart shifted in his seat. "We have offensive capabilities."

Bethany Anne put down her teacup. "So, what you mean is that you're happy to defend yourselves, but not to do the right thing when your weaker, less technologically-advanced neighbors are in need?"

Stewart reddened. "What do you want us to do? Divert

our own resources for the good of everyone? That's the kind of socialist thinking we left to avoid."

Tabitha strode forward and placed her hands on the arms of Stewart's chair. She allowed her emotion to show in the red flare of her eyes. "Then you're a bunch of fucking idiots, no matter how much tech you have."

Bethany Anne agreed with Tabitha's sentiment. "I think we're done here." She got to her feet and looked at Stewart with utter disgust. "I can see why your group didn't stay with the rest of humanity. I have no time for anyone who chooses to ignore those in need when they have the ability to act and save lives."

She held up a hand to Stewart, putting an end to his weak protests about charity beginning at home. "If I'd taken that tack, humanity would be a distant memory, or slaves to the Kurtherians right now. You deserve everything that's coming to you." *ADAM, get me everything on their systems. I want to know who these wastes of oxygen have left to die.*

>>**Already done,**<< he replied. >>**Sayomi is anxious to leave, so I had her decouple her ship from the airlock. I didn't think you would want to stick around for the exit rigmarole.**<<

You thought right.

Bethany Anne spared a hard look for Stewart. "Enjoy your isolation while it lasts. You can expect a Federation party here within the week to supervise your learning curve. No more isolation. No more selfish fucking decisions. You are the power out here, so you'd better get fucking used to the responsibility that goes with it."

She had a few more choice words for Stewart and his

kind before she placed her hands on John's and Tabitha's shoulders and took the three of them back to the *Sayomi* via the Etheric.

Tabitha pulled Bethany Anne into a brief hug when they came out on the bridge of the *Sayomi*. "You okay? I know how badly selfish snotweasels like him get to you."

Bethany Anne shrugged. "What can I do except make sure they learn their lesson and do better in the future?" she asked.

"Sayomi, get us the hell out of here before my ability to restrain my temper runs out."

22

QBS *Sayomi*, Skaine Space

The *Sayomi* emerged in an area of space that looked nothing like the place they'd just left, the main difference besides the visible star being the permanent Gate illuminating the dark side of a smallish planet tucked up against the system's red dwarf star.

Sayomi wisely chose to feed the system data through the console rather than risk annoying Bethany Anne. "It appears that the planet is tidally locked. There is a large settlement that rings the horizon, where the temperature is stable and some natural light is available."

John peered at a dark gap in the habitation. "Looks like they've been attacked recently."

Tabitha indicated the Gate with a jerk of her chin. "The people in this system can't catch a break. What are we going to do about *that?*"

Bethany Anne raised an eyebrow. "The Gate that has no business being here? Destroy it, of course. After we've ascertained what's on the other side."

John shook his head. "I'm sticking by what I said. Anyone choosing to live outside of the protection of either the Federation or the Interdiction can't be choosing it for any good reason." He adjusted his chair into the upright position as the holoHUD retracted into his headrest. "You want us to go in and investigate?"

Bethany Anne shook her head. "Send a few drones for now. Keep them at a safe distance, and make sure they log anything that crosses in either direction. We're going straight down to the planet, so I can find out for myself why the Skaines are fleeing."

Tabitha tossed each of them a heavy cloak. "Don't want the remaining colonists to die of fright before we get a bead on what scared the rest of them away."

Bethany Anne put on the cloak with a flourish. "Being Skaines, I'd expect they're going to be more bothered about you than me."

John chuckled as he pulled up the hood of his cloak. "Yeah, I can see that happening. Tabitha walks in, the Skaines run out screaming."

Tabitha narrowed her eyes. "What is this, pick-on-the-hot-chick day?" She waved her hands in annoyance. "Jeez. You spend a hundred measly years kicking the slaving tendencies out of a species, and all you get for your efforts is shit from your friends."

"We have arrived," Sayomi announced, putting an end to the teasing.

Bethany Anne transferred them through the Etheric to an alley off the main street of the quarter Tabitha had identified as being most likely to have the colony's leadership buildings. The colony was as expected for a Skaine settlement, uniform buildings made from metal. There were no decorations and no art. All in all, it was a place that did very little for the imagination, despite being perfectly practical.

Tabitha took point, being the expert on the Skaine way of life and therefore, best suited to finding what they were looking for in the metal maze. She led them into the heart of the built-up area surrounding the spaceport, being careful to keep her identity concealed under the hood of her cloak.

Nevertheless, the Skaines they passed on the streets must have known on some base level that their scourge was among them because they gave the three humans a wide berth.

Bethany Anne skimmed the thoughts of the Skaines as they walked. She mostly got a sense of the pervasive dread that blanketed the community, fear of being stolen from their beds and taken who-knew-where for a purpose they could only guess.

John felt disquiet at the flood of thoughts. He glanced at Bethany Anne, wondering once again how she coped with the constant barrage in a crowd.

You'll learn to filter it out, Bethany Anne told John, speaking directly into his mind. *It's just a hell of a lot harder to block it out when it's the hopes and fears of the innocent.*

John did what he could to put up a mental barrier, but he agreed. This was an entirely different situation to the one where he'd had an enemy to subdue. The only enemy here was fear, and he had no clue how to put an end to that unless the boogeymen presented themselves so that he could tear them limb from limb in front of the Skaines.

Bethany Anne felt his turmoil. *Take it easy. We'll get to the bottom of this, and then you can work that frustration out on the root cause of these people's fear.*

That's how you cope, John replied. *Two hundred years, BA. Christ. No wonder when you snapped, you snapped all the way. Your self-control has to be tight.*

My mental abilities aren't even the strongest, Bethany Anne reminded him. *You want to see self-control, speak to Michael. Or Barnabas. Hell, talk to Akio. I've never seen him so much as raise his voice.*

Self-control is overrated. Tabitha had nothing else to add on the subject since she was happy to fess up to whatever was bothering her and apply her foot to the balls of the problem. She paused and read the street signs before taking them through a huge, empty square to a building that was slightly larger and better maintained than the others bordering the open space. *This is just an accounting office, but it's the closest they'll have to a government seat,* she explained as they mounted the stairs to the front entrance. *If there is anyone in charge, this is where we'll find them. Don't mind the title "overseer," if that's who we find. It's a title, not a functional description.*

Bethany Anne murmured her surprise. "This is the first time I've had reason to come to a Skaine world," she admitted out loud. "They don't go in much for individual-ity, huh?"

"Yeah, no. Unless you count the financial and military institutions," Tabitha told her as she pulled the door open. "It's why you don't see so many of them inside Federation borders. Those who can follow the rules get on just fine, but the majority are bent on keeping to the old ways."

She paused to reconsider as they entered the atrium. "Except for the slavery, of course."

"Yes, well," a voice interrupted. "You put an end to that as the basis of our economy, didn't you, Ranger Two?"

Bethany Anne shrugged. "Looks like your disguise plan fell short of the mark." She pushed back her hood to gasps from the Skaines behind the counter. "You're the Skaine in charge around here?"

The one who had spoken came forward with his head bowed. "Empress. Forgive me, I did not realize you accompanied the Ranger." He spat the word "Ranger" like it tasted bad. "My name is Slater, and I am the governor here. How may I be of service?"

Bethany Anne raised an eyebrow. "You can start by dropping the attitude. The Rangers have been disbanded for over a decade. You can't still be sore, surely?"

John chuckled. "Wanna bet?"

The Skaine didn't quite dare to answer. His face, however, spoke volumes.

Tabitha shoved a finger in Slater's face. "An economy built on the backs of others is not how decent people operate. It served the slavers right to be shut down. If I find that this colony is operating a slave trade, you're going to be sorry we came here to help."

Slater's lips drew back in a snarl. "We obey the law here. As for your help, what help do we need from *you*? We do not take slaves here, so I can only assume you're here to fuck things up for us."

Bethany Anne held up a hand before it got heated,

knowing Tabitha was—quite rightly—like a dog with a bone on the slavery issue. "That's not why we're here, although Tabitha is right about us shutting you down if you're harboring a slave trade." She paused while ADAM confirmed that there was nothing to indicate the colony was making income from people-trafficking. "Now that I'm assured you are innocent, I want to know why people from this quadrant are leaving in such large numbers, and I want to know how and why there is an unauthorized Gate in this system."

The Skaines at the counter looked away quickly, and the atmosphere switched from one of mild anger to one of utter distress.

Slater half-turned and extended an arm to indicate the door to the back rooms. "If you will join me in my office?"

Bethany Anne strode past him. "Don't mind if I do."

Slater closed the door of his office, eyeing John warily as he did so. "Take a seat. I won't be a moment setting up a secure space."

Bethany Anne waved a hand to enclose the room in a bubble of Etheric energy, which she commanded to block all signals going in or out. "No need. I make my own secure space that can't be matched by any technology."

Slater frowned, giving away a touch of displeasure at the information.

"Including the recording devices you have set up in here," Bethany Anne told him firmly. She took a seat in his guest chair, and John and Tabitha moved to flank her.

Slater's shoulders dropped at the information that he wouldn't be getting a record of Bethany Anne's appearance. "Very well, we will get straight to business if that's how you want to do this." He took his seat and laced his fingers on the desk. "Two months ago, that Gate appeared. Who placed it there is a mystery we haven't been able to solve. However, since its arrival, there have been numerous disappearances that can't be explained. Always the strongest and healthiest. They never take the weak, the young, or the old."

"How do you mean?" Bethany Anne inquired. "You must know when these kidnappings are happening. You're not exactly technologically challenged."

"Speaking of which," Tabitha cut in. "Are you aware of the human colony the next system over?"

Slater's distress was real. "We see no one, and we can't track any technology being used. In short, we are powerless to detect the kidnappers and I'm clueless as to how to prevent them from taking my people." He twisted his hands fretfully as he spoke. "We don't have the capability to take out the Gate without causing extensive damage to our planet."

"Sounds like maybe Saint Payback owns the Gate," Tabitha muttered darkly.

Bethany Anne considered all the information. "Okay, here's what we're going to do. I'm going to have another ship come here. You're going to find me somewhere suitable to set up base on the colony. I have a sneaking suspicion I know exactly who is behind all of this, and I don't intend to let the slippery fuckers get away with another raid."

The next day, not one, but three ships Gated into the system.

"What the shiny fuck is *that?*" Bethany Anne almost choked on her Coke as they watched the *Penitent Grand-daughter* slide into place between the *ArchAngel* and the *G'laxix Sphaea* on the viewscreen in Slater's office. "Please tell me that hunk of rust isn't the ship Nickie has been running my logistics network from?"

Tabitha gave the old Skaine battleship an unconcerned glance. "Oh, yeah. But don't stress it. The ship was completely overhauled by Jean. It has all the capabilities of a QBS, plus the Skaine weaponry was tweaked to give her the advantage over any pirates she runs across on the transport routes."

Bethany Anne's lip curled as the ship made from odd angles and bulging holds grew larger on the screen. "But it's so *ugly!*" She looked at Tabitha while pointing at the screen. "How does she look at that ship and not puke?"

Slater made a sound of disapproval. "Skaine ships are built to cause destruction, not to win beauty contests." His forehead creased as a thought occurred. "I have heard of the Grimes-who-would-be-a-Ranger. She was instrumental in making the Federation's borders a no-go area for any Skaines who were foolish enough to get in her way."

John flashed a grin at the Skaine. "Yeah. I'm very proud of my granddaughter. She's really stepped up and lived up to the family name these last few years."

Slater wisely kept his mouth shut, having a bone-deep feeling that criticizing the theft of the ship would end in those very bones getting broken by the Grimes *nobody* wanted to fuck with.

Bethany Anne snickered softly. Her own opinion on the youngest Grimes had shifted radically since Nickie had decided to quit whining and embrace her destiny as a protector. "My people will be arriving shortly. This won't take long to resolve."

Dan, Kael-ven, and Kiel arrived just ahead of Nickie and Grim.

Kael-ven blustered into the meeting room, taking in the Skaine overseer with a distrustful look before bowing his head minutely to Bethany Anne. "You command, I serve. But did you have to choose this location for your base?"

Bethany Anne lifted a finger. "These are good Skaines, if you can get over the irony in that statement, and they need our help to stop their people from being stolen by whoever owns that Gate."

Kiel managed to keep his thoughts to himself for once. He did, however, exchange a wry glance with Tabitha.

"Where's Natalia?" Bethany Anne inquired when Dan's right hand did not appear behind him.

"She stayed aboard with Darryl," he replied with a wink. "I disrupted her leave to rush over here, but I didn't have the heart to drag her down to the colony when she and Darryl have been apart for so long."

Bethany Anne held up a hand. "Enough said. Do not desire TMI."

John brightened at the sight of his old pupil. "Grim'zee!"

Grim, for his part, swelled with pleasure as he side-stepped Dan and Kiel to reach his hero. "Always good to see you, my friend."

John clapped the Yollin on the back with fervor. "I hope Nickie isn't working you into the ground."

Grim cupped his mouth with a hand and dropped his voice to a stage whisper. "Mentally, yeah. But you know my stamina when it comes to dealing with fiery females."

Nickie snorted. "Yeah, that's why you're terminally single. Grim the lover loves his food too much to settle on one female for longer than it takes to eat dinner."

Grim gave her a mock-pained look and put his hand on his chest. "You see the abuse I have to deal with?" he asked John. "There's just no respect for a Yollin of my age and experience. You'd think she would be grateful she's not eaten cold food out of a can since I showed up, but no. She just takes her moods out on her closest friend."

Slater looked at the group in confusion as they all laughed at Grim's good-natured grumbling.

Bethany Anne met his stare and shrugged. "I guess humor is subjective." She clapped to get everybody's attention. "Take your seats, people. Let's get this meeting underway, starting with an update on what the drones we left at the Gate have picked up so far."

Tabitha flourished a hand for effect, and the screens that wrapped the meeting room lit up with the drone data. "Nothing has crossed the Gate yet," she informed them. "Now that we have Dan, Kael, and Nickie here, we should think about going over there and taking the fight to whoever is doing the kidnapping."

"We all fucking know it's Gödel," Nickie interrupted. She looked at the doubtful faces. "What? Which other llama-sniffing dictator could it be?"

"I can't argue. You're probably right," Bethany Anne

conceded. "Okay, send one of the drones in to get a closer look. We'll wait for the results before making a decision as to whether we go in or destroy the Gate outright. We all know the Seven have no access to the Bakas and will need to replace their genetic material with some from a species who likes to fight without thinking."

"Hey!" Slater protested.

"You most definitely resemble that remark," Tabitha deadpanned. "And you're a hell of a lot less likely to fight back than say, the Shrillexians. I'd buy it. Hell, I'm surprised she didn't just send someone to negotiate a price with you."

Slater's eyes widened, and his mouth fell open. "I don't believe it."

Bethany Anne fixed Slater with an icy stare. "You're going to tell me that actually happened?"

Slater nodded vigorously, looking at Bethany Anne with dawning horror in his eyes. "A mercenary company came through here recruiting a couple of months back. There were a few takers, mostly post-adolescents with too much testosterone and something to prove." He eyed her, worry on his face. "You think there's a connection?"

Bethany Anne lifted her shoulder. "Don't expect them to come home. It looks to me like you gave the Seven a free sample of your genetics, and they liked what they saw." She shook her head and sighed. "I expected to have a little longer before we were faced with a new flavor of Ookens to contend with. Unfortunately for Gödel, we already know what the Skaines' weaknesses are."

"What is an Ooken?" Slater asked, hardly daring to hear the answer.

MICHAEL ANDERLE

Bethany Anne thought for a moment before deciding to tell him. "The Seven's answer to fighting at a distance. For the last few years, they've been creating them from three species of people who are now under my protection. Now that they have no access to one of the species, they're looking to replace them so they can continue building the numbers to cause me a damned headache."

Nickie leaned back in her chair with a thoughtful expression on her face. "Yeah, but Skaines with nanocytes? That's going to be uglier than a bag of smashed assholes."

"Nickie," John cautioned. "Be helpful or be quiet."

Nickie pouted. "Whatever, Grandad. I'm with Aunt Tabbie. Let's go blow up whatever's on the other side of that Gate."

Slater closed his eyes and rubbed his temples with his fingers. "I hate to agree with a Ranger by any name, but they're speaking sense." He frowned as he tried and failed to process the bigger picture. "I cannot understand how we got caught up in this. We're just a small colony." He waved an agitated hand. "Nothing to do with the politics of the wider universe."

Kael-ven shook his head in sympathy. "Be glad. Everyone is aware of how my people were tricked into believing filthy Kurtherian lies for centuries until Bethany Anne came along. If any of your people are still alive, we'll get them back."

Dan had been quiet throughout the conversation so far. Bethany Anne saw he had something formulating and turned her attention to Kael-ven. "What do you think?" she asked. "You've been fighting the Ookens all over the Interdiction this last year."

288

Kael-ven considered the question a moment before replying. "If this is Gödel, we have to assume she has a factory on the other side of the Gate. That makes it our duty to cross the Gate and dismantle it." He frowned. "After we rescue their prisoners, of course."

"That's horrifying," Kiel exclaimed. "The prisoners you and Michael rescued last time have all needed extensive therapy, along with Pod-doc time to heal the physical damage done by the Ookens using them in their experiments."

They're not experimenting," Bethany Anne reminded them. "They are building. The only purpose of those factories and the Ookens operating them is to produce more programmable soldiers."

"Meaning that there will be more than the missing Skaines in trouble," Dan put in, concern creasing his features. "We can guarantee we'll find at least one or two Collectives, and likely a number of Bl'kheths, plus whoever else they have captive. If that's the case, the only option is to go in and take the whole operation down."

Bethany Anne nodded. "That's my thinking as well."

Tabitha let out a surprised squeak. "I have an update. The drone has crossed the Gate." She lifted a finger and the image on the wallscreens switched to show a rolling view of the other side. "Everyone agrees that looks like an Ooken factory, right?"

Bethany Anne recognized the crystalline structure easily. A wave of anger caused her heart and stomach to contract. She stood and leaned on the table with her hands clenched into fists. "We're going in."

Slater didn't know what he was seeing onscreen, but

the red light from Bethany Anne's eyes stirred something in him that he'd never expected to feel—the urge to fight for whoever was trapped in that structure. "Wait for me," he asked, getting to his feet.

Bethany Anne narrowed her eyes as Slater crossed to a console embedded in the wall by the door.

He pressed a button and spoke in a tone that brooked no protest. "This is your overseer. Every Skaine fit to fight will report for duty. We will be joining Empress Bethany Anne in her attack on the Kurtherians who have taken your sons and brothers. Do not falter. There will be a severe penalty for any able-bodied Skaine whose name does not appear on a ship roster in the next hour."

Slater dropped his hand, squeezing it tight to get control of the rage running through his veins. "These are my people who have been taken prisoner," He looked at Bethany Anne. "And you say there will be others who are victims of this atrocity? We may have been slavers until we were educated, and we may be sore about the methods the Rangers used to teach us the lesson, but we are not heartless. We will not stand idly by while anyone, no matter their species, is subjected to torture."

Tabitha shot Slater a double-thumbs up. "You have come a long way from the miserable excuses for sentient life I had to kick into shape."

Nickie laced her hands behind her head. "Don't count on it. These guys might be all friendly, but I can tell you right now that there are still plenty of cannibal scumbag Skaines around, too."

Bethany Anne shot Nickie a look that shut the youngest

Grimes up and turned her attention to Tabitha. "I might give you shit, but you've done good, girl."

Tabitha slung an arm around Slater's neck. "What can I say? Just call me the HR expert around these parts."

Nickie laughed, deep and throaty. "All that means is that you *can* polish something a bit...turd-like...if you've got the patience."

Tabitha shook her head and groaned.

John rolled his eyes. "Trust you to say something to ruin the moment."

Bethany Anne ignored Nickie. "Let's go."

23

Kurtherian Space, QBS *ArchAngel*

"Empress on board," ArchAngel announced from every display when Bethany Anne boarded the ship.

Bethany Anne headed down the corridor to the bridge with Dan at her side. Her heart swelled at the shining faces of the crew lining the corridor. She waved to the crewmembers she recognized and smiled warmly at the new faces in the impromptu receiving line.

It was almost overwhelming to be back aboard the *ArchAngel* and see her restored to her former glory after so many years as a derelict. Bethany Anne had hated to leave her in the Straiphus System and had been beyond happy to have her retrieved and repaired.

This ship held a special place in her heart as the one that most embodied her spirit.

Her father's idea to have Dan take *ArchAngel* out into the border systems as a lone point of defense against incursions had been a wise one, given that the Ookens were showing up out there more often since Bethany Anne had cut off Gödel's access to the Bakas.

Bethany Anne allowed the surge of memories to wash over her as she walked onto the bridge, captured by the reminder that so many of them had been created in times of victory dragged from the jaws of defeat.

ArchAngel's was the only face Bethany Anne saw when she entered the bridge.

The AI filled the main viewscreen, backlit with a glow that spoke to Bethany Anne of pure joy. "Welcome back, Mother."

Tears welled in Bethany Anne's eyes at the warm welcome. "Thank you, ArchAngel. For the welcome, and for everything you have done to protect the Federation in my absence. It's good to see you, too."

ArchAngel returned a mirror image of Bethany Anne's smile. "It pleases me to have you aboard my ship for this assault." Her eyes flared red, and her fangs gleamed as she spoke. "I have longed for nothing more than for us to ride together into battle, Valkyries into the fire."

"You and I both." Bethany Anne's eyes blazed as she took her position in the captain's chair. She leaned to the left as she crossed one leg over the other and rested her chin on her hand. "Give me the fleet. It's time to begin."

ArchAngel opened communications to the *Sayomi*, the *G'laxix Sphaea*, the *Penitent Granddaughter*, and the fifty-seven Skaine ships that had joined them at Slater's order. Her face shifted, becoming altogether more vampiric as she settled into bitch-AI-ready-for-war mode. "May I have the honors?" she asked.

Bethany Anne waved a hand, giving ArchAngel a warm

smile. "You are and have always been an extension of my will. Go ahead and give the order."

ArchAngel's hair whipped in a wind that did not exist as she appeared on every screen across every ship in the fleet. "The only thing to fear today is being the enemy who is unfortunate enough to fall under our regard. Let the Kurtherians and their allies learn that to fuck with innocence earns a death sentence that will be carried out immediately—and without mercy."

Red light flared from her eyes, washing the space around her avatar the color of blood. She opened her arms and tilted her chin, flashing her fangs in a dazzling smile that sent chills down the spines of everyone watching. "Go forth and be victorious."

Bethany Anne got to her feet as ArchAngel withdrew from all but the main screen. "Perfect. I wish I could take you with me, ArchAngel, but I know you will be ready and waiting to blow the shit out of that atrocity the moment we have the prisoners safe."

She took a moment to be still and connect to the mind-space, looking for a certain mental signature. Finding what she was searching for was both a relief and a source of pain. "Fuckdammit," she muttered.

"What was that?" ArchAngel asked, catching an echo of the Collectives' cry.

"They are my allies," Bethany Anne told her, emotion cracking her voice as the cry receded. "The Collectives, who I have sworn to set free and avenge. They are in pain, and I won't fucking stand for it." She opened a channel to Kael-ven. "Be ready for me to transfer the Collectives they have in there. I can't tell how many there are or what state they're in physically, but their minds are broken. I can only hope they respond well to the Conduit."

Kael-ven shook his head, his features hardening in a mixture of sympathy and anger on the Collectives' behalf. "Of course. I'm sure bringing the Conduit along was the right thing to do, but how will you get them to agree to the transfer if they are broken?"

"I'm not going to ask their permission to *move* them," Bethany Anne told him solemnly. "The Conduit's presence will help, but I will have you Gate them to QT2 as soon as they are aboard. It's likely you'll have to increase shielding around the tank in case they react in distress."

Kael-ven nodded. "We had the hold reinforced with Dukes technology before the kelp and water were added," he assured her. "It will take whatever they can dish out, and the Conduit has its own space to retreat to if it gets too violent in there, as you ordered."

"Good to know." Bethany Anne dropped the link and pressed the button on her armor's collar to activate her helmet before turning to Dan. "I'll see you on the other side of this. Make sure anyone waiting in the transfer bay is not in the way of any large group I bring over." She made to step into the Etheric, then paused as a thought hit her. "And no matter what, do *not* let any Bl'kheths loose aboard this ship. I won't have them harmed in any way, but this ship is precious to me."

Dan repressed his mental image of the *ArchAngel* arriving at QT2 with more holes than a slice of swiss cheese in her hull. "That was your experience?" he asked somewhat uncertainly.

Bethany Anne nodded. "Those guys are ninety percent

aggression, ten percent logical thinking, and 10 percent hangry," she told him. "Their keepers will have them too starved to fight back, so they will be wild and hungry." She smiled. "And yes, I'm aware that is more than a hundred percent."

Dan nodded and leaned over his console for a moment. "I have the information on the Bl'kheths from ADAM. I'll have Natalia prepare a good meal and suitable quarters for them."

Bethany Anne smiled, appreciating Dan's foresight. She placed a hand on his shoulder briefly. "I missed this. Me, ready to kick ass. You, there to back me up. Good times. Good memories."

Dan grinned, similarly warmed by the return to their easy rhythm when working together. "Here's to making a few new ones. Now go kick some ass, already. I'm getting old waiting here."

Bethany Anne hopped to the *Penitent Granddaughter* to grab Nickie.

Her appearance on the bridge brought a couple of nervous screams from the more sensitive members of the crew.

Nickie rolled her eyes and took the hand Bethany Anne held out to her.

"Can they run the ship without you?" Bethany Anne asked once they were in the Etheric.

Nickie snorted. "Yeah, sure. Don't be fooled by their reactions. My crew is a tight team, and they don't let shit slide when it comes down to it."

Bethany Anne's next step took them out of the Etheric

and onto the *Sayomi*, where they picked up John and Tabitha and made the trip to the dark crystal platform.

Bethany Anne brought them out of the Etheric on the lowest level of the structure and turned to them with fire in her eyes. "You three need to take out the Ookens working the nanocyte production and destroy any nanocyte stores they have down here. I don't want to give our Skaine friends any reason to fall into temptation once this place has been blown to shards."

Tabitha pressed her lips together in distaste. "I think we need to be ready in case they turn on us once the factory has been secured," she warned Bethany Anne. "I know they can't do much against our ship tech, but you never know if they'll be stupid enough to think they can win because they have the numbers advantage."

"Where's the advantage?" Bethany Anne responded. "All that means is that if they turn, they're placing me in a target-rich environment."

Tabitha lifted her hands. "What can I say? Stupid is knowing the consequences and doing it anyway. I beat the ignorance out of them as a species, so I know for a fact they're aware we can't be beaten."

Bethany Anne's mouth twitched in amusement. "I'll keep that in mind."

"Gotcha," John affirmed. "Ladies, shall we?"

Nickie lifted her Jean Dukes Specials with a slightly manic grin fixed on the production line. "You know me, Grandad. Let's throw a few spanners in their works and see what happens."

Tabitha pointed at one of the huge machines nearby, and a wisp of smoke rose from it as the internal workings ground to a painful-sounding halt. "Who needs to waste time on that?" She jerked her head in the direction of the worker Ookens farther down the production line. "You guys take care of them while I concentrate on figuring out what they're doing with this machinery while I get in there and break it all."

Bethany Anne looked at the glass wall, a shiver passing down her spine as the identical layout of the floor reminded her that there would be close to a million Ookens on the surface. She opened a link to the *ArchAngel*. "We're here. Have the Skaines start their distraction."

The crystal vibrated as the surface bombardment began. Dan had point for the fleet, along with instructions on how to breach the platform's shielding.

There was no reason to have anyone except Bethany Anne's team set foot on the platform, and whether or not the Ookens required an atmosphere to survive wasn't a concern.

"The only good Ooken is a dead one," Bethany Anne murmured after dropping the link. She stepped through the Etheric again, this time only walking far enough to circumvent the glass wall and get into the tank beyond.

She emerged and walked slowly along the floor of the tank while she got her bearings and adjusted her mass to best travel through the water. The Collectives were easy enough to locate since there was none of the vegetation they preferred to live in to obscure them from her sight.

Bethany Anne made her way around the ring, searching out the group mind as she walked. The curving wall led her to the opposite side of the factory floor, which was where she found the Collectives.

Their condition was pitiful. Bethany Anne stopped in her tracks, needing to gather herself. She felt their agitation at the awareness of her presence. However, they did not react violently. She felt the reason before she saw it. Their misery was absolute, and Bethany Anne had to work hard not to be sucked into their emotional miasma.

Their skin was pale and sagged around their frames. They clung to each other, their tentacles entwined for comfort, and what little protection they could afford themselves from the ministrations of their torturers. It was hard to make out where one Collective ended and another began.

Bethany Anne cursed, feeling a gnawing in her stomach that did not belong to her. They were beyond hungry. Worse than the physical starvation was the mental agony they were suffering from. Being cut off from the group mind was utter hell for a Collective, and these were relatively young compared to her guests. She didn't know how they hadn't reached the point of giving up already.

These beings thrived on community, and they were dependent on close contact with each other. They were only whole when they were together as part of a much larger whole.

Bethany Anne paused to process her rage on their behalf. Her anger was not going to help these Collectives. They needed a kind touch. They needed a strong mind to hold them close and cleanse them of hurt that had been done to them.

She attempted to connect with the Conduit, thinking its presence in her mind would be more than useful to keep them calm while she moved them to the *G'laxix*

Sphaea. However, the distance must have been too great because the attempt failed.

Bethany Anne wondered briefly what that would mean for her in terms of how much it was going to cost in energy to take the Collectives across that distance.

More than I'm comfortable with, TOM told her flatly.

Not much I can do without moving the **G'laxix Sphaea** *into the line of fire.*

Oh, no, TOM snarked. **Kael-ven's ship might get a scratch on the paintwork.**

>>**Well, not really,** << ADAM interjected. >>**But it would create a gap in the destruction of the towers, which means there would be a fuck-ton of Ookens free to make their way down to BA.**<<

Look at you with your accurate estimations, TOM remarked icily. **You do remember it's our place to help Bethany Anne to survive these encounters, not to enable her to hero herself into a grave?**

Quit bitching, the pair of you, and get ready to make sure the day I go to my grave is in the very, **very** *distant future.* Bethany Anne breathed calm into herself and pushed Etheric energy out of her palms to act as jets. She sped toward the knot of tentacles with resolve and empathy as her weapons in the fight against despair. *ADAM, you're up. Make sure I land in the center of the* **G'laxix Sphaea's** *tank.*

ADAM fed her the tank's precise location. >>**You good?** <<

As I'll ever be. Here's hoping they don't decide to hug me to death. Bethany Anne reduced her speed as she came up on the clustered Collectives, sending calming thoughts into the group mind as she approached and moving her body through the water to miss a misshapen and sad tentacle.

Without a thought for herself, she drew massively on the Etheric and locked the Collectives inside a bubble of water.

They reacted with fear as Bethany Anne screamed with the effort the transfer took. The Collectives' cries of confusion were briefly accompanied by flailing tentacles as they rearranged their protective huddle before becoming still.

Bethany Anne fed them her love and her promise to be their salvation from the hurts that had been done to them. She showed them her guests aboard the *Helena* and those beneath the Hexagon. The effort of maintaining a mindlink on top of pulling the Collectives and her battle armor through the Etheric set her nose bleeding, but she ignored the trickle even when it turned to a steady flow.

She exerted her control over the floating bubble of water and pushed on regardless.

Just keep going. I've got your brain, TOM murmured so as not to distract her from the herculean effort of pulling five-plus tons of Collective plus the metal she wore over the miles between the factory and the *G'laxix Sphaea.*

It's a fucking good thing I'm not put off by the prospect of hard work, Bethany Anne joked, pushing away the realization that she would have to do this many more times before everyone from the cells was safe aboard one of her ships.

Her armor dragged, weighing only half as much as the burden of her responsibility for the lives of the Collectives. She gritted her teeth and forced herself to pick up the pace. She focused on what mattered, which was saving lives, and grunted out her pain as she pulled the whole squirming bunch to the *G'laxix Sphaea* at a speed that even she had not known she could attain.

>>**BA**,<< ADAM called, stirring her from the state of autopilot she'd fallen into. >>**You almost went past your exit point.**<<

Thanks. Bethany Anne left the Etheric after checking she hadn't completely overstepped her target landing point. Seeing she had stopped inside the tank's boundaries, she made the transfer and let the bubble around the Collectives go.

She staggered as the resistance from the Etheric vanished. Her heart pounded in her chest from the sheer effort of transferring that much mass. The Collectives remained entwined despite being released from the bubble.

Bethany Anne managed to reach out and call for the Conduit with what little mental energy she had remaining.

The Collectives screamed inside their minds, too traumatized by the move to realize they were in a better place.

The Conduit's voice filled the mindspace, its voice a calming song that interrupted the cacophony of panic the rescuees were emitting. They began to unfurl, curiosity at the new voice in their group mind drawing them out of their terror.

Bethany Anne had no energy left to help. She had her armor keep her weighted to the floor of the tank while she bent to rest her hands on her knees and pulled energy from the Etheric to assist TOM with repairing the damage to her entire body.

Good job, TOM soothed. **Keep drawing energy so I can repair your internal organs.**

Shit, how much damage is there to repair? Bethany Anne knew it wasn't good. She'd never felt so drained, or so much like a dried-out sponge left in the sun. *Fix me faster. I have to get back and transfer the rest of the prisoners to the ArchAngel before the Ookens make it down there to kill everyone before we can get them to safety.*

TOM paused before replying. **This was not as bad as the damage you've sustained after repairing a rift, but nevertheless, I had to concentrate on keeping your mind whole, and your body began to cannibalize itself.**

How. Fucking. Long? she demanded as the pain of his rapid repairs wracked her body. She growled in frustration. *I need a better solution before we hit the rest of the factories. If this is almost killing me, it's going to be a damn sight worse for anyone else doing the transfers.*

Just keep pulling the energy, TOM repeated, concern lacing his words. **I'll tell you the moment you can make the transfer without collapsing.**

He gave her the all-clear a few minutes later. **The others will not take so much to transfer since they can move under their own power. I'll be monitoring you.**

The last thing Bethany Anne saw before she left for the battle was the Collectives untangling from each other to welcome the Conduit. She felt their amazement at the Conduit's presence and the lush kelp that caressed their tired bodies.

Thank you, Bethany Anne, the Conduit told her. *You were true to your word, and I am glad to be here for my kin.*

Take care, Bethany Anne replied. *I'll see you guys back at QT2 when this place is no more than ashes on the solar wind.*

She returned to the factory floor to find the equipment

up in flames. The worker-Ookens had scattered, and she felt the telltale energy of the fighting kind in the mindspace. Bethany Anne assumed that some sense of self-preservation in their programming must have kicked in and drawn the fighters from the surface.

Bethany Anne wondered where Tabitha, John, and Nickie had gotten to.

There was a whoop from up ahead, which was followed by the appearance of Tabitha riding a worker-Ooken like a damned horse as she fired her Jean Dukes Specials at the bulk of the mass of fighter-Ookens chasing her.

She threw up a hand to wave at Bethany Anne. "I wish you'd taken me with you last time!" she yelled over the crackling flames and screeching Ookens. "This is *fuuuun!*"

John and Nickie stood on top of the machines, taking out Ookens out with cold efficiency from their respective angles.

"We found the vats," John called. "We destroyed them, no nanocytes left. Just these tons of sick fuckers to go, and we'll be there to help with the cells."

Bethany Anne decided they had things under control on this level, so she leapt onto the nearest machine on her left and activated the software she'd had Eve install in her neural chip. She reached into the mindspace once again as she made a run for the cells' locking mechanism.

With the nanocurtains over the cells down, she darted back to the open part of the factory floor and made the leap up to the level where the prisoners were being kept. *Is there a Seian here?* she called. *Or any Bl'kheth of higher rank?*

The mindspace fell silent. Bethany Anne wasn't about

to be put off by the reticence they were feeling. She increased the strength of her mental voice, making sure the translation software was broadcasting her thoughts as well as her speech. *My name is Bethany Anne Nacht, but you may know me better by my Kurtherian name—Death. I am here to set you free. Do not run for the Etheric since I can't protect you if you do. I have food and a safe place for you to recover from your ordeal while my ship takes you to the home I have created on my planet for your kind.*

Silence stretched for a long moment as the images telling the story of Sean's group filtered into their minds. What followed was a rising babble that filled the mindspace.

Bethany Anne heard a complexity of voices arguing about whether to trust this stranger who nevertheless had managed to communicate with them when no other had ever tried. She followed the sound, which was limited to the cells on the other side of the circular walkway.

John, Tabitha, and Nickie joined her, each moving in a different direction to get the prisoners organized into groups for transfer. Many of the Skaines refused to come out of their cells at the sight of Tabitha.

They soon realized she was there to help.

Sometimes an outstretched hand and a genuine smile were all that was needed to repair a misconception.

Bethany Anne moved faster than most of the prisoners could see, stopping only when she came to four cells containing the Bl'kheths. The thing that struck her much like her first encounter was that despite their malnourished state, these people had not allowed their spirits to be crushed.

They stared at Bethany Anne proudly despite the fear she felt in their shared thoughts.

She knelt and opened her arms wide. *Honored Bl'kheths. I owe six of your people a debt I can never repay. All I can do is offer you safety and swear that you will be returned to your home and your people once I have freed every Bl'kheth the Seven are holding hostage against the rest of your world.*

The Bl'kheths did not reply except to express surprise that Bethany Anne also knew their history.

I know you must be wary after being used for so long. Search my mind and see that I'm telling you the truth. She opened her memories of Sean's group again, adding her emotional reaction to their sacrifice and her vow to protect the innocent from Gödel's evil. *Will you come willingly?* she asked. *Will you help me to fight the Seven?*

The Bl'kheths conferred among themselves again. The rising murmurs in the mindspace first went in favor of running, then shifted as the Bl'kheths saw that Bethany Anne was trusted by Sean—and that she was fully capable of doing the things she was promising them.

A female extracted herself from the group in the second cell. *We will go with you,* she agreed on behalf of the group. *We find you to have honor, and the staunch heart needed to give up your own needs for the good of your people.*

We will follow you, Bethany Anne Nacht.

Bethany Anne let out a breath she hadn't realized she'd been holding. She understood that these pint-sized warriors had already earned a special place in her heart due to their refusal to be ruled by anything but right. *That's all I wanted to hear. Just no suicides, okay? Nobody needs to die to win this war except the Seven and their fuckpuppets. Take my hands, and I'll get you out of here.*

The Bl'kheths gathered around Bethany Anne, each placing a hand on her body.

Bethany Anne drew on the Etheric and transferred them to the bay aboard the *ArchAngel,* where the crew was waiting to receive them. She pointed out Natalia and Darryl, who both wore the headsets needed to communicate with the Bl'kheths.

Go with my people, she instructed gently. She held up a finger before they left. *Darryl and Natalia will take you to an enclosed space where there is plenty of food waiting.* She eyed them. *Under no circumstances are you to eat any part of my ship.*

24

The next hour went by in a blur of factory-Etheric-*Arch-Angel*-repeat.

Bethany Anne took group after group to the *ArchAngel*, exhausting herself further with each trip. She ignored the pleas to rest between groups, choosing instead to keep increasing her draw on the Etheric and push through the pain while TOM did his repairs on her body.

Darryl tried to hold her back when she arrived with the first group of Skaines and he saw her nose had been bleeding again.

Bethany Anne shrugged him off and stepped back into the Etheric.

It might not be the worst idea to take a break, TOM ventured. **A few minutes isn't going to make much of a difference.**

Bethany Anne exited into the factory and found that John, Tabitha, and Nickie were holding back an increasing tide of Ookens filtering down from the wreckage on the surface. *Tell that to everyone who's dying right now.*

By the time Bethany Anne had gotten all of the prisoners to the ship and made the final jump with John, Tabitha, and Nickie, the Skaines had finished slaking their thirst for revenge with their blanket bombardment of the surface, and they were all ready to withdraw and commence the last stage of taking the factory down.

Bethany Anne took one last trip through the Etheric to the bridge of the *Sayomi*. She exited at a stagger, completely drained from the effort of carrying out the whole rescue effort.

Her next step turned out to be beyond her capability.

John dashed over to catch her before she hit the floor. "I told you."

Bethany Anne blinked back the dark spots in her vision and pushed John away. "I'm fine."

Her knees buckled a second time as the darkness crashed down.

Kurtherian Space, QBS *ArchAngel*, Ready Room

Dan had his chair scooted back against the wall in order to get a better view of the ships in play and the damage they were doing to the Kurtherian factory in the center of the battle zone.

Part of his attention was on the small screen embedded in his desk, where John was giving him a rundown of Bethany Anne's condition.

"It was transferring the Collectives that caused her to collapse. That and her refusal to stop and let TOM heal her completely before she took on rescuing everyone else."

"But she's going to be okay, right?" Dan asked, his eyebrows meeting in worry.

"Yeah, she's in the Pod-doc," John told him. "Sayomi has the helm while we wait for her to heal. How are the prisoners doing?"

"As well as can be expected," Dan replied with a sigh. "Natalia and Darryl have a team working with them to take care of them until we can take them somewhere safer."

"Got you." John nodded stoically. "Good luck out there."

"Same to you, my friend." Dan closed the video link and immersed himself in the battle. His concentration was on ArchAngel's projection of the system in miniature. Planning a battle in the three dimensions of space was no easy feat.

ArchAngel flitted from screen to screen, spooling endless data to Dan as she set the fleet's positions in relation to the satellite stations around the factory platform.

Dan switched the projection view so that their ships became green markers of varying shapes and sizes, and the Kurtherian drones and satellites were transformed into red triangles. He found the traditional layout easier to keep track of than the scaled-down versions of each ship Arch-Angel had given him to work with.

ArchAngel was able to process, predict, and therefore react so much faster than Dan could even *think* that it was she who was running the fleet, not him. All Dan had to do was allow her access to his inner observations via his neural chip while he took care of his part.

This was their way of working. In the years they had been patrolling the forgotten reaches of space, they had built a trust with each other that allowed them to operate together to produce the best results. His long experience as a tactician gave him a perspective that would be near-impossible to duplicate, even for an AI. He believed it was his human touch, combined with her speed, precision, and accuracy, that made them the formidable team they'd become.

They lost three Skaine ships to an unexpected complement of drones that came bursting out from the underside of the factory. Dan cursed vehemently at the loss, but ArchAngel had already instructed Meredith to take the drones out before they had the chance to strike again.

Dan had no time to reflect. He remained the physical contact for the fleet captains, keeping them informed of their orders while ArchAngel did what she could through the digital entities aboard the Skaine ships. Messages flew thick and fast between the *ArchAngel* and the fleet as he instructed them as to where ArchAngel wanted them.

The difference between this experience and other recent battles Dan had lived through was that the Skaines did not allow their digital entities to control their ships. Consequently, the outcome of the battle depended on the Skaines' ability to keep up with the steady stream of commands he and ArchAngel were sending.

Dan had already given up trying to keep up with the conversation between ArchAngel, Sayomi, and Meredith, but then, they were all veterans of war with the Ookens.

The three ships moved in complete synchronicity, which made up for the lag caused by communicating with the weapons and navigation systems on the Skaine ships via their organic operators. This version of Meredith was no surprise, beyond the quirks she'd developed from prolonged contact with Nickie. He had been wary of Sayomi until the recalcitrant AI had bowed to the experience of ArchAngel, making the three ships more comparable to three parts of a whole.

The Kurtherian defenses were in full swing, giving Dan the opportunity to test the *ArchAngel's* newfound durability when it came to attacks. While they lacked anything like a BYPS, they had the numbers game down to an art. The projection showed many multiples of red Kurtherian assets compared to the relatively small number of green ships on the board.

The main point of concern for Dan had been whether the sheer number of Kurtherian drones would be a factor when it came to their efforts to penetrate the shields. However, ArchAngel kept the shield phasing tight enough to ensure that no drone got through. Even so, Dan noted she had just over two thousand armed bots stationed on the hull, each one programmed to be ready to destroy anything that managed to make it past them.

"I'm not going to get bitten in the ass twice," ArchAngel assured Dan, pulling him from his introspection.

"I can't imagine you would," Dan told her distractedly. "We need to take out the satellites."

"Already on it," ArchAngel replied. "The Skaines are taking care of them."

They received a distress call from another of the Skaine ships. This one looked to have gotten caught between a thick swarm of drones and the platform.

Dan frowned. "What are they doing out of position?"

"They're right where they're supposed to be," Arch-Angel answered. "That distress call is fake. I'm using the Skaine ship as bait to draw out the ship I know is guarding that platform."

Just when it appeared that the Skaine ship was going to be destroyed, two ships decloaked. One was the *Sayomi*. The other was the Kurtherian ship ArchAngel had predicted.

"Only one?" Dan asked.

"Just wait," ArchAngel told him with a serene smile.

The *Sayomi* destroyed the drones in a burst of flame, then vanished again as the Skaine ship shot out of there.

Dan found himself on the edge of his seat as the Kurtherian ship came around to the *Sayomi's* last location. Explosions peppered the void as the *Penitent Granddaughter* released a number of guided missiles that homed on the Kurtherian ship while the Skaines she was covering took out the satellite stations and put a stop to their ability to replace the drones.

The Kurtherian ship responded by sending out a tidal wave of small pods.

"Ookens," ArchAngel told Dan offhand. "They can't beat us with technology. It's almost comical that they'd try this way."

"You mean, target practice," Dan replied, typing furiously to warn the Skaines to take the pods out before they reached them. "If they get aboard any of our ships, we can consider them lost. These are unenhanced Skaines, not Guardians."

"Ah. Yes." ArchAngel appeared to be dancing, but Dan

knew better than to assume that. "I can do something about it."

Each movement of her hands preceded the release of a round of pucks from her stores. Dan was grateful his crew were so dedicated to their duty. He could almost see them down in the belly of the ship, working in unison to keep the supply coming.

ArchAngel's intervention saved the Skaines from imminent destruction—but it also drew the attention of the Kurtherian ship,

The ship turned its weapons on the *ArchAngel*. Bright blue light filled the void between them as the Kurtherian ship loosed its plasma weapons plus a spread of missiles in their direction.

The plasma licked harmlessly at the shields. However, the ArchAngel shook as the missiles impacted along her flank.

"Damage report," Dan called.

"No damage," ArchAngel told him. "Shields are still at optimal performance levels. What you felt was me moving the ship with the impacts to reduce stress on the shields."

"Pretty expensive light show if you ask me," Dan commented as he watched ArchAngel's return fire speed toward the Kurtherian ship. "Good call."

ArchAngel's Etheric-enabled missiles raked the Kurtherian ship. The unstable energy stored within them caused a burst of explosions when she scored a hit on weak points in their defenses.

"My show is worth the ticket price," ArchAngel told Dan with a smile.

Dan waited for the large explosions to follow, but the

ship's shielding held. It came about again, putting the damaged flank out of reach for the moment. A large number of pods detached from the top of the ship. These did not spread out like the first wave but rather clustered around certain points of the ship.

"I don't think there's a Kurtherian aboard that ship," Dan ventured. "They're reacting too predictably."

"I have a plan for them either way," ArchAngel replied. "See how the Ookens have been placed? They might believe that will give them an extra layer of protection when I strike again, but they are wrong. Now I know where to press to make my point. It would be wise for the Skaines to withdraw to a safe distance. You know I've been dying to test some of the Dukes weapons that were included in my refit."

Dan felt his mouth turn up despite the seriousness of the situation they were in. The video he'd seen of the ADAM-created, Dukes-modified missiles being tested had taken his breath away with their potential for utter destruction. "Take it away. I'm as excited as you are to see what those suckers can do now they've had the kinks worked out."

ArchAngel conferred with Meredith and Sayomi while Dan instructed the Skaines to return to the Gate and prepare to exit the system.

The Skaine overseer requested a video link.

Dan put him up on the desk screen. "What's the problem?" he asked curtly. "You have your orders."

Slater scowled in response. "No problem. But we're not going to run away. This is our fight as much as it is yours."

Dan lost his friendly look. "You can get out of the way, or you can get fried along with the Kurtherians. I have an AI who is extremely focused on removing the threat, and she won't wait to coddle your hurt feelings about not being needed at this point."

Slater paled when ArchAngel appeared on his viewscreen.

"That ship is filled with Ookens," ArchAngel stated. She folded her arms and fixed Slater with a look that brooked no protest. "So get out of my way. What I'm about to unleash will take out any ship in range, whether it belongs to friend or foe. I don't want your people to die, but neither do I want there to be any survivors on the enemy side."

Slater took into consideration *ArchAngel's* continued assault on the drones the entire time they'd been fighting, and that she'd already used technology beyond anything he had available to him. "What do you expect us to do?" he demanded.

Dan recognized that the Skaine's defiance had nothing to do with being difficult and everything to do with his desire to get some payback for what had been done to his people. "I expect you to keep your people alive long enough to enjoy their reunion with the people Bethany Anne rescued." He gave Slater an understanding look. "You should work on keeping the Gate clear. Once ArchAngel lets loose, they're likely going to try to take out your home as revenge."

Slater's face hardened. "Over my dead body!" he exclaimed.

"Then do not make that your reality," ArchAngel told him. "Protect your people. I will take care of the rest."

Slater relented at last. "Make sure you don't leave a single one of them alive," he told her in a grim tone.

ArchAngel inclined her head a fraction. "That is my plan."

The *Penitent Granddaughter* provided the Skaines with cover while the *Sayomi* took care of what drones still remained. The last remaining barrier to destroying the factory platform was the Kurtherian ship blocking them with everything it had.

Missiles, plasma, and plain old kinetics streaked across the void at the three ships under ArchAngel's command.

The *ArchAngel* bore the attack with little strain. Her shields lit up with every impact, but she remained unscathed. The *Penitent Granddaughter* fared much the same. As for the *Sayomi*? Well, they couldn't hit what they couldn't see.

Dan held his breath as ArchAngel launched one of ADAM's gifts from each ship. He waited for the telltale streak to show the progress of the missiles. "What happened?" he moaned when the missiles did not appear on his projection.

"You cannot see them," ArchAngel informed Dan. "These weapons travel through the Etheric, guided by the programming I gave them prior to launch."

"How will we know if they worked?" Dan asked with some confusion. "The video I saw had them travel partly in our dimension."

A huge explosion lit the projection. Then another. Then a third.

"That's how you know," ArchAngel replied. "Going off your supposition that the ship was unmanned, I calculated its most likely course and had the missiles exit the Etheric inside the ship."

Dan couldn't argue the effectiveness of ArchAngel's tactics. Neither could any of the Ookens since they had been obliterated when their ship exploded in a rain of molten metal. "Any losses on our side?" he asked.

"No," ArchAngel informed him. "The Skaines made it to the Gate and are clearing up a group of drones that followed them. Otherwise, all the Kurtherian assets have been destroyed except the factory itself."

Dan slapped the desk with both hands. "That's music to my ears. Let me get John or Tabitha onscreen. I want to know if Bethany Anne has made it out of the Pod-doc yet. I don't want her to miss this if she can help it."

It was Tabitha who appeared on the desk screen. "Nice work with the missiles," she told him as greeting. "Shame Bethany Anne wasn't awake to see it."

Dan's face crumpled in concern. "She's still in the Pod-doc?"

Tabitha shook her head, the light accentuating the heavy luggage she was carrying under her eyes. "She's out, but she's not awake yet."

Dan's frown deepened. "Why not? It healed her, right?"

"Yeah," Tabitha confirmed. "But she pushed herself so far beyond her limit, it's going to take a while for her to fully recover. TOM thinks she'll probably be out for another few hours at least."

Dan sucked in a breath, wondering just how close Bethany Anne had been to pushing herself completely over the edge. "Shit. Well, I guess we'd best get this wrapped up without her."

"Sounds good to me," Tabitha replied, stifling a yawn. "You don't need us for this part, right?"

Dan smiled softly. "No. You get some shuteye. Arch-Angel and I will take care of the factory."

Tabitha let out a hollow laugh. "The chance would be a fine thing. We're gonna escort the Skaines back to the colony, and make sure none of the drones snuck through while our backs were turned."

Dan nodded. "Just make sure you take care of yourselves as well as everyone else. You might be superhuman, but it doesn't preclude you from needing to sleep."

Tabitha snickered. "Doesn't my tired ass know it. It's been a hell of a long day."

She dropped the link, leaving Dan and ArchAngel alone in the ready room.

"Shall we?" ArchAngel noted Dan's tight shoulders as she sent instructions for her full complement of ADAM's missiles to be loaded. "You appear to be tense. We will be done here soon, and then we can get back to what we do best. Are you ready?"

Dan nodded. "Almost. Let everyone else get through the Gate before you take out the factory." He stretched, feeling the strain in the small of his back from being seated for so long. "Then we can get the hell out of this system and destroy that damned Gate."

ArchAngel tracked the exodus of the fleet through the Gate. She released Sayomi and Meredith as the last of the Skaine ships returned to their own system. "That's everyone," she informed Dan.

Dan lifted a hand and waved it in a circle. "Then have at 'em, ArchAngel." He got to his feet and sighed, glad to be done with the whole mess.

ArchAngel zoomed the viewscreen in on the factory, returning the projection to the realistic representation she had originally displayed at the same time. "It would be my pleasure. The payload has been delivered."

A few moments later, there were a series of explosions all over the factory platform.

The shattered crystal was flung violently outward in a microfine spray.

Dan's eyes remained fixed on the screen until the ring of dust slowed and was pulled apart by the gravitational influences of the other bodies in the system. A smile touched his lips as the majority was pulled unerringly toward the star. "You know," he murmured, partly to Arch-Angel, mostly to himself, "we're going to be seeing more of these places."

ArchAngel returned his distracted smile with a raised eyebrow. "You bet your ass we will. Especially when I get my way and Bethany Anne gives us the green light to search them out." She looked off to the side and raised her eyebrows. "Oh. Well, that changes things."

Dan knew ArchAngel didn't get surprised often. "What is it?"

ArchAngel's mouth turned up at the corner. "ADAM has the location of every one of the Kurtherian factories. We can skip the searching and go straight to the destruction."

Dan liked the sound of that. "What are you waiting

for?" he asked. "The sooner we take out that Gate and get our passengers to Devon, the sooner we can get started."

"About that," ADAM cut in over the speaker system. "Bethany Anne has another task in mind for you two. Report to the *Baba Yaga* once you've handed over the rescued prisoners."

25

The Interdiction, Open Space, QBS *Sayomi*

Tabitha was at Bethany Anne's side when she opened her eyes again. "Hey, Sleeping Beauty. I was starting to think you were gonna sleep the rest of the century away."

Bethany Anne put a hand to her throbbing head, not quite daring to sit up in her bed. "Guess I went down good, huh?" She licked her lips but found her tongue had all the usefulness of sandpaper in the desert. "Where are we?"

Tabitha poured a glass of water and held the straw to Bethany Anne's lips. "We're almost home."

Bethany Anne paused before accepting it. "The Collectives? Everyone else?"

Tabitha gave her a stern look. "Drink first, questions after. It was downright reckless of you to push so hard," she chided gently. "Everyone is fine. Dan and ArchAngel dealt with the factory and the Gate after we got everyone back into the Skaine system. He's somewhere behind us. Kael-ven is already at Devon since he messaged to ask permission to take the Collectives there instead of to QT2. Something the Conduit requested."

Bethany Anne sipped the water as Tabitha ran through the post-op report, grateful for the sensation returning to her parched mouth. "Probably because the habitat in Eve's lab is larger," she surmised. "Give me some room."

She waved for Tabitha to move back and pushed herself into a sitting position. "Fuck!" She grabbed her head and cursed some more as the brass band inside her skull kicked up its enthusiasm a notch.

Tabitha's eyebrows went up as she moved in to steady Bethany Anne. "You okay?

Bethany Anne nodded carefully as Tabitha propped her up with pillows. "Yeah. It's just been a while since I've been this weak. You're right, I pushed too hard, and I'm paying for it. I'll be fine as soon as I've eaten something." She moved her hair out of the way before focusing on Tabitha again. "What happened after I went down?"

Tabitha grinned as she counted off the remaining points on her fingers. "The Skaines were happy they got their people back. The delegation from the Federation you requested to fix Stewart McAssface's wagon reported for duty, and I gave them an intro to Slater."

Bethany Anne lifted a hand to halt Tabitha's retelling. "Slow down. Intro? To Slater? Why?"

Tabitha's grin widened. "Oh, yeah. I made Slater the governor of this quadrant and had him sign a treaty with the Federation on behalf of his people." She shrugged at the look Bethany Anne gave her. "What did you want me to do? You were busy napping, so I acted for you. Slater isn't so bad."

She lifted a finger when Bethany Anne smirked at her. "*Don't* tell him I said that," she warned.

"You did good," Bethany Anne conceded. "Has Dan had any trouble getting the people we rescued taken care of?" She surprised both of them with a huge yawn that erupted without warning.

Tabitha shook her finger at Bethany Anne. "You haven't even asked how you're doing. You need to rest. Sleep. We'll talk when we get home."

Bethany Anne closed her eyes as weariness stole over her. *TOM? Do I want to know what I did to myself?*

TOM considered whether knowing she'd been inches from death would be helpful. Then again, not telling her wouldn't work out so well for him. **You cut it pretty fine,** he admitted. **But I knew there was no reasoning with you while you were so focused. You did what you had to do to save those people's lives.**

Bethany Anne was hit by a huge yawn. *Thank you for keeping me alive. You're a good friend.*

TOM didn't quite know how to respond to that.

He had not expected to care so deeply for Bethany Anne when he had made the decision to merge himself with her, but today had taught him something new about himself. If it had come down to it, he would have burned out his own mind to save hers without hesitation.

Thank you, he managed to tell Bethany Anne, despite being overcome with relief that she'd pulled through.

Bethany Anne's reply was a murmur before he received a soft snore.

· · ·

Devon, The Hexagon, Eve's Sublevel

Tina pushed her datapad away with a tired smile on her face. "Progress," she murmured. "I thought it was *never* going to happen."

Marcus looked up from his simulation. "You solved the formula?"

Tina frowned, missing his meaning. "Formula? Oh, for the E-BYPS. No. This is something else Bethany Anne had me thinking about." She sent the file she was working on to Marcus, William, and Bobcat with a smile. "How to extend the BYPS in our reality to cover the Federation."

Bobcat and William shared a glance before the two of them focused on her again.

"I don't think even Bethany Anne can afford the expense of that," Bobcat blurted. "Just getting that many satellites into place would bankrupt her."

"Unlikely," Tina replied. "Since I designed this to be a cost-efficient model instead of a spendathon. No satellites. We're going to turn each individual point of defense on the Federation borders into a piece of a network that will cover the whole, like a crocheted blanket."

William's brow furrowed as he tried and failed to picture the end result. "So, there will be gaps?"

"Yes," Tina confirmed. "It was something Bethany Anne said about the armor project that got me thinking. The Bl'kheths providing a security blanket, or something like that. So yes, there will be physical gaps, but they are only figurative because CEREBRO will be present throughout the network. The first thing I considered was the impossibility of producing that many individual BYPS systems. The second was how to get around the sheer distance between some of the locations. My solution is to use the infrastructure that's already there. Upgrading the offensive capabilities is just a question of bootstrapping. We don't even need a ton of people to make it work since CEREBRO can take care of the programming."

William looked at Tina skeptically. "You can't get *all* of it accomplished using EIs."

Tina inclined her head. "No. Don't get me wrong, most of the physical labor can be taken care of using bots and printer tech, but there does need to be some input from the people at the locations."

"Have you taken the strain on CEREBRO into account?" Bobcat questioned. "It's not omniscient and omnipresent, and...uh..." He glanced at William. "A little help?"

"Omni-something?" William replied, delivering a shrug with his answer.

"Not much help," Bobcat eyed him. "I should have called in Marcus. What was I thinking?"

"I've no idea," Marcus agreed. "If you need a drinking buddy, you call William. If you need a word starting with 'omni,' such as 'omnipowerful,' you tag me."

William pointed at Marcus. "Yeah, the mistake was with your selection."

Tina ignored the three of them with practiced ease. "Yes," she replied to the question of strain on the system. "We incorporate the EIs in each location on the network into CEREBRO, which gives the whole a boost in processing power for each core added. By the time we've done that, CEREBRO will have unmatched computational power."

,"Meaning they will be able to react in sync across galaxies," Marcus marveled. "This is ambitious, but I think you're on to something."

Tina lifted her hands. "We'll see. This is all just theory until we test it. I'm not done figuring out all the potential snags to the project's success yet. There are bound to be a few locations where the distance is too great for them to connect, which we'll have to take care of by placing boosters at the relevant point—or points—between them to make up for the shortfall."

William began scribbling as an idea took him. "We'll have to come up with a safe way to do that." He waved his stylus. "We don't want to be leaving a bunch of backdoors into our defense system lying around in open space for just anyone to find."

"Valid," Tina agreed. "Can any of you think of other potential pitfalls? I'm relying on you guys to tear this plan to shreds and identify everything that could go wrong.

Bobcat tilted his head. "Bethany Anne will want this system up yesterday. We have to be clear that it can't just be thrown up like wallpaper."

"True," Tina agreed. "We need to build a simulation and test this 'blanket' to destruction before we can rely on it to be the protection she wants the Federation to have."

Marcus' eyebrows rose in appreciation for his wife's fine mind. "I would say that this is unbelievable, but you have been doing the impossible your whole life." He gathered his belongings. "I'll get started on building the sim."

Tina squeezed Marcus' hand. "Be harsh," she told him. "Make the conditions stringent enough to be certain we won't fail once we roll it out across the Federation."

"You've got it," Marcus promised, touching her shoulder before he left for his private office, where he could work in silence.

Bobcat grinned as he popped open a beer. "Looks like it's time to crank up the power on our thinking caps. I make that," he looked up a moment, "three urgent and impossible projects we have on our hands." He took a sip and placed his can in the one empty spot on the table in front of him. "What d'you say to having dinner brought to us?"

"I say bring on the cheese pizza," Tina replied. "My stomach thinks my throat's been cut."

Bobcat turned to William. "Pizza good with you?"

William nodded. "Sounds like a plan. Make mine a meat feast. We'll keep chipping away at the E-BYPS problem while you do your thing."

Devon, The Interdiction, QSD *Baba Yaga*

Bethany Anne strode down the corridor to the lower bridge access, her mind on her next steps now that she was back at full strength.

Michael insisted on remaining by her side in case she relapsed, although Bethany Anne thought that had more to do with his absence when she had gone down.

"You can quit fussing over me," she told him as they approached the bridge door. "Shit happens. I'm over it."

Michael released a patient breath. "You can hardly blame me for being concerned when I know for a fact that we're walking to the bridge right now because you don't want to draw on the Etheric. You should have called for me."

Bethany Anne fixed him with a knowing look. "What, so you could leave our children here? When I would have had to pull your ass through the Etheric in that old armor? I don't think so. I told you, I'm fine."

Michael put an arm across the bridge door to prevent Bethany Anne from entering. "You almost *killed* yourself transferring those Collectives. Then you risked your life again and again, transferring the rest of the prisoners instead of stopping to get the care you needed. What if you had died, Bethany Anne?"

His face was caught between loss and rage, which made Bethany Anne angry. "You mean like *you* did when you decided to try to outrun a backpack nuke?"

"That was different," Michael refuted. "We didn't have children who would have been left without a parent." His face softened as dawning realization crossed her face. "Promise me you won't go to extremes like that again."

Bethany Anne wished she could make that promise. "You know that's not how it works," she told him. "I could promise, but it would be a lie. I have a larger duty to consider. I could die if I come up against someone more powerful than me. I face the prospect every time I step up to take care of the Seven's latest move. Our enemies don't care that we have children, Michael."

Michael dropped his arm. "What happens then? Do you think our son and daughter would sit back?" He shook his head. "Don't forget how they reacted to Addix's death. They would throw themselves into taking their revenge, and there would be nothing I could do to prevent it."

Bethany Anne understood what he was suggesting, and the thought of her children in any kind of danger proved to be too much to bear. The ship shook violently, listing in the outpouring of Etheric energy of which she was the epicenter.

The bridge door opened, and John peered through it. "BA, you okay?"

Bethany Anne nodded. "I'm good."

John looked at her skeptically. "You don't look so good to me." He pointed at the shaking corridor. "You don't generally start shaking the ship to pieces when everything's peachy."

Bethany Anne gritted her teeth and narrowed her eyes at John. "We'll be in shortly."

John flicked a glance at Michael before closing the door.

"We will talk about this another time," Michael told Bethany Anne, understanding her fight to retain control of her reaction. "Preferably somewhere you can't destabilize with an Etheric storm. I think we need to have a serious discussion about it."

Bethany Anne breathed hard, riding the wave of inexplicable emotion that threatened to swamp her entirely with continued difficulty. "Nothing is going to happen to our children," she ground out. "If one of us dies, the other won't have the luxury of losing their shit since we will have them to think about."

The ship ceased its rocking as she reaffirmed her grasp on logical thought and clamped down on the energy buildup.

Michael captured her darting eyes. "Do you have it

under control?"

"Yes." Bethany Anne met Michael's eyes with determination. "We have a responsibility above and beyond most parents'. We may be left with no choice at some point, but I swear on all that's good and right I won't allow my children to risk their lives for something as stupid as revenge."

Bethany Anne entered the bridge without another word and headed for the small room on the upper level.

Michael had known Bethany Anne long enough to understand when to give her time to think. She understood he was coming from a place of love and not a desire to control her choices. Or at least, he hoped she did.

Bethany Anne's heels on the stairs announced her arrival before she opened the ready room and walked past John and the guys, who were seated on the right-hand side of the table. She nodded at Tabitha, Dan, and Kael-ven and took her seat at the head of the table. "I'd say let's get straight to business, but we appear to be a few people short of a full meeting."

Izanami looked up from the console she was sitting at and Lance appeared on the wallscreen. "Team BMW is almost here," the AI informed Bethany Anne. "They appear to be having a debate about whether they should have brought an antigrav cart."

"Hey, Dad." Bethany Anne smiled at Lance and tapped her nails on the table while they waited for Tina, Marcus, Bobcat, and William.

They filed in a few minutes later with their arms full of cartons.

"Sorry we're late," Tina apologized as she put her stacked boxes on the table and took a seat next to Tabitha.

"We had a breakthrough last night and wanted to be ready before we presented the concept to you."

Bethany Anne waved the others in, glad of getting some good news before they'd even begun the meeting. "Now that we're all here…" The view on the wallscreen split to make space for Jean. "Now we're *all* here…" she corrected.

Bobcat placed his boxes in the space between the table and the door and unhooked the cooler from his arm. "I figured this was going to be a long meeting, so I brought refreshments." He opened the cooler and handed out the Cokes he had on ice in there. "We didn't forget to bring the good stuff. Nathan sends his regards."

Bethany Anne smiled as she twisted the cap off her bottle. "Bobcat, you're an ass, but you're a thoughtful ass."

William chuckled dryly. "Don't thank him yet. You haven't heard what we're about to propose."

"It will have to wait," Bethany Anne told him. "Take your seats and check your HUDs for the notes ADAM has prepared to help you keep up. The first item on today's agenda is the Plan. That's 'plan' with a capital P. By the time it's complete, there won't be a single fucking resource left that the Seven can bring against us or anyone else."

She nodded at Izanami, who activated the HLP while everyone who was hearing about the crystals for the first time scanned their notes for details. "The attack on Devon wasn't random. It was a diversion put in place so the Kurtherian calling herself 'Gödel' could break into my home and take back the memory crystals Michael and I recovered before Qu'Baka was destroyed."

Everyone at the table shifted to watch as the spindles moved above their heads and a large 3D window made from hard light came into being. It showed a huge swath of space containing a number of galaxies, with a dark area along one edge. The spindles moved again, and the galaxies were steadily populated with tiny white geotags.

Bethany Anne got to her feet once the projector had finished whirring and set the window to turn slowly so that everyone got to look at the whole projection. "What you are looking at is called a galaxy map. It's Kurtherian technology, gained from the one crystal we were able to read before Gödel pulled her stunt. The blank space is Federation territory. Using this, we've been able to pinpoint the location of close to eight hundred holdings belonging to Gödel. A number of those locations are the factories where the Ookens are mass-grown in Pod-doc equivalents."

The window shifted in response to Bethany Anne's deft hand movements. The dark area was discarded, and a number of the tags in the populated area turned red. "These are our targets. Every one of these factories is identical. Each is capable of producing millions of Ookens." She paused to let the information sink in. "Worse than that, each of those factories is also a prison, where the only escape for the inmates is worse than death."

Bethany Anne sensed the shift toward anger in the room. She dismissed the galaxy map with a wave and took her seat again. "We are going to take out all these factories, and we're going to do it in one go."

"How?" John asked. "They're spread out across galaxies we didn't even know existed."

There was a murmur of agreement around the table.

Bethany Anne held up a hand. "We aren't in this alone.

We have Federation support." She saw Lance's question before it left his lips. "My Plan includes rolling out an upgrade for everyone who takes part in this operation. We'll work the fine details out, but just like I'm not willing to take any of you into this without protection, neither am I willing to send people to die unnecessarily."

Lance furrowed his brow. "You weren't kidding, then."

Bethany Anne shook her head. "I don't fuck around when it comes to the lives of the people fighting for me. This is going to be the single biggest military operation there has ever been, and the most dangerous. I want them prepared."

Michael shifted in his seat. "You all know what the Ookens are capable of. What we don't know is how many the Seven have in reserve, or how many millions more they're going to make in the time it takes us to prepare for this incursion."

"How long do we expect it to take?" Lance asked. "I can guarantee that as shit-hot as Federation troops are, they haven't encountered anything as nasty as the Ookens."

Bethany Anne's mouth curled at the corner. "That's not strictly true, is it? I have Terry Henry's group in mind. They've seen some hairy shit since we picked them up from Earth."

That raised eyebrows around the room.

Bethany Anne waved a hand. "We'll get to them. I've decided to formally ally the Interdiction planets with the Federation, since my intention is to take the ArchAngel on a tour of the Federation, and I'm guessing the Federation council will freak at the thought of me setting foot there unofficially."

Lance sat back in shock. "You're sure about that?" he asked. "That would give the council room to place political pressure on you."

Bethany Anne raised an eyebrow. "In what way? I'm suggesting a simple military alliance, most of the details of which were already agreed to when we met on Red Rock. The only question, is where the hell do we station all of the troops?"

Tina jumped to her feet. "*That's* what I was missing!" she exclaimed. She shook her head when everyone turned to stare at her. "Let me tell you about our security blanket."

EPILOGUE

Bethany Anne and Michael made their way from the bridge to Demon's den after the meeting had broken up.

"What did you think of Tina's idea?" Bethany Anne asked as they turned into the corridor Demon's room was off.

Michael shrugged. "I think if it works, then we have a viable system for keeping everyone inside the Federation safe. I won't pretend I understood how they intend to repurpose Tabitha's NARCS drones for boosting CERE-BRO's ability to communicate over long distances, but it certainly sounds like they can make it work for us."

Bethany Anne nodded. "That's my hope. Jean seems to be close to getting the formula for the Etheric-capable metals down."

"I think that woman lives for being under pressure that would make most people run screaming," Michael told her with a dry chuckle. "Has she even slept since she received the bodies of Sean's group?"

"Who knows?" Bethany Anne replied. "I've never seen it

happen." She flashed a grin at Michael. "Hey. Maybe she's a vampire."

Michael remained silent as they entered Demon's room. There were dark times ahead of them, and he for one was grateful for the light of new birth to give them hope.

Demon and Sam were nestled on the boxed-in sleeping pallet, their bodies pressed together like yin and yang to protect their kittens while the four of them slept.

Sam raised his head when they walked in. He noted who had arrived, then laid back down and closed his eyes.

"Lazy cat," Bethany Anne teased.

Demon made a sound of contentment as she flowed to her feet to come and greet Bethany Anne and Michael. *What brings you here?* she inquired.

"No reason," Bethany Anne replied, accepting the face bump Demon offered. "We just got out of a long meeting and wanted to spend some time with you all."

Michael offered his hand for Demon to rub her face along. "How are the kittens doing? They should be opening their eyes soon, right?"

Demon sat back on her haunches and nodded. *Eve says ten days to two weeks is usual for earthborn felines, but also that my kittens have a mixture of genetics from Sam and me, and it may be longer if their nanocytes have altered the natural course of development.*

Bethany Anne wasn't too surprised to hear that might be a factor. "So, any day now, right?"

Demon inclined her head. *It is my hope.*

Bethany Anne peered into the nest. "They've grown. They've almost doubled their birth weight, I'm guessing."

Demon's reply was forestalled by a shift in the atmosphere of the room.

Bethany Anne manifested an energy ball in each hand to match the fiery blade that appeared in Michael's grip. "Izanami!"

"It's not the Kurtherians," Izanami informed them. She appeared in full armor by the pallet. "It's the exotic energy again. The one Loralei picked up. Whoever the invader is, they're not getting aboard this ship."

Michael noted that Sam had woken up.

Contrary to the male cat's usual defensive reaction to anything new that occurred near his young, he was purring.

Michael nudged Bethany Anne. "Why isn't he more bothered?"

Bethany Anne couldn't have guessed.

The air in the room crackled, and suddenly there was a redheaded human woman standing in the room with them. She ignored the energy ball Bethany Anne was ready to throw at her.

She looked around until her eyes landed on Sam. "There you are! She crouched and pulled Sam in for a hug.

Bethany Anne recognized that voice. "Who the fuck are you, and what are you doing on my ship?"

The woman tipped a wink at Bethany Anne. "Sure, and that's a fine welcome from an old friend." She put a hand on her hip and pouted at Bethany Anne. "Now I know exactly why I've had the devil's own time locating my lost familiar. Thanks for keeping my Samhain safe, Bethany Anne."

Michael eyed Bethany Anne. "You know this woman?"

"I… Yessss." Bethany Anne blinked as the cognitive dissonance she was experiencing melted and the woman's name surfaced in her memory. "Amanda, right?"

"You got me," Amanda replied, flashing a saucy grin. "So this is your universe, huh?"

The missing piece of the puzzle fell into place for Bethany Anne. "Bob's Bar, right? Until now, I'd believed those memories were nothing more than a dimensional dream."

Amanda chuckled. "It was as real as can be." Amanda chuckled, cuddling Sam again before standing up.

Bethany Anne had an idea something was up when Amanda put her hands on her hips and faced her and Michael with a look she'd seen too many times before. *What do you think?* she asked Michael. *She needs help, or she thinks I need help?*

My money's on the former, Michael replied. *Bonus if she brings the cat into it.*

Amanda faced Bethany Anne with sincerity. "Bethany Anne, I'm here to *warn you about an imminent danger to your life!*"

Bethany Anne waved the energy ball away as Michael's fiery blade disappeared.

"Amanda," Michael sounded more exasperated than annoyed at her sudden appearance. "That's a normal Tuesday around here."

FINIS

Thank you for reading our stories!

Right now, I'm in the middle of the 3rd 20Booksto50K® Las Vegas convention and trying to wake up with lots of sugar and caffeine as I'm talking story with Chrishaun Keller Hanna and Natalie Roberts.

Yesterday, I celebrated the adulthood (if you will) of this group of Indie authors when IngramSpark and Publishers Weekly joined us in Las Vegas and are supporting and recognizing 20Books in an awesome way.

Further, Amazon brought fourteen people! (That is *AWESOME*.)

Google Play brought six people and so many other companies are here helping us learn how to work our business interests and (I suspect) will allow us to bring our stories to more locations around the world.

Ok, that's enough of the business side, let's chat STORY.

We receive a lot of questions of 'where did XYZ go? Will we see this character again' and we want to answer them, but sometimes we don't always get the how and why and implement it in a way all readers appreciate.

For example, some readers love nothing but explosions, and others are happy when I provide popcorn watching scenes with the ladies talking.

I happen to love both types of scenes.

As we draw to the conclusion of The Kurtherian Endgame, we will have a lot of antagonistic conversations ending in aggressive throwing of lead and lasers to decide who wins the conversation.

Now THAT is what I call adult conversation!

Thank you, again, for reading and loving Bethany Anne and her cohort of crazy friends working to save the Universe.

One ass-kicking at a time.

Ad Aeternitatem,

Michael

P.S. – I would LOVE to thank fellow Author Marc Stiegler for taking time to talk through some of the tech stuff with us! If you love well crafted stories that integrate the science into your stories, please check out some of Marc's books on Amazon!

PREVIEW OF A BITCH OF A PARADOX

BY ANDREW DOBELL & MICHAEL ANDERLE

Amanda appeared in her suite. She stood in the middle of the spacious living area and sighed. It was the end of another long day of meetings, and frankly, she felt shattered.

The formation of the Terran Foundation had fractured

the Nexus and war with the Accord had begun, which in turn had led to countless problems the fledgling Foundation had to deal with.

Luckily, Amanda was spared most of the tedium, leaving the majority of it to Elden, Trevelyan, and the others, but during these quieter days, she did what she could to help out.

Nearby, Sam lay in front of the sleek fireplace in the center of the room, enjoying its heat.

Amanda walked over to her familiar and rubbed the big cat's head, enjoying the feel of his soft, honey-colored fur. "No, no, don't get up," she muttered.

Sam lifted his head, his golden eyes peering up at her as the light from the fire danced along his huge saber teeth. He grunted and laid his head back down.

"Smart arse," she replied.

Amanda stood up and walked to the kitchen. She pulled the plate with the half-eaten baked vanilla cheesecake from the fridge, cut herself a slice and moved it to a separate plate, then put the rest back in the cooler.

She picked it up and turned to see that Sam had sat up and was looking at her with his head cocked to one side. "Don't you look at me like that. It's been a long day."

Sam grunted again.

"Shut it, you," Amanda replied good-naturedly.

Sam didn't talk, but she always knew what he was saying with his chuffs, coughs, and grunts due to her close relationship with her familiar. He'd been her companion for over eight hundred years now, ever since she'd first created him, and she loved him dearly.

She walked back into the living space of her suite and

dropped into the welcoming embrace of the sofa, then carved off a bite of the cheesecake with her fork.

Essentia flared in the room just meters from her.

Amanda jumped up from the sofa and dropped the plate and loaded fork to the coffee table with a clatter as she turned to face the surging energy.

Her suite was protected by a powerful Aegis, so no one should be able to Port into the room. However, just a few meters from her, three figures snapped into existence inside her Aegis, which, she noted, was still intact.

Backing up from the figures, Amanda dumped more Essentia into her personal Aegis.

Sam rose from the rug he'd been lying on, his hair standing on end as he growled at the intruders.

Amanda recognized the lead figure. He wore a black trench coat and had long dark hair that was slicked back behind his ears. The man's blue eyes swept the scene from beneath his heavy brows before he focused on Amanda.

"Morden," Amanda muttered the man's name.

Morden looked at her and smiled. "At least you recognize me."

Amanda pressed her lips together in consternation. She knew now why they'd been able to bypass her Aegis. They'd Ported in from outside the universe and could appear anywhere, even inside shields as powerful as Amanda's. She'd need to see if there was a way to stop that from happening, but now wasn't the time.

"Come for another ass-whupping?" Amanda asked.

Morden smiled. "Cute. It's one against three, though. Are you sure it will go the same way as last time?"

Amanda remembered the fight she, Jessica, and

Cheeky'd had with Morden on board *Sabrina* when Morden and the other Reavers had attempted to steal their Stasis Shield tech. He'd been a slippery foe that day, but she was on her home turf now, and had a few new tricks up her sleeve.

"Why are you here?" Amanda asked, bored with the back and forth.

"Why do you think? I'm not going to stand for some trumped-up witch like you messing with my missions," he answered, stepping forward.

Sam growled deeper at the implied threat.

"Oh, really? Well, you just might have to, because I'm not going anywhere."

The two Magi who flanked Morden stepped sideways, spreading out.

With her Aetheric Sight, Amanda could see the Magical energies they were pulling in as they readied themselves for a fight.

Amanda smiled. She'd already split her mind using the multitasking effect and boosted her Aegis.

Apparently, Morden had also tired of the witty repartee. Essentia surged around him and he released the bloom of energy, lashing out at Amanda.

Amanda Ported several meters to her right, dodging the Essentia strike before releasing a flash of electrical and explosive energy. Lightning lashed out at the three Magi, backed up by Kinetic rams that slammed into them.

The one on the far left staggered when Sam leapt on him, clawing at the Reaver as he knocked the man to the floor.

Morden weathered the blast from Amanda, but his

Aegis was badly damaged from the strike. On Amanda's right, the third Magus, a woman in dark similar clothing to Morden's, had been sent sprawling to the ground.

Essentia lanced out from both of them and crashed against Amanda's Aegis. The energy in the attacks hit her Aegis hard. It felt like Morden was letting loose and hitting her with everything he had. Amanda landed on her feet in a crouch but steadied herself with one hand, looking up at Morden, who was staring at her with a mix of fury and frustration.

Standing, Amanda allowed a grin to play over her face. "Regretting coming here?"

Morden stood up a little straighter and puffed his chest out. "No," he answered, and with a flick of his fingers, an invisible force knocked Sam off his companion.

Sam hit the wall with a whimper, but was back on his feet and looking more pissed than ever a second later.

Amanda could see he was merely bruised.

"My curiosity is satisfied," Morden replied.

Morden's companion rose from where Sam had pinned him, his wounds Magically healing, and scowled at Sam. "Mangy shit," he muttered and spat at the cat.

Sam charged forward and slammed into the Reaver as Morden Ported.

Amanda worked her own Magic and reached out, trying to pull Sam back.

The air snapped as the Magic ran its course. Essentia flashed, and the Reavers were gone.

So was Sam.

Amanda stood staring at the spot where the Reavers had been, shock and disbelief washing over her. "Sam?"

Amanda called. She looked around, but he was nowhere to be seen. "Sam, don't be an idiot now. Where are you?"

Essentia flared in her suite once more.

"What the... What now?" Amanda asked.

Amanda spotted the floating chrome figure that had just appeared.

She was surrounded by silver fractals that warped reality around her.

"Void," Amanda exclaimed.

Void's echoing, strangely-pitched voice filled the room. "Reavers?"

"They took Sam." Amanda felt a little lost without her familiar.

"I saw," Void replied.

"I have to find him," Amanda insisted.

"I know. Let me see what I can find," Void told her, and with another snap, she was gone.

Amanda frowned. She needed to be ready. Concentrating, she worked her Magic and Ported out of the universe and into her Quantum Realm, appearing on the main deck of her ship, the *Arkady Mark II*.

"Jesus," Matt exclaimed, clutching his chest. "Don't do that."

"Sorry," Amanda apologized with a conciliatory smile. "But I'm going to need the ship."

Matt was sitting beside Liz on the nearby sofas. "Oh?" he asked. "Where are you headed?"

"Another mission for Void," Amanda answered.

"For Void? You mean, you're going to another universe again?"

Amanda nodded. "I was just attacked by Reavers in my suite at the Union Spire."

"Are you all right?" Liz asked.

Amanda nodded. "I'm fine, but they took Sam."

"What?" Matt asked, coming up off the sofa.

"No!" Liz added.

"I'll get him back come hell or high water," Amanda stated. Essentia flared behind her. She recognized the Magical signature and turned to face Void. "Any news?"

"He's alive," Void answered.

"And *you* couldn't get him?" Amanda asked.

"There are Magi who even *I* would struggle to stand against, Amanda. Some of those are within the Reavers. But I believe I know where he's going. There's a Reaver operation going on, and he stowed away on a scouting ship. If you focus on him, I believe you might find him, and be able to foil it."

"All right, good. I'm going."

"Me, too," Liz called.

"I'll come too," Matt added. "If you'll allow me to join you."

Amanda shrugged. "Sure, why not? The more the merrier."

"I will take my leave of you," Void said, fading from view.

"So, what happens now?" Matt asked.

"Follow me," Amanda instructed. She led the pair through the main deck and onto the bridge, where she took her place in the command chair. "Be ready for anything."

Amanda closed her eyes and took a few seconds to calm

her mind and body, breathing deeply as she summoned an image of Sam. She focused on him, building up her mental image of who he was and the memories they shared until he was crystal-clear in her mind's eye.

Then she reached out.

She hunted for him, pressing her mind and Magic out into the multiverse.

As she did so, she called on her Magic and willed herself, her ship, and her friends to go there. To find him and appear close to him. In space, but close.

Then she had him. She felt his presence, and knew she could reach him. Forcing Essentia into her Magical working, the colossal energies surrounding her fluoresced and rushed in.

Light flashed behind her eyes as the ship and everyone on it Ported. They jumped universes, and the Magic faded.

Amanda nearly collapsed into her chair as the effort of the crossing took its toll. She felt like she'd just finished a triple marathon and almost fell out of her chair.

"We're here," Matt called. "Wherever here is. I don't recognize anything out there, except they have a *lot* of defenses. Those I recognize just fine."

"We're not in Kansas anymore," Liz agreed.

"I have a planet on my scans," Matt announced. "There are dead ships, too. Looks like the remains of a battle."

Amanda sat up and focused on her breathing. She'd need a few moments to gather herself together and get her energy back, so she concentrated on that and allowed the comments of her friends to wash over her. She listened as they called out their findings, wondering if she'd recognize anything.

"There's life on that planet. Three...no, four large cities. Something's down there, that's for sure," Matt continued.

Amanda took another deep breath as her energy returned. She opened her eyes.

"Are you okay, Mandy?" Liz asked.

Amanda smiled reassuringly. "I'm fine. It just takes a lot out of me to make these crossings."

"As long as you're sure."

"I am. Right, hold on. Let me see," she muttered as she focused on Sam once more and tried to locate him. Right away, she could feel his presence. He was close. She concentrated and conjured a set of Magical senses—vision, hearing, and smell—and willed them to manifest close to Sam.

In her mind, the image of a room appeared, with Sam sitting beside another cat and a small litter of kittens. Nearby were two figures, one of whom she recognized.

Amanda gasped. "Well, I'll be jiggered!"

"What is it?" Matt asked.

"I know where we are," she replied, getting up from her chair. "Stay here. I'm going to pop over and say hi."

Amanda worked her Magic and Ported across space and into a room on a nearby ship. She appeared with a snap.

"There you are!" Amanda cried, focusing on Sam for the time being. She crouched and pulled him in for a hug.

"Who the fuck are you, and what are you doing on my ship?"

Amanda smiled on hearing that familiar, foul-mouthed voice.

Amanda turned her head. "To be sure, and that's a fine

welcome for an old friend. Now I know why I've had the devil's own time locating my lost familiar. Thanks for keeping Samhain safe for me, Bethany Anne."

"You know this woman?" the man asked Bethany Anne, brandishing a sword made from exotic energy.

"I... Yessss." Bethany Anne blinked as the cognitive dissonance she was experiencing melted and the woman's name surfaced in her memory. "Amanda."

"You got me," Amana replied, flashing a grin. "So this is your universe, huh?"

The missing piece of the puzzle fell into place for Bethany Anne.

"BOB's Bar, right?" Bethany Anne raised an eyebrow. "Until now, I'd thought those memories were nothing more than a dimensional dream."

Amanda chuckled. "It was as real as can be."

Amanda remembered how those memories had felt to her after her trip to the bar. She gave Sam one last hug before standing up and turning to face Bethany Anne and Michael.

Bethany Anne seemed like quite a dramatic person, so maybe she'd appreciate a little melodrama. She put her hands on her hips. "Bethany Anne, I'm here to *warn you about imminent danger to your life!*"

Bethany Anne waved the energy balls away as Michael's fiery blade disappeared.

"Amanda." Michael sounded more exasperated than annoyed by her sudden appearance. "That's a normal Tuesday around here."

And you," Amanda added, pointing at Sam. "You've got

some explaining to do." Her eyes flicked to the nearby female mountain lion and the kittens she was protecting.

Sam cocked his head sideways and gave a questioning grunt.

Pre-order now at Amazon.com

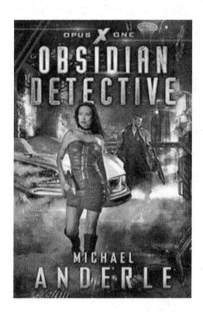

Available now at Amazon and through Kindle Unlimited

Two Rebels whose Worlds Collide on a Planetary Level.

On the fringes of human space, a murder will light a fuse and send two different people colliding together.

She lives on Earth, where peace among the population is a given. He is on the fringe of society where authority is how much firepower you wield.

She is from the powerful, the elite. He is with the military.

Both want the truth – but is revealing the truth good for society?

Two years ago, a small moon in a far off system was set to be the location of the first intergalactic war between humans and an alien race.

It never happened. However, something was found many are willing to kill to keep a secret.

Now, they have killed the wrong people.

How many will need to die to keep the truth hidden?

As many as is needed.

He will have vengeance no matter the cost. *She will dig for the truth. No matter how risky the truth is to reveal.*

Available now at Amazon and through Kindle Unlimited

Made in the USA
Coppell, TX
30 July 2020